Majesty
A Novel

by

Louis Couperus

Majesty
A Novel
by Louis Couperus

Copyright © 2023

All Rights reserved.

ISBN: 978-93-60465-30-8

Published by

DOUBLE 9 BOOKS

2/13-B, Ansari Road
Daryaganj, New Delhi – 110002
info@double9books.com
www.double9books.com
Tel. 011-40042856

ABOUT THE AUTHOR

Louis Marie-Anne Couperus was a Dutch author and poet who lived from June 10, 1863, to July 16, 1923. Lyric poems, psychological and historical novels, novellas, short stories, fairy tales, feuilletons, and sketches are just some of the types of writing he has done. Couperus is thought to be one of the most important people in Dutch writing. He was given the Tollensprijs (Tollens Prize) in 1923. Couperus and his wife took many trips in Europe and Asia, and he later wrote a series of travel books about those trips that came out every week. Louis Marie-Anne Couperus was born on June 10, 1863, at Mauritskade 11 in The Hague, Netherlands. She came from an Indo family that had been in the Dutch East Indies for a long time and was part of the colonial landed class. He was the eleventh and youngest child of Catharina Geertruida Reynst (1829-1893) and John Ricus Couperus (1816-1902). John Ricus Couperus was a well-known colonial official, lawyer, and landheer or lord of the private domain (particuliere land) of Tjikopo in Java. He was a great-grandson of Governor of Malacca Abraham Couperus (1752-1813) and Governor of Ambon Willem Jacob Cranssen (1762-1821). His father was related to them through a female line that goes back to the middle of the 18th century.

CONTENTS

PREFACE

The betting-book in one of London's oldest and most famous clubs contains a wager, with odds laid at one hundred sovereigns to ten, that "within five years there will not remain two crowned heads in Europe." The condition—"in the event of war between Great Britain and Germany"—was imposed by the date of the wager, for one member was venturing his hundred to ten at a moment when another was dining with him to kill time before the British prime minister's ultimatum took effect: the imperial German government had to deliver its reply before midnight, by Greenwich time, or eleven o'clock, by Central European reckoning.

Since the fourth of August, 1914, the King of the Hellenes, the Czar of Bulgaria, the Emperor-King of Austria-Hungary, the German Kaiser and a host of smaller princes have abdicated and sought asylum in countries left neutral by the war; the Czar of All the Russias also abdicated, but was executed without an opportunity of escape. Thus, though republican and royalist may protest that the wager was too sanguine or too pessimistic, the challenger must have taken credit for his prescience, as three of the great powers and two of the lesser converted, one after another, their half-divine sovereign into their wholly material scapegoat; by no great special pleading he might claim that the bet was won in spirit if not in fact when the morning of Armistice Day shewed monarchy surviving only in Spain, Italy, Roumania and Greece, in the small liberal kingdoms of Scandinavia and the Netherlands, in the minute principality of Monaco, in the crowned republic of Great Britain and Ireland and in the eternal anachronism of the Ottoman Empire. And the time-limit of five years had been exceeded by only three months.

In the peaceful period, four times longer, between the publication of *Majesty* in 1894 and the outbreak of the Great War, historians were kept hardly less busy with their record of fallen monarchs and extinguished dynasties: King Humbert of Italy was assassinated in 1900; King Alexander of Servia, with his queen, in 1903; King Carlos of Portugal, with the heir-apparent, in 1908; and the Sultan Abdul Hamid was deposed and imprisoned in 1909. Before the year 1894 no ruler of note had removed himself or been removed since the assassination of the Czar Alexander II in 1881; this study of "majesty" in its strength and, still more, in its weakness was published at a time when even the autocrat was more secure on his throne than at any period since "the year of revolution," 1848.

If *Majesty* is to be regarded as a *roman à clef*, there is a temptation, after six and twenty years, to call Couperus 'prophetic:' to call him that and nothing else is to turn blind eyes to the intuitive understanding which is more precious than divination, to ignore, in one book, the insight which illumines all and to overlook the quality which, among all the chronicles of kings, penetrates beyond romance and makes of *Majesty* an essay in human psychology. So long as the fairy-tales of childhood are woven about handsome princes and the fair-haired daughters of kings, there is no danger that the setting of royalty will ever lose its glamour; so long as "romantic" means primarily that which is "strange," the writer of romance may bind his spell on all to whom kings' houses and queens' gardens are an unfamiliar world; so long as the picturesque and traditional hold sway, the sanction and titles of kingship, the dignities and the procedure, the inhibitions and aloofness of royalty will fascinate, whether they like it or not, all those in whose veins there is no "golden drop" of blood royal. A romance of kingship, alike in the hands of dramatist, melodramatist and sycophant, is certain of commercial success.

The strength of this temptation is to be measured by the number of novels written round the triumphs and intrigues of kings, their amours and tragedies, their conflicts and disasters: King Cophetua and "King Sun," Prince Hal and Richard the Second, Louis the Eleventh and Charles the First, a king in hiding, a king in exile, a king in disguise; so long as he is a king, he is a safe investment for the romantic writer. But the weakness of those who succumb to this temptation is to be measured by their failure to make kings live in literature. Those few who survive beyond the brief term of ephemeral popularity survive more by reason of their office than of themselves and Jan de Witt makes little show beside Louis the Sixteenth; their robes are of so much greater account than their persons that the feeblest German prince cuts a more imposing figure than the strongest president of the Swiss Confederation.

Those who stand out in despite of their romantic setting, the human, perplexed Hamlets and vacillating, remorseful Richards, are inevitably few; and few they are likely to remain so long as the frame outshines the picture and the prince is labelled and left a celestial being apart, or labelled and dragged into passing sentimental contrast with men less exalted; it would seem that to regard a king first as a man and afterwards as an hereditary office-holder was to waste his romantic possibilities. This, nevertheless, is what Couperus has set himself to do in *Majesty*; he presents his family of kings as a branch of the human family; their dignity ceases to be stupefying when all are equally high-born; they wear their uniforms and robes as other men wear the conventional clothes of their trade; and, stripping them of their titles and decorations, he paints his group of men and women who have been born to rule, as others are born to till the soil; to marry for love or reasons of state, as others marry for love or reasons of convenience; to experience such emotions as are common to all men and to face the special duties and dangers apportioned to their caste by the organization of society:

"... *The Gothlandic family*," says Couperus, "... *lived [at Altseeborgen] for four months, without palace-etiquette, in the greatest simplicity. They formed a numerous family and there were always many visitors. The king attended to state affairs in homely fashion at the castle. His grandchildren would run into his room while he was discussing important business with the prime minister.... He just patted their flaxen curls and sent them away to play, with a caress.... From all the courts of Europe, which were as one great family, different members came from time to time to stay, bringing with them the irrespective nuances of different nationality, something exotic in accent and moral ideas, so far as this was not merged in their cosmopolitanism.*"

To this "one great family" the organization of society apportioned with one hand special privileges and exemptions, with the other special hardships and dangers. Revolution, to these professional rulers, was what successful trade rivalry is to a store-keeper; assassination was a daily risk to which store-keepers are commonly not exposed:

"... *Such is the life of rulers: the emperor lay dead, killed by a simple pistol-shot; and the court chamberlain was very busy, the masters of ceremonies unable to agree; the pomp of an imperial funeral was prepared in all its intricacy; through all Europe sped the after-shudder of fright; every newspaper was filled with telegrams and long articles....*

"*All this was because of one shot from a fanatic, a martyr for the people's rights.*

"*The Empress Elizabeth stared with wide-open eyes at the fate that had overtaken her. Not thus had she ever pictured to herself that it would come, thus, so rudely, in the midst of that festivity and in the presence of their royal guest....*"

It is to be understood, none the less, that she had always expected it to come: assassination is one of the special risks attaching to majesty at all times when one form of kingship or the whole institution of kings is debated and criticized. "*When the intellectual developments or culture of a race*," wrote Heine, in *The Citizen Kingdom in 1832*, "*cease to accord with its old established institutions, the necessary result is a combat in which the latter are overthrown. This is called a revolution. Until this revolution is complete, so long as the reform of these institutions does not agree at all points with the intellectual development, the habits and the wants of the people, during this period the national malady is not wholly cured and the ailing and agitated people will often relapse into the weakness of exhaustion and at times be subject to fits of burning fever. When this fever is upon them, they tear the lightest bandages and the most healing lint from their old wounds, throw the most benevolent and noble-hearted nurses out of window and themselves roll about in agony, until at length they find themselves in circumstances or adapt themselves to institutions that suit them better."*

So much for the race, in the gripe of growing-pains; but what of the nurses? How little benevolent or noble-hearted soever they be, nurses are bound by the honour of their profession and by personal pride not to forsake their patients. In one passage of *Majesty* the crown-prince is shaken by fundamental doubts of his own inherited right to rule; he questions and analyses until he is brought to heel by his imperial father who remembers that an excess of "victorious analysis" rotted the intellectual foundations of the old order and prepared the way for the logical French revolution. In another passage the boy realizes without any qualification that he at least is unfitted for the burthen of empire and that it is better to abdicate in favour of his brother or to commit suicide than to play Atlas with a world that he cannot sustain; once more, his imperial father silences any admission that his own flesh and blood can be too degenerate for the task of majesty. And so, at the moral sword-point, this hereditary nurse is held to the duty and privilege of standing by an hereditary patient whom he cannot relieve with "the most healing lint" and who may at any moment throw him out of window.

Not even in thought may majesty abdicate: a prince inherits his philosophy as he inherits his title.

"Life is so simple," proclaims the collectivist Zanti.

"'As you picture it, but not in reality,' objected Herman.

"Zanti looked at him angrily, stopped still, to be able to talk with greater ease, and, passionately, violently, exclaimed:

"'And do you in reality find it better than I picture it? I do not, sir, and I hope to turn my picture into reality. You and yours once, ages ago, made your picture reality; now it is the turn of us others: your reality has lasted long enough....'

"Othomar, haughtily, tried to say something in contradiction; the old man, however, suddenly turned to him and, gently though roughly, with his penetrating, fanatical voice which made Othomar shudder:

"'For you, sir, I feel pity!... Do you know why? Because the time will come!... The hour will come. Perhaps it is very near. If it does not come in your father's reign, it will come in your reign or your son's. But come it will! And therefore I feel

pity for you. For you will not have enough love for your people. Not enough love to say to them, "I am as all of you and nothing more. I will possess no more than any of you, for I do not want abundance while you suffer need. I will not rule over you, for I am only a human being like yourselves and no more human than you." Are you more human? If you were more, then you would be entitled to rule, yes, then, then.... See here, young man, you will never have so much love for your people as to do all this, oh, and more still and more! You will govern and possess abundance and wage war. But the time will come! Therefore I have pity for you ... although I oughtn't to!'"

The dead weight of inheritance, always a psychological fascination for Couperus, becomes doubly fascinating when one generation after another inherits an undwindling legacy of divine, ironic whim. As, in *The Books of the Small Souls* and in *Old People and the Things that Pass*, the children and grandchildren are born with minds tainted by prenatal memories, so, in *Majesty*, a prenatal influence has ordered the life and determined the fate of an infant who first draws breath as Count of Lycilia, eldest son of the Duke of Xara, himself crown-prince and eldest son of the Emperor of Liparia. There is no escape, no lack of heirs to the ironic inheritance: *"'If it's a son,'"* says the empress mother, on the morrow of her husband's assassination, *"'it will be a Duke of Xara....'*

"And then the Emperor of Liparia ... lost his self-restraint. In one lightning-flash, one zig-zag of terror, he saw again his life as crown-prince, he thought of his unborn son. What would become of this child of fate? Would it be a repetition of himself, of his hesitation, his melancholy and his despair?..."

If *Majesty* be a *roman à clef*, "this child of fate," with his father and mother and sisters, had his short spell of hesitation, melancholy and despair ended in 1918 by the revolver-shots of his gaolers. If Othomar be not a portrait of the Czar Nicolas II., it is hard to believe that the character was not suggested by him; though the Czar Alexander III. died a natural death, he would seem to have supplied a parallel for the Emperor Oscar, as Alexander II. supplied one for the liberal emperor, Othomar XI. The fanatical Zanti has his model in Count Tolstoi; and even the tragic romance of Prince von Lohe-Obkowitz has its historical counterpart.

But the interest and value of the book do not lie in any fancied resemblance, among the characters, to living or dead kings; the study of Prince Othomar does not depend on any likeness to the Czar Nicolas II.; Couperus succeeds or fails not as a court painter, but as a great sympathetic and imaginative artist who does or does not create, in the unfamiliar atmosphere of a court, first the collective life and spirit of a caste long trained to formalize its life and suppress its emotions, then a group of human characters who stand out compelling and vital against the posturing, shadowy kings and queens of romance.

To the composition of *Majesty* go the understanding and the historic sense, the irony and tenderness that enable Couperus in later books to draw with unfaltering touch his exquisite portraits of old age and youth, of men and women, in their moments of solitude and in their reactions upon one another. Few men have stepped so lightly and surely across the confines of the centuries and the continents; his intuition makes him equally at home in Alexandria and the Hague, with women and men, in the second century and in the twentieth; and it is not benumbed by the surface inhumanity of a court. When the Archduchess Valérie had lost her lover, the crown-prince could not understand her being able to talk as usual at dinner.

"It irritated him, his want of penetration of the human heart: how could he develop it? A future ruler ought to be able to see things at a single glance.... And suddenly, perhaps merely because of his desire for human knowledge, the thought arose within him that she was concealing her emotions, that perhaps she was still suffering intensely, but that she was pretending and bearing up: was she not a princess of the blood? They all learnt that, they of the blood, to pretend, to bear up! It was bred in their bones."

Perhaps it was bred in his bones, perhaps it was his mere desire for human knowledge that gave Couperus his penetration into the emotions which they of the blood were taught to conceal. In none of his books has he lavished more sympathy than in his painting of Prince Othomar's vacillation and passionate good-will, his timidity and desperate courage; nowhere has he used greater tenderness than in his sketch of the chivalry and gratitude which did duty for love in the passionless union of Valérie and the crown-prince.

STEPHEN MCKENNA.

LINCOLN'S INN, LONDON, 7 *October*, 1920.

CHAPTER I

1

Lipara, usually a city white as marble: long, white rows of villas on a southern blue sea; endless, elegant esplanades on the front, with palms whose green lacquer shimmered against an atmosphere of vivid blue ether. But to-day there drifted above it, heavily, a sombre, grey sky, fraught with storm and tragedy, like a leviathan in the firmament. And this grey sky was full of mystery, full of destiny, of strange destiny: it precipitated no thunder, but remained hanging over the city, merely casting faint shadows over the brightness of its palaces, over the width of its squares and streets, over the blue of its sea, its harbour, where the ships, upright, still, anxious, raised their tall masts on high.

White, square, massive, amid the verdure of the Elizabeth Parks, in the more intimate mystery of its own great plane-trees—the celebrated plane-trees of Lipara, world-famed trees—stood the Imperial, the emperor's palace, quasi-Moorish, with white, pointed arcades: it stood as the civic crown of the capital, one great architectural jewel, separated from the city, though standing in its very midst, by all that park-like verdure.

The empress, Elizabeth of Liparia, sat in the private drawing-room of her apartments in the right wing; she sat with a lady-in-waiting, the Countess Hélène of Thesbia. The windows were open; they opened on the park; the famous plane-trees rose there, knotty with age, wide-spreading, anxious, motionless with their trimmed leaves, between which a dull-green twilight shimmered upon the lawns which ran into the distance, rolling softly and smoothly, like tight-stretched velvet, into an endless violet vista, with just here or there the one strident white patch of a statue.

A great silence buzzed its strange sound of stillness indoors from the park; it buzzed around the empress. She sat smiling; she listened to Hélène reading aloud; she tried to listen, she did not always understand. A nervous dread haunted her, surrounded her, as with an invisible net of meshes, unbreakable. This dread was for her husband, her children, her elder son, her daughters, her younger boy. This dread crept along the carpet beneath her feet; it hung from the ceiling above her head, stole round about her through the whole room. This dread was in the park: it came from afar, from the violet vistas; it swept over the lawns and climbed in through the open windows; it fell from the trees, it fell from the sky, the grey, thunder-laden sky. This dread trembled through Liparia, through the whole of Liparia, through the whole empire; it trembled in, in to the empress, enveloping her whole being....

Then Elizabeth drew a deep breath and smiled. Hélène had looked up to her at a certain sentence with a light stress of voice and eyes, pointing the dialogue of the novel; this made the empress smile and she listened afresh. The anxiety smouldered in her, but she extinguished it with abounding acquiescence, acquiescence in what was to happen, in what must happen.

The novel which Hélène was reading was *Daniële Cortis,* a work that was in vogue at court because the Princess Thera had liked it. The countess read carefully and with great expression; the rhythm of the Italian came from her lips with the elegance of very pointed Venetian glass, flowery and transparent. And the empress wondered that Hélène could read so beautifully and that she did not seem to feel the anxiety which nevertheless stole about everywhere, like a spectre.

There was a knock at the door leading from the anteroom; a flunkey opened the door; a lady-in-waiting appeared between the hangings and curtseyed:

"His highness Prince Herman," she announced in a voice that hesitated a little, as though she knew that this hour of the afternoon was almost sacred to the empress.

"Ask the prince to come in," replied the empress: her voice, with all its haughtiness, sounded kind and attractive and sympathetic. "We have been expecting the prince so long...."

The door remained open, the lady-in-waiting disappeared, the flunkey waited at the hangings, motionless, for the prince to come. His firm tread sounded, approaching quickly, through the anteroom; and he made a pleasant entrance, with friendliness in his healthy, red face and the joy of meeting in his large grey eyes, with their gleaming black pupils. The flunkey closed the door behind him.

"Aunt!"

The prince stepped towards the empress with both hands outstretched. She had risen, as had Hélène, and she moved a step towards him; she took his two hands and allowed him to kiss her heartily on both cheeks.

Hélène curtseyed.

"Countess of Thesbia," said the prince, bowing.

"So you have come at last!" said the empress, with jesting discontent. She shook her head, but could not but look kindly at his pleasant, handsome, healthy face. "Why did you not telegraph for certain when you were coming? Then Othomar would have gone to the station, but now...."

She shrugged her shoulders with a smile of regret, as much as to say that now it could not be helped that his reception had only been *tel quel....*

"But, aunt," said Herman—the tone of his voice implied that he would never have demanded this of Othomar—"I have been excellently received: General Ducardi, Leoni, Fasti, our worthy minister and Siridsen...."

"Othomar will be sorry all the same," said the empress. "He is out driving now with Thera. Thera is driving her new bays. I can't understand why they went; it is sure to rain!"

The empress resumed her seat, with an anxious look at the weather outside; the prince and Hélène likewise sat down. A cross-fire of enquiries after the two families was kindled between the empress and her nephew; they had not seen each other for months. There was much to be discussed; the times were full of disaster; and the empress showed a long telegram which the emperor had sent from Altara about the inundations. Her fingers shook as they held the message.

She was still a woman of remarkable beauty, in spite of her grown-up children. But the charm of her beauty was apparent to very few. In public that beauty acquired a hardness as of a cameo: fine, clear-cut lines; great, cold, brown eyes, without expression; a cold, closed mouth; before people her slender figure assumed something stiff and automatic; she even showed herself thus before the more intimate circles of the court. But when she was seen, as now, in the seclusion of her own drawing-room, with no one except her nephew, whom she loved almost as much as her own children, and one little lady-in-waiting whom she spoilt, then, in spite of the dread which she repressed deep down in her heart, she became another woman. In her simple grey silk—she was in slight mourning for a relation—what was stiff and automatic in her figure changed into a gracious suppleness of carriage and movement, as spontaneous as the other was studied; the cameo of her face became animated; a look almost of melancholy came into her eyes; and, above all, a laugh about that cold, hard mouth was as a gleam of sympathy that rendered her unrecognizable to one who had seen her for the first time cold, stiff and austere.

Prince Herman of Gothland was the second son of her sister, the Queen of Gothland. A tall, sturdy lad in his undress uniform as a naval lieutenant, with the healthy, Teutonic fairness of the house of Gothland: a firm neck, broad shoulders, the swelling chest of an athlete, the determined quickness of movement of a lively nature, more than sufficient intelligence in his large grey eyes with the black pupils and with now and then a single pleasant, soft note in his baritone voice, a note that caused a momentary slight surprise and rendered him attractive when it sounded gently in the midst of his virility. And now that he sat there, easily, simply, pleasantly and yet with a certain dignity that did not permit him an absolute excess of joviality; now that he spoke, with his sweet voice, of his father, his mother, his brothers and sisters and asked after his uncle, the Emperor Oscar of Liparia, asked after Othomar, Thera: now, yes, now he aroused in the empress a delicate feeling of family affection, something of a secret bond of blood, a very solid support of relationship amid the isolation of their respective grandeurs, the grandeurs of Liparia and Gothland. Yonder, at the other side of Europe, far, far away from her and yet so near through the magnetism of this delicate feeling, she felt Gothland lying as one vast plain of love, whither she could allow her thoughts to wander. She was no longer giddy with melancholy and dread in that she was so high together with those whom she loved, her husband and her children, for she was not high alone: in her highness she leant against another highness, Liparia against Gothland, Gothland against Liparia. It brought moist tears to her eyes, it brought a melancholy that was like happiness clinging to her breath. The spectre of dread had disappeared. She could have embraced her nephew; she would have liked to tell him all this: his mere presence gave her this feeling, a feeling of comfort and of strength; she had not known it for months.

2

The door was opened; the flunkey stood stiff and upright, with a fixed look that stared straight before him, in the shadow of the hangings. Princess Thera and Othomar entered. The princess went up gaily and kindly to her cousin, they kissed; Othomar also embraced Herman, with a single word. But, in comparison with the natural utterances of the empress and of Thera, this single word of the Duke of Xara sounded studied and smilingly cold, not intimate, and carried a needless air of etiquette. It failed to conceal a translucent insincerity, a transparent show that made no effort to simulate affection, but seemed quite simply what at this moment it could not but seem, a greeting of feigned kindness between two cousins of the same age. Prince Herman was accustomed to this: there was no intimacy between him and Othomar; and this was the more striking when they saw each other for the first time after several months; it affected the empress keenly, disagreeably.

The conversation again turned upon the inundations in the north. The empress showed her children the latest telegram, the same that she had shown to Herman; it mentioned fresh disasters: still more villages swept away, towns harassed by the swollen and overflowing rivers, after a month of rain that had resembled the Flood. It had caused the emperor to proceed three days ago to the northern provinces; but they at court were now every moment expecting his orders that the crown-prince should replace him there, as he himself was returning to Lipara because of the cabinet crisis.

The crown-prince discussed all this a little coldly and formally. He was a young man of twenty-one, slender and of short stature, very slightly built, with delicate, melancholy features and dull, black eyes, that generally stared straight before him; a young moustache tinted his upper lip as with a stripe of Indian ink. He had a way of drooping his head a little on his chest and then looking up from under his eyelids; he generally sat very quiet; his hands, which were small and broad but delicate, rested evenly upon his knees; and he had a trick of carrying his left hand to his eyes and then—he was a little short-sighted—just peering at his ring. He was tightly girt in the blue-and-white uniform of a captain in the lancers, the uniform which he generally wore in public: its silver frogs lent a certain breadth to his slenderness; on his right wrist he wore a narrow, dull-gold bracelet.

"This is the first letter," said the empress. "Read it out, Thera...."

The princess took the letter. The emperor wrote:

"It is heartrending to see all this and to be able to do so little. The whole district south of the Zanthos, from Altara to Lycilia, is one expanse of water; where villages stood there now float the remains of bridges and houses, trees, accumulations of roofs, dead cattle, carts and household furniture and, as we were going along the Therezia Dyke, which—God be praised!— still stands firm at Altara, a cluster of corpses was slowly washed straight before our feet in one gigantic embrace of death...."

The crown-prince had suddenly turned pale; he remained sitting in his usual attitude, peering at his ring, with the trick that was his habit. Thera read on. When the crown-prince looked up he met his mother's eyes. She nodded to him with her eyelids, unseen by the others, who were listening to the letter; he smiled—a smile full of heartbreaking melancholy—and answered her with the same invisible quiver of the eyelids; it was as though he understood that gentle greeting and drew a scrap of comfort from it for a mysterious, silent sorrow that depressed him within himself, that lay on his breast like an oppression of the breath, like a nightmare in his waking life.

But Prince Herman was already talking about the ministerial crisis: it was momentarily expected that the authoritative government, rendered powerless, since the new elections, in the house of deputies with its majority of constitutionals, would proffer its resignation to the emperor.

The question, as always, was that of a revision of the constitution, which the constitutionals desired and the authoritatives—taking the side of the emperor—opposed. The Empress Elizabeth heaved a sigh of fatigue: how often had not this question of a revision of the constitution, which in Liparia always meant an extension of the constitution and a restriction of the imperial authority, come looming up during their twenty years' reign as a personal attack upon her husband! Resembling his long line of Liparian ancestors, hereditarily autocratic, Oscar could never forgive his father, Othomar XI., for allowing a constitution to be passed in his more liberal reign. And now, at this crisis, it was no small thing that they were asking, the constitutionals. The house of peers, hereditary and authoritative, the emperor's own body, which cancelled every proposal of a too constitutional character sent up from the house of deputies, was no longer to stand above them, hereditary and therefore, because of its hereditary nature, invariably authoritative: they wanted to make it elective! Even Othomar XI., with his modern ideas in favour of a constitution, would never have suffered this attack upon one of the most ancient institutions of the empire, an attack which would shake Liparia to its foundations....

While Herman was debating this, casually, his words lightly touching this all-important question, it seemed to Othomar as though he were turning giddy. A world passed through his head, rushing with rapid clouds through his imagination; and out of these clouds visions loomed up before him, pale-red, quick as lightning, terrible as a kind of apocalypse, the universe ending in a dynamite explosion. Out of these clouds there flashed up for an instant a scene, a recollection of the history of his imperial inheritance: an emperor of Liparia murdered centuries ago by one of his favourites at a court festival. Revolutions in other countries of Europe, the French revolution, flickered up with a blood-red reflection; the strikes in the quick-silver mines of the eastern provinces grinned at him out of them, out of the clouds, the world of clouds storming through his thoughts.... And so many more, so many more, all so rapid, with the rapidity of their lightning-flashes; he could not grasp them, the ruddy lightning-flashes; it all just flickered through him and then away: it flickered away, far away!... And it seemed strange to him that he was sitting there, in his mother's drawing-room, with the stately park swarming behind the plate-glass windows, with tints of old, medieval gold-leather, now, in the lowered gleam of the sun-rays; with his mother opposite him, so sweet, so daintily gentle in the intimacy of this short, uninterrupted meeting: his cousin talking and his sister replying and the little lady-in-waiting listening with a smile.... How strange to sit like this, so easily, so peacefully, so serenely, in the seclusion of their palace, as though Liparia were not shaking like an old, crazy tower!... Yes, they were talking about the crisis, Herman and Thera, but what did talking amount to? Words, nothing but words! Why this endless stringing together of words, beautiful, empty words, which a sovereign is obliged to string together and then utter to his subjects, now on this occasion, now on that? No, no, they were not in his province, speeches! For what, after all, were they supposed to express, this or that? What was right, what was just, what was right and just for their empire, this or that? How could one know, how could one be certain, how could one avoid hesitating, seeking, groping, blind-folded? Even if he had a thousand eyes all over the empire, would he be able to see everything that might happen? And, if he were omniscient, would he always be able to know what would be right? The constitution: was it good for a country to have a constitution or not? In Russia: was it good in Russia? A republic: would a republic be better? And who was right? Was his father right in wanting to reign as an absolute monarch, with his hereditary house of peers, in which he, Othomar, now recalled his admission, as Duke of Xara, at his eighteenth year, with the ducal crown and the robes and chain of the order of the Imperial Orb? Or was the house of deputies right? Would it be a good thing to place a restriction upon absolute sovereignty? It was difficult to decide.... The inundations: "It is heartrending to see all this and to be able to do so little.... An expanse of water all the way to Lycilia, a cluster of corpses in the embrace of death...."

It lightened.

Dull, heavy rumblings rolled through the sky; thick drops fell hard as liquid hail upon the leaves of the plane-trees; the whole park seemed to shiver, dreading the threatening cloud-burst. Hélène rose and closed the open window.

Then Othomar heard a strange sound: Syria.... Had they ceased talking of the house of peers? Syria, Syria....

"The king and queen were to have come next week, but they have now postponed their visit," said the empress.

"Because of the inundations," added Thera. "They are going to Constantinople first. I only wish they would remain with the sultan...."

"This visit seems to me at least to be something of an infliction," said Herman, laughing. "And how long do they stay, aunt?"

The empress raised her shoulders to say that she did not know: the approaching visit of the King and Queen of Syria pleased neither her nor the emperor, but it was not to be avoided.... However, not wishing to say much on this subject before Hélène, she replied:

"All the court festivities are now postponed, as you know, Herman, because of these terrible disasters. You will have a quiet time, my boy. You had better go with Othomar to Count Myxila's this evening...."

Count Myxila, the imperial chancellor, was that day keeping his sixtieth birthday. He was the emperor's principal favourite. That morning he had been to the empress to receive her congratulations. The crown-prince was, by the emperor's desire, to appear for a moment at the reception in the chancellor's palace.

Prince Herman glanced at Othomar enquiringly, as though expecting a word from him too.

"Of course," the Duke of Zara hastened to say. "Myxila will reckon on seeing Herman...."

3

When, at half-past ten in the evening, Othomar and Herman returned from the chancellor's palace in a downpour of rain, it was known among the empress' entourage also that the government had resigned; the princes had met the ministers at Count Myxila's; the crisis had thrilled through the outward ceremonial of the reception like a threatening shudder of fever. Also there was a telegram from the emperor for the Duke of Xara:

"I wish your imperial highness to proceed to Altara to-morrow.

"OSCAR."

The telegram did not come as a surprise, but was the natural consequence of the resignation of the government and of the emperor's return, for the emperor did not wish to leave the scene of the disasters without the consolation that the heir-apparent was about to replace him.

After a moment spent with the empress, Othomar withdrew to his own apartments. He sent for his equerry, Prince Dutri, and consulted with him shortly and in a few words, after which the equerry hurried away with much ado. In his dressing-room Othomar found his valet, Andro, who had been warned by one of the chamberlains and was already busily packing up.

"Don't pack too much," he said, as the valet rose respectfully from the trunk before which he was kneeling. "It would only be in the way...."

So soon as he had said this, he failed to see the reason. Nor did the valet seem to take any notice of it: kneeling down again before the trunk, he continued to pack what he thought fit. It would be quite right as Andro was doing it, thought Othomar.

And he flung himself into a chair in his study. One of the windows was open; a single standard lamp in a corner gave a dim light. The furious downpour raged outside; a humid whiff of wet leaves drifted indoors.

The prince was tired, too tired to summon Andro to pull off his tight patent-leather boots. He was wearing the white-and-gold uniform of a colonel of the throne-guards, the imperial body-guard; the chain of the order of the Imperial Orb hung round his neck; other decorations studded his breast. The reception at the imperial chancellor's still whirled before his eyes; in his brain buzzed, mingling with the rain, the inevitable conversations about the crisis, the government, the house of peers. He saw himself the crown-prince, always the crown-prince, always too condescending, too affable, not sufficiently natural, not simple, not easy like Herman; and he saw Herman moving easily through the rooms of the chancellor's palace, asking quite simply to be introduced to the ladies, now by Count Myxila and again by an equerry. And he envied his cousin, who was a second son. Herman did not cause the atmosphere around him to freeze at once, as did he, with the cold imperial look of his crown-princedom.

He saw the ministers, the ministers who were about to retire, each with his own interests at heart instead of those of Liparia. He suspected this from their humble attitudes before him, the crown-prince, when he had spoken to all of them.... He felt that they were only playing a part, that there was much in them that they did not allow to transpire; and he suddenly asked himself why, why this should all be so, why so much show, nothing but show.... And he was suffering now, deep in his breast; the tightness of his uniform, loaded with decorations, oppressed him....

He saw old Countess Myxila and some other ladies, whom he had seen curtseying amid the crackling of their trains and the sudden downward glitter of their diamonds, whom he had seen flushing with pleasure because the Duke of Xara had taken notice of them. And the wife also of the court-marshal, the Duchess of Yemena, who had so long been absent from court in voluntary exile at her estate in Vaza: he saw her approaching on Prince Dutri's arm. For he did not know her: years ago, when she was at court, he was a boy of fifteen, undergoing a strict military education, seldom with the empress and never at the court festivals; he had never seen the duchess at that time.

Now, in the twilight of that one lamp, with the weather raging outside, he saw her once more and she became as it were transparent in the lines of the rain; she looked strange, seen through the rain, as through a curtain of wet muslin. A tall woman, voluptuously formed, half-naked under the white radiance of her diamond necklace, that was how she approached him: her hair blue-black with a gleam in it, her face a little pale under a thin bloom of rose powder; she came nearer, slowly, hesitating, in her yellow-gold figured satin, edged with heavy sable; she bowed before him, with a deep, reverential curtsey before the imperial presence: her head sank upon her breast, the tiara in her black hair shot forth rays, her whole stature curved down as with one serpentine line of grace in the material of gleaming gold that shone about her bosom and seemed to break over the thick folds of her train with a filagree of light. He had spoken to her. She rose from the billows of her reverential grace; she replied, he forgot what; her eyes sparkled upon his like black stars. She had made an impression upon him. He thought it was because he had heard her much spoken of as a woman with a life full of passion, a thing that was a riddle to him. His education had been military and strictly chaste, his youth had remained uncorrupted by the easy morals of the court, perhaps because his parents, after a long and secret separation, known to none but themselves, had come together again from a need of family-life and mutual support; the Empress Elizabeth had forgiven the Emperor Oscar and submitted to his infidelities as inevitable. Round about him Othomar had never had occasion to observe the life of the senses. At the university of Altara, where he had studied, he had never taken part, except officially, in the diversions of the students; he had always remained the crown-prince, not from haughtiness, but because he was unable to do otherwise, from lack of ease and tact.

And something in the duchess had made an impression on him, as of a thing unknown. He felt in this woman, who curtseyed so deeply before him with her sphinx-like smile, a world of emotion and knowledge which he did not possess; he had felt poor in comparison with her, small and insignificant. What was it that she possessed and he not? Was it a riddle of the soul? Were there such things, soul-enigmas, and was it worth while to try to fathom them? Such a woman as she, was she not quite different from his mother and sisters? Or did his equerries, among themselves, speak of his sisters too as they spoke of the duchess? And this life of passion, this life of love for so many, was that then the truth? Did they not slander her, the equerries, or at least did they not make truth seem different from what it was, as they always did in everything, as if the truth must always be made to seem other to a prince than to a subject?

He felt tired. And he sat on, striving in vain to drive from him the whirl of the strange figures of that reception seen through a transparency of rain. Before him, as though in his room, they all walked through one another: the ministers, the equerries, Count Myxila and the duchess....

A knock, a chamberlain:

"Prince Herman is asking whether he may intrude on your highness for a minute."

He nodded yes. After a moment Prince Herman entered.

"You are always welcome, Herman," said Othomar; and his voice sounded cold in spite of himself.

"I have come to ask you something," said Herman of Gothland. "I should much like to go with you to Altara to-morrow; but I want to be certain that you don't mind. I would not have asked it of my own accord, if my aunt hadn't spoken of it. What do you think?"

Othomar looked at Herman; Othomar did not like his cool voice:

"If you do so out of sympathy, because you happen to be at Lipara, by all means," he began....

"Let me tell you once more: I am doing this chiefly because of ... your mother."

His voice sounded very emphatic.

"Do it for her then," replied Othomar, gently. "It will give me great pleasure if you go with me for my mother's sake."

Herman realized that he had been unnecessarily cool and emphatic. He was sorry. The empress had asked him to accompany Othomar. He had hesitated at first, knowing that there was a lack of sympathy between Othomar and him. Then he had yielded, but had not known how to ask Othomar. His usual ease of manner had forsaken him, as it always did in Othomar's presence.

"Very well, then," Herman stammered, awkwardly.

Othomar put out his hand:

"I understand your intention perfectly. Mamma would like you to go too, because she will then be sure that there is some one with me whom I can trust in everything. Isn't that it?"

Herman pressed his hand:

"Yes," he said, pleased, contented, feeling no annoyance that Othomar had had the best of the conversation, delighted that his cousin took it like this. "Yes, just so; that's how it is. Don't let me detain you now: it's late. Good-night...."

"Good-night...."

Herman went. It was still pouring with rain. Othomar sat down again; the chill of the rainy night pressed coldly into the room and fell upon his shoulders. But he remained staring motionlessly at the tips of his boots.

Andro entered softly:

"Does your highness wish me to...."

Othomar nodded. The valet first closed the window and drew the blind and then knelt before the prince, who, with a gesture of fatigue, put out his foot to him and rested the heel of his boot on the man's knee.

4

The downpour ceased during the night; but it was raining again in the morning. It was seven o'clock; a sultry moisture covered the colossal glass roof of the station, as though it had been breathed upon from end to end. The special train stood waiting; the engine gave short, powerful snorts, like a discontented, tired beast. A great multitude, a buzzing accumulation of vague people filled the glass hall; a detachment of infantry—two files, to right and left; the uniforms, dark-red and pale-grey; above, a faint glitter of bayonets—drew two long stripes of colour diagonally through the sombre station, cut the crowd into two and kept a broad space clear in front of the imperial waiting-room.

Dissatisfaction hovered over the crowd; angry glances flashed; rough words crackled sharply through the air, mingled with curses; a contemptuous laugh sounded in a corner.

There was a long wait; then a cheer was heard outside: the prince had arrived in front of the station. The waiting-room became filled with uniforms, glistening faintly in the morning light; brief sentences were exchanged in a low voice.

Othomar entered with Herman and the Marquis of Dazzara, the governor of the capital, the highest military authority, whose rich uniform stood out against the simpler ones of the others, even against those of the princes; they were followed by adjutants, Liparian and Gothland equerries, aides-de-camp. The mayor of the town and the managing director of the railway stepped towards Othomar and saluted him; the mayor stumbled through long phrases before the two princes.

"Why wasn't the approach to the platform closed to the public?" asked General Ducardi of the director, after the adjutant-general had glanced at the platform through the lace curtains, curious about the humming outside.

The director shrugged his shoulders:

"That was our first intention; it was done in that way when the emperor left," he replied. "But a special message was received from the Imperial, urgently requesting us not to shut off the platform; it was the Duke of Xara's wish."

"And how about all those soldiers?"

"By command of the governor of the capital. An aide-de-camp came and told us that a detachment of infantry was coming as a guard-of-honour."

"Was that aide-de-camp also from the Imperial?"

"No, from the governor's palace...."

Ducardi shrugged his shoulders; an angry growl fluttered his great, grey moustache. He walked straight up to the crown-prince:

"Is your highness aware that there is a detachment of infantry outside?" he said, interrupting the mayor's long sentences.

The governor heard him and drew nearer.

"A detachment?... No," said Othomar, in astonishment.

"Did your highness not command it, then?" Ducardi continued.

"I? No," Othomar repeated.

The governor bowed low; the general's loud, gruff voice unnerved him.

"I thought," said the governor, urbanely, but mumbling, stammering—and he tried to be at once humble before the prince and haughty towards the general—"I thought it would be well to safeguard your highness against possible ... possible unpleasantness, especially as your highness desired ... desired that the platform should remain open to the public...."

Othomar looked out as Ducardi had done; he saw the infantry drawn up and the crowd behind; angry, murmuring, drab, threatening:

"But, excellency," he said, aloud, to the governor, "in that case it would have been better to shut off the platform entirely. This is quite wrong. The police would have been sufficient to prevent any crowding."

"I was afraid of ... of unpleasantness, highness. Troubled times, the people so discontented," he whispered, fearing to be overheard by the equerries.

"Quite wrong," repeated Othomar, angrily, nervously excited. "Let the infantry march off."

"That's out of the question now," Ducardi hastened to say, with an unhappy smile. "You understand that that can't be done."

The conversation had been carried on aside, in a half-whispering tone; yet everybody seemed to listen. All eyes were gazing on the group surrounding the princes; the others were silent.

"Then let us prolong this regrettable situation as little as possible; we may as well go," said Othomar; and his voice quivered high, young and nervous in his clear throat.

The doors were opened; Othomar, in his hurry, stepped out first; the equerries and aides-de-camp did not follow him at once, as they had to make way for Prince Herman, who happened to be a little behind. Herman hurried up to Othomar; the others followed.

The princes made a movement of the head to left and right as though to bow; but their eyes met the fixed, round eyes of the soldiers, who had presented arms with a flash; they saluted and walked on to their compartment a little quickly, with an unpleasant feeling in their backs.

Under the colossal glass roof of the station, behind the files of soldiers, the crowd stood as still as death, for the humming had almost ceased; there was no curse nor scornful word heard, but also no cheer, no loud, loyal hurrah sweet to the ears of princes.

And the faces of those vague people, separated by uniforms and bayonets from their future ruler, remained gazing fixedly with dull, hostile eyes, with firmly-closed lips, full of forced restraint, as though to stare him out of existence in the imperial compartment.

The princes waved their hands from the windows to the dignitaries, who stood on the platform bowing, saluting. The engine whistled, shrieked, tore the close atmosphere of humidity under the dome; the train left the station, drove into the early morning, which was lighter outside the glass roof, glided as it were over the rainy town upon viaducts, with canals, streets, squares beneath it; farther on, the pinnacles and spires of the palaces and churches; the two marble towers of the cathedral, with the doves nestling in the renascence tracery of the lace-work of its steeples, standing out pale-white against the sky, which was now turning blue; then, in the centre of the town—green and wide, one oasis—the Elizabeth Parks, the white mass of the Imperial and, behind that, the gigantic bend of the quays, the harbour with its forest of masts, the oval curve of the horizon of the sea, all wet, glittering, raining in the distance.

Othomar looked sombrely before him. Herman smiled to him:

"Come, don't think about it any more," he advised him, adding with a laugh, "Our poor governor has had his appetite spoilt for to-day."

General Ducardi muttered an inward curse:

"Monstrously stupid," Herman heard him mumbling.

"I wanted to show them," said Othomar, suddenly.... He had intended to say, "that I am not afraid of them." He threw a glance around him, saw the eyes of Prince Dutri, his equerry, fixed upon him like a basilisk's and let his voice change from proud to faint-hearted; sadly he concluded, "that I love them and trust them so completely. Why need it have happened like this?..."

His voice had sounded faint, to please Prince Dutri; but it displeased the general. He first glanced aside at his crown-prince and then at the Prince of

Gothland; he drew a comparison; his eye continued to rest appreciatively, in soldierly approval, on the smart naval lieutenant, broad and strong, sitting with his hands on his thighs, bending forward a little, looking back at the white capital as it receded before his eyes through the slanting rainbeams....

After four hours' travelling, Novi, in the province of Xara. The train stops; the princes and their suite alight, consult clocks, watches. They express surprise, they walk up and down the platform for half an hour, for an hour. Prince Herman engages in a busy conversation with the station-master. It is still raining.

At last the special from Altara is signalled. The train glides in and stops; the Emperor Oscar alights from the imperial compartment. He is followed by generals and aides-de-camp: their uniforms, the emperor's included, have lost something of their smartness and hang in tired creases from their shoulders, like clothes worn a long time. The emperor, still young, broad and sturdy and only just turning grey, walks with a firm step; he embraces his son, his nephew, brusquely, hastily. The imperial party disappear into the waiting-room; Ducardi and one of the Gothlandic officers follow them. The interview, however, is a short one: in ten minutes they reappear on the platform; brief words and handshakes are exchanged; the emperor steps back into his compartment, the crown-prince into his. The prince's train waits until his father's passes it—a last wave of the hand—then it too steams away....

Care lies like a cloud upon Othomar's forehead. He remembers his father's words: in a desperate condition, our fine old city. The Therezia Dyke may be giving way; so little energy in the municipal council; thousands of people without a roof to cover them, fleeing, spending the night in churches, in public buildings. And his last word:

"Send some of them to St. Ladislas...."

Othomar reflects; all are silent about him, depressed by the after-sound of the emperor's words, which have painted the disaster anew, brought it afresh before their eyes: the eyes of Ducardi, who knows himself to be more ready with sword in war than with sympathy in cases of inundation; the eyes of Dutri, still filled with the mundane glamour of the incomparable capital. Some part of their self-concentration falls silent; a thought of what they are about to see crosses their minds.

And Othomar reflects. What shall he do, what can he do? Is it not too much that is asked of him? Can he, *can* he combat the stress of the waters?

"Oh, this rain, this rain!" he mutters, secretly clenching his fist.

Five hours' more travelling. The towers of the city, the crenulated outline and Titanic plateaus of St. Ladislas, with its bastions, shoot up on the horizon, shift to one side when approached. The train stops, in the open country, at a little halting-place; the princes know that the Central Station is flooded; the whole railway-management has been transferred to this halt. And suddenly they stand in the presence of the smooth, green, watery expanse of the Zanthos, which has spread itself into one sea of water, broad and even, hardly rippled, like a wrath appeased. A punt is waiting and carries them through ruins of houses, through floating household goods. A dead horse catches on to the punt; a musty odour of damp decay hovers about. At an over-turned house, men in a punt are busied fishing up a corpse; it hangs on their boat-hooks with slack arms and long, wet hair, the pallid, dead head drooping backwards; it is a woman. Herman sees Othomar's lips quiver.

Now they float through a street of tall, deserted houses in a poor suburb. This part has been flooded for days. They alight in a square; the people are there; they cheer. Louder and louder they cheer, moved by the sight of their prince, who has come across the water to save them. A group of students shout, call out his name and cheer and wave their coloured caps.

Othomar shakes hands with the mayor, the minister for waterways, the governor of Altara and other dignitaries. His heart is full; he feels a sob welling up from his breast.

From among the group of students one steps forward, a big, tall lad:

"Highness!" he cries. "May we be your guard-of-honour?"

Etiquette hardly exists here, though the dignitaries look angry. Othomar, remembering his own student days, not yet so long ago, presses the student's hand; Prince Herman does the same; and the students grow excited and once more shout and clamour:

"Hurrah! Hurrah! Othomar for ever! Gothland for ever!"

Behind this square the city is perceived to be in distress, a silent distress from yet greater danger threatening: the old coronation-city, the city of learning and tradition, the sombre monument of the middle ages; she looks grey compared with white Lipara, which lies laughing yonder and is beautiful with new marble on her blue sea, but which does not love her sovereigns so well as she does, the dethroned capital, with her gigantic Romanesque cathedral, where the sacred imperial crown with the cross of St. Ladislas is pressed on the temples of every emperor of Liparia. Though her masters are faithless to her and have for centuries lived in their white Imperial over yonder and no longer in the old castellated fortress of the country's patron saint, she, the old city, the mother of the country, remains faithful to them with her maternal love and not because of her oath, but because of her blood, of her heart, of all her life, which is her old tradition....

But, like his father, Othomar was not this time to go to the Castle of St. Ladislas: the fortress lay too high and too far from the town, too far from the scene of disasters. Open carriages stood in waiting; they stepped in, the students flung themselves on horseback; the princes were to take up their residence in the palace of the cardinal-archbishop, the primate of Liparia, in the Episcopal, which, together with the cathedral and the Old Palace, formed one colossal, ancient, grey mass, a town in itself, the very heart of the city.

They rode quickly on. The people cheered; they look upon them as a train of deliverers who, they thought, would at last bring them safety. Between the departure of the emperor and the arrival of the prince a depression had reigned which, at the sight of Othomar, changed into morbid enthusiasm.

It became suddenly dark, but not through the sun's setting—it was only five o'clock in the month of March in the south—it became dark because of the clouds, the ships in the sky carrying in their tense, bowl-shaped, giant sails water which already was beginning to trickle down again in drops. Under that grey sky the cheering of the people rose in a minor key, when suddenly, as though the swollen clouds were bursting open with one rent, a flood dashed down in a solitary, perpendicular sheet of water.

Othomar was sitting with Herman and Ducardi in the first carriage.

"Would not your highness prefer to have the carriage closed?" asked the old general, helping the prince on with his cape.

Othomar hesitated; he had no time to answer the general; the crowd increased, became thicker, cheered; and he bowed in acknowledgement, saluted, nodded. The heavy rain clattered straight down. The hard rainbeams ran down the princes' and the general's necks, down their backs, soaked their knees. The crowd stood sheltered under an irregular roof of umbrellas, as though grouped under wet, black stars, filled the narrow streets of the old city, pressed in between the outriders and the carriage: the coachman had to drive more slowly.

"Won't you have the carriage shut?" Herman repeated after Ducardi.

Othomar still hesitated. Then—and he himself thought his words a little theatrical and did not know how they would sound—he answered aloud:

"No, do not let us be afraid of the water; they have all suffered from the water here."

But Ducardi looked at him; he felt something quiver inside him for his prince....

The carriage remained open. In one of the landaus following, Prince Dutri looked round furiously to see how much longer the Duke of Xara meant to let himself be saturated with rain and his suite with him. In the narrow, high streets near the cathedral they had to drive almost at a walking-pace, right through the cheering of the crowding populace. Soaked to the skin, the Crown-prince of Liparia with his following arrived at the cardinal-archbishop's; they left a trail of water behind them on the staircases and in the corridors of the Episcopal.

5

In changed uniforms, a short dinner with the high prelate; a few canons and minor ecclesiastics sit down with them. The room is large and sombre, barely lighted with a feeble glimmer of candles; the silver gleams dully on the dressers of old black oak; the frescoes on the walls—sacred subjects—are barely distinguishable. A silent haste quickens the jaws; the conversation is conducted in an undertone; the servants, in their dark livery, move as though on tiptoe. The cardinal, on either side of whom the princes are seated, is tall and thin, with a refined, ascetic face and the steel-blue eyes of an enthusiast; his voice issues from low down in his throat, like that of an oracle; he says something of the Lord's will and makes a submissive gesture with both hands, the fingers lightly outspread, as Jesus does in the old pictures. One of the priests, the cardinal's private secretary, a young man with a round, pink face and soft, white hands, laughs rather loudly at a joke of Prince Dutri, who, sitting next to him, tells a story about a countess in Lipara whom they both know. The cardinal casts a stern glance at the frivolous secretary.

After the hurried dinner, the princes and their suite ride into the town on horseback, cheered wherever they go. The water already mounts close to the cathedral and the Archiepiscopal Palace. Groups of men, women and children, sobbing, flow towards the prince, as he rides across the dark squares; they carry torches about him, as the gas is not everywhere lighted; the ruddy flares look strange, romantic, over the ancient dark mass of the walls and are reflected with long streaks of blood in the water lying in the narrow alleys. A large house of many storeys and rows of little windows appears to have suddenly gone under: a sudden mysterious pressure of water, filtering from the foundations through the masonry of the cellars, making its treacherous way through the least crack or crevice. The inhabitants save themselves in skiffs, which pass with little red lights through the black, watery town; a child cries at the top of its voice. They are poor people there in hundreds, living, packed as in boxes. The princes alight and step into a boat and are rowed to the spot; it becomes known who they are; they themselves help an old woman with three children, all wet to the waist, to climb on to a raft; they themselves give them money, shout instructions to them. And they point to the old fortress of St. Ladislas as a refuge....

But a cry arises, farther on, a cry at first not clearly perceived in the darkness of the evening, then at last distinctly audible:

"The Therezia Dyke! The Therezia Dyke!..."

The princes want to go there; it is not possible on horseback; the only way is in boats. Prince Herman himself grasps the sculls; in the next boat Dutri declares to Von Fest, one of the Gothlandic equerries, that, taken all round, he thinks Venice more comfortable....

"The Therezia Dyke! The Therezia Dyke!..."

The dyke lies like the black back of a great, long beast just outside the town, on the left bank of the Zanthos, and protects the whole St. Therezia district, the eastern portion of the city, which stands tolerably high, from the river, which generally overflows in springtime. The boats glide over the water-streets; a landing is possible in the Therezia Square; lanterns are burning; torches flare, ruddy scintillations dart over the water. The square is large and wide; the houses stand black round about it and surround it in the night with their irregular lines of gables and chimneys, with the massive pile of the church of St. Therezia, whose steeples are lost in the dark sky; in the centre of the square rises a great equestrian statue of a Liparian emperor, gigantic in motionless bronze, stretching one arm, sword in hand, over the petty swarming of the crowd.

Othomar and Herman have sent their three equerries, Dutri, Leoni and Von Fest, for whom horses have been found and saddled, to the dyke, which protects a whole suburb of villas, factories and the St. Therezia railway-station against the waters of the Zanthos, which has already poured its right bank over the country and is drowning it. The princes stand in the middle of the square on the steps of the pedestal of the statue; they would have liked to go on farther, but the mayor himself has begged them to stay where they are: farther on mortal danger threatens at every moment.... All that could be done has been done; there is nothing more to do but wait.

Quarters of an hour, half-hours, pass. This waiting for terrible news calms them; they hope afresh. The officers ride to and fro; the villas and factories yonder are deserted: a whole town lies empty, forsaken. Prince Dutri, turning his horse, which he has ridden out of breath, assures them that the embankment will hold firm; after he has spoken with the princes, he is surrounded: it is the occupiers of the villas, the manufacturers, who overwhelm him with questions, fortified by the self-assurance of the imperial equerry. Dutri gallops off once more.

Now the doors of the church are opened wide, quite wide; at the end of the vista, between the pillars, the tiny lights glitter on the altar; a procession files out slowly: a mitred bishop, priests, acolytes, singing and carrying banners and swinging clouds of smoke from their censers; behind the upraised crucifix, the relics of St. Therezia, in their antique shrine of medieval gold and crystal and precious stones, round or roughly cut; it is borne under a canopy and in the shimmering gleam of candles it glitters and sparkles like a sacred jewel, like a constellation, across that sombre square, through that black night of disaster; flicker the giant emeralds, glitters the precious chased gold and before the Most Holy the crowded populace draws back on either side and falls upon its knees. This is the fifth time to-day that the procession goes its round, that the reliquary is borne on high, to exorcize the calamity. It passes the statue, the princes kneel down; the Latin of the chant, the gleam of the relics in their shrine, the cloud of the incense pass over them with the blessing of the bishop....

The procession has brought stillness to the square, but a murmur now approaches as from afar.... The crowd seems to surge as though in one wave, nobody is now kneeling; the very procession is broken up and confused. Through the throng rushes the report: the dyke has given way!...

They do not yet believe it; but suddenly from above the fort of St. Ladislas, which spreads its ramparts about the castle, a shot thunders out and vibrates over the black city and shakes through the black sky as though its rebound were breaking against the lowering clouds. A second shot thunders after it, as with giant cymbals of catastrophe, a third ... the whole town knows that the Zanthos has broken the dyke.

The whole square is in confused motion, like a swarm of ants; troops of tardy fugitives still come thronging in, poor ones now and indigent, who had not been able to fly earlier, who had been still hoping; through the crush Prince Dutri, panting, cursing, on horseback, terror in his eyes, strives to reach the statue; the distant murmur as of a sea comes nearer and nearer. Men scatter along the streets, on foot or in boats; the disordered procession, with the glitter of its reliquary, seeming to reel on the billows of a human sea, scatters towards the church.

"Is not even the square safe?" asks Othomar.

He can hardly speak, his chest seems cramped as it were with iron, his eyes fill with tears, an immense despair of impotence and pity suffuses his soul.

The mayor shakes his head:

"The square lies lower than the suburbs, highness; you cannot remain here. For God's sake go back to the Episcopal in a boat!..."

But the princes insist on remaining, though the murmur grows louder and louder.

"Go into the church in that case, highnesses: that is the only safe place left," the mayor beseeches. "I beg you, for God's sake!"

The square is already swept clean, the torch-bearers lead the princes to the steps of the church; the Zanthos comes billowing on, like a soft thunder skimming the ground.

Inside the church the organ sounds; they sing, they pray all through the night. And the whole night long everything outside remains chaotically black, gently murmuring....

When the first dawn pales over the sky, which begins in the distance to assume tints of rose and grey, faint opal and mother-of-pearl, Othomar and Herman and the equerries emerge on the steps of the church.

The square stands under water; the houses rise out of the water; the statue of Othomar III. waves its bronze arm and sword over a lake that ripples in the morning breeze.

From the Therezia Square to the Cathedral Square everything lies under water.

6

"TO HER IMPERIAL MAJESTY THE EMPRESS OF LIPARIA

"THE EPISCOPAL,
"ALTARA,
"—*March*, 18—.

"MY ADORED MOTHER,

"Your letter reproaches me with not writing to you two days ago, without delay; forgive me, for my thoughts have so constantly been full of you. But I felt so tired yesterday, after a busy day, and I lacked the strength to write to you in the evening. Let me tell you now of my experiences.

"You describe to me the terrible impression produced at Lipara by the telegram from here about the breach in the Therezia Dyke and how none slept at the Imperial. We too were up all night, in St. Therezia's Church. No such fearful inundation has been remembered for fifty years; at the time of that which my father remembers in his childhood, the Therezia Square was not flooded and the water only came as far, they say, as the great iron-factory.

"How can I describe to you what I felt that night, while we were hoping and waiting, hoping in turn that God and His Holy Mother would ward off this disaster from us and waiting for the catastrophe to burst forth! We stood on the pedestal of the equestrian statue, unable to do anything more. Oh, that impotence about me, that impotence within me! I kept on asking myself what I was there for, if I could do nothing to help my people. Never before, dearest Mother, have I felt this feeling of impotence, of inability to counteract the inevitable, so possess my soul, until it was wholly filled with despair; but neither have I ever so thoroughly realized that everything in life has its two sides, that the greatest disaster has not only its black shadow but also its bright side, for never, never have I felt so strongly and utterly, through my despair, the love for our people, a thing that I did not yet know could exist in our hearts as a truth, as I then felt it quivering all through me; and this love gave me an immense melancholy at the thought that all of them, the millions of souls of our empire, will never know, or, if they did know, believe that I loved them so, loved them as though my own blood ran in their veins. Nor do I wish to deceive myself and I well know that I should never have this feeling at Lipara, but I have it here, in our ancient city, which gives us all her sympathy. I feel here that I myself am more of a Slav, like our Altarians, than a Latin, like our southerners in Lipara and Thracyna; I feel here that I am of their blood, a thing that I do not feel yonder.

"No doubt much has been said and written in the papers about the want of tact of the Marquis of Dazzara, with his foolish guard-of-honour at the station at our departure; be that as it may, I felt great sadness in the train to think that, in spite of their having come to see me leave, they did not seem to love me. I know you will again disapprove of this as false sensitiveness on my part, but I cannot help it, my dear Mother: I am like that, I am hypersensitive to sympathy in general and to the utterances of our people in particular. And for that reason too I love the people here, very simply and childishly perhaps, because they show that they love me: enthusiasm everywhere, genuine, unaffected enthusiasm wherever we go; and yet what are we able to do for them, except give them money! I find this sympathy among the lowest: workmen and labourers whom I had never seen before to my knowledge and to whom I could only speak three or four words of comfort—and I can never find much else to say, it is always the same—and among the soldiers, although they must feel instinctively, in spite of never seeing me except in uniform, that I am no soldier at heart; and also among the students, the priests, the civic authorities and the higher functionaries. Yesterday we went round everywhere, to all the places appointed as refuges: not only the barracks and shops and factories, but even some of the rooms at the law-courts, two of the theatres and the prison, poor souls! And also St. Ladislas. From the Round Tower we had a view of the surrounding country: towards the east there was nothing but water and water, like a sea. My heart felt as though screwed tight into my breast.

"We went to the university also. I remembered most of the professors from two years ago, when I was here as an undergraduate.

"It was a terrible scene outside the town. Oh, Mamma, there were hundreds, there were thousands of corpses, laid out side by side on a meadow, as in a mortuary, before the burial, for identification! I saw harrowing scenes, my heart was torn asunder: troops of relations who sought or who, sobbing, had found. A terrible air of woe filled the whole atmosphere. I felt sick and turned quite pale, it required all my energy to prevent myself from fainting, but Herman put his arm through mine and supported me as well as he was able without ostentation, while a couple of doctors from among the group of physicians to whom I was speaking gave me something to smell. Oh, Mamma, it was a terrible spectacle, all those pallid, shapeless, swollen corpses, on the green grass, and, above, the sky, which had become deep blue again!

"I have informed the municipal council, in accordance with your wish and my father's, that you are each of you presenting a personal donation of a million florins and I presented my own at the same time. The whole world seems in sympathy with us; money is flowing in from every side, but the damage is like a pit that cannot be filled up. As you say, the donation of our Syrian friends is truly princely and oriental.

"What more have I to tell you? I really do not know; my brain is confused with a nightmare of ghastly visions and I have difficulty in thinking logically. But I promise you, my dear Mother, to do what I can and to do it with all my might; and all I ask is that you will send me a single word to tell me that you are not too dissatisfied with your boy.

"As my father desires, I will stay here another week; it seems to do the people good to see us, they love us so. They were enraptured when it was announced that after my departure you and Thera were coming to Altara. You with your soft hand will be able to do so much that we have omitted. How they do love us here! And why are we not always at St. Ladislas? Though the fortress is sombre, it is bright with their sympathy.

"But do not let me write to you so poetically in these distressful days, in which we should be practical. Herman's society does me a deal of good and I can do more when he is by my side. General Ducardi is a fine, indefatigable fellow, as always. The others have all been very willing and practical; and, if I may be allowed respectfully to differ from my Father, I am inclined to think that the municipal council does what it can. It is true, an English engineer told me that with better precautions and a more thorough supervision the Therezia Dyke would perhaps have held out; however, I don't know.

"Herman will accompany me on my journey through the provinces. We shall go to Lycilia and Vaza and so far as possible to the lowlands. These are of course in the worst case.

"I have just received the telegrams: the Marquis of Dazzara dismissed and the Duke of Mena-Doni—I don't like that man—governor of the capital! Lipara under martial law! And will my father succeed in preserving our house of peers by this dissolution of the house of deputies?

"Dearest Mother, his eminence has just sent to ask me to receive him. I do not want to keep him waiting and therefore close my letter hurriedly; with a fond embrace, I am, with fondest and most respectful love,

"your own boy,
"OTHOMAR."

CHAPTER II

1

The Province of Vaza also, lying to the north of the Altara Highlands, the Alpine range of the Gigants, was harassed in parts by the Zanthos. The capital, Vaza, was flooded. In the neighbourhood of the mountain-slopes the province had been spared. There vast terraces of vineyards lay, alternating with forests of chestnut-trees and walnut-trees and olives. The glittering white snow-line of the mountain-tops surged up against a dazzling blue sky, piercing it with its crests and biting long pieces out of the deep azure in ragged lines; it seemed to whet ice-teeth, gleaming white fangs, against the metal of the firmament, which was like burnished steel. There, enthroned on its rocks, twelve miles from the town, stood old Castel Vaza, the castle of the dukes of Yemena and counts of Vaza, surrounded by parks and woods, half castle, half citadel, strong, simple, medieval, rough in outline, with its four towers and its square patches of battlements, rounding off the horizon about it on every side and keeping it aloof. Near at hand, a swarm of little villages; in the distance, the towers and steeples, the huddled roofs of Vaza; still farther, in the circle of panorama that broadly girt the towers, the wide Zanthos, winding down to hurl itself into the sea, and Lycilia, white in the sun with its little squares of houses, set brilliantly on the blue of the water; then a second sea: the mountain-tops, surging away in snowy vistas and distant mists. And, also glittering in the sun, those strange lakes on the Zanthos: the water which the full river had vomited, the inundations....

The square castle, enclosing a courtyard in its four wings, has two more wings added at the back, in a newer style of more elegant renascence, and looking on the park, in which lie the ornamental basins, like oval dishes of liquid silver, set in emerald lawns. The fallow deer graze there, dreaming, as it were, and graceful, roaming slowly on slim legs: sometimes, suddenly, extending themselves, their heads thrown back, their eyes wild, they run some distance, a number of them, fleeing before an unseen terror; others, calmer, graze on, laconically, philosophically.

The dukes of Yemena and counts of Vaza are one of the oldest families of the empire; and their ancestral tree is rooted ages back, before the time of the first emperor of Liparia. The present duke, court-marshal and Constable of Liparia, has three children of his first marriage: the heir to his title, the young Marquis of Xardi, aide-de-camp to the emperor, and two daughters, younger, girls still, at a convent.

The duchess is alone at the castle. She is sitting in a large boudoir, built out with a triangular loggia, and looking over the park, the basins, the deer. A breeze is blowing outside; and the rapid clouds, which, like flaky spectres, like rags hidden beneath diaphanous veils, chase one another through the clear blue sky, trail their shadows, like quick eclipses, across the park, just tinting it with passing darkness, which darkens the deer in their turn and then makes them gleam brown again in the sun. It is silent outside; it is silent in the castle. The castle stands secluded; within, the servants move softly through the reception-rooms and corridors, speaking in whispers, in expectation of the august visitors.

Lunch is over. The duchess lies half-out-stretched on a couch and gazes at the deer. She is not yet dressed and wears a tea-gown, loose, with many folds: *vieux rose broché*, salmon-coloured plush and old lace. When she is alone, she likes plenty of light, from a healthy need of space and air; the curtains are drawn aside from the tall bow-windows and the shrillness of the spring sky comes streaming in. But the light does not suit her beauty; for, though her hair is still raven black, her complexion has the dullness of faded white roses; her eyes, which can be beautiful, large, liquid and dark, look full of lassitude, encircled with pale-yellow shadows; and very clearly visible are the little wrinkles at the side, the little grooves etched around the delicate nose, the lines that have lengthened the mouth and draw it down.

The duchess rises slowly; she passes through a door that leads to her bedroom and dressing-room and stays away for a few moments. Then she returns; in both hands, pressing it to her, with difficulty, she carries an obviously heavy casket and sets it on the table in front of the couch. The casket is of old wrought silver enriched with gilt chasing and great blue turquoises, of that costly renascence work which is not made nowadays. She selects a little straight, gold key from her bracelet and unlocks the casket. The jewels glisten—pearls, brilliants, sapphires, emeralds—and catch in their facets all the spring light of the sky, blue, white and yellow. But the duchess presses a spring unclosing a secret drawer, from which she takes two packets of letters and some photographs.

The photographs all show the face of a man no longer young, a strange face, half-dreamy, half-sensual, filled with great mystery and great charm. The photographs show him in the elaborate uniform of an officer of the throne-guards, in fancy-dress as a medieval knight, in flannels and in ordinary mufti. The duchess' eyes pass slowly from one to the other; she compares the likenesses, a sad smile about her mouth and melancholy in her eyes. Then she unties the ribbons of the letters, takes them out of the carefully preserved envelopes, unfolds them and reads here and there and reads again and refolds them....

She knows by heart the phrases that still tell her of a strange passion, the most fervent, the truest, the simplest and perhaps for that reason the strangest that she has ever felt, that has surrounded her with fairy meshes of fire. Though her eyes look out again at the deer—the sunshine streams like fluid gold over the park—between her and the peaceful landscape there rise up, transparent, in tenderly gleaming phantasmagorias, remembrances of the past, the pictures of that love, and it seems to her as though sparks are dancing before her eyes, as though brilliant curves and scintillations of light are swarming on every hand. She lives through past events in a few moments; then she closes her eyes, draws her hand over her forehead and thinks how sad it is that the past is nothing more than a little memory, which flies like dust and ashes through our souls which we sometimes endeavour, in vain, to collect in a costly urn. How sad it is that one cannot go on mourning, though one wish to, because life does not permit it! Nothing but that dust and ashes in her soul ... and those letters, those photographs....

She locks them away again and now gazes at the jewels. And she looks well into her own heart, sees herself exactly as she is, for she knows that she has been loyal, always, loyal to him and to herself: loyal when their love broke like a glittering rainbow of sparkling colours on a wide firmament and she became unwilling to see or to exist and withdrew from the court into this castle and let it be rumoured that a lingering illness was causing her to pine away. And she mourned and mourned, first sobbing and wringing her hands, then calmer in despair, then ... The deer had gone on grazing there, as though they always remained unchanged. But she....

She had been loyal, always: in her despair and also in what followed, in the abatement of that despair. Then she was saddest of all, because despair was able to abate. Then sad, because she still lived and felt vitality within her. Then ... because she began to grow bored. Because of all this a great despair had filled her strange soul, luxuriantly, as with the morbid blossoms of strange orchids. She hated, despised, cursed herself. But nothing changed in her. She was bored.

She led a solitary life at the castle. Her husband and her stepson were at Lipara; her stepdaughters, to whom she was much attached, were finishing their education at a convent, of which an imperial princess, a sister of the emperor, was abbess.

She was alone, she never saw anybody. And she was bored. Life awoke in her anew, for it had only slumbered, she had deemed it dead, had wished to bury it in a sepulchre around which her memories should stand as statues. Within herself, she felt herself to be what she had always been, in spite of all her love: a woman of the world, hankering after the glamour of imperial surroundings, that court splendour which fatally reattracts and is indispensable to those who have inhaled it from their birth as their vital air. And, at moments when she was not thinking of her despair, she thought of the Imperial, saw herself there, brilliant in her ripe beauty, made much of and adored as she had always been.

Then she caused her stepson, the Marquis of Xardi, to spread the rumour that she was convalescent. A month later, in the middle of the winter season, after a great court festival but before one of the intimate assemblies in the empress' own apartments, she requested an audience of Elizabeth.

Thus she beheld herself in true, clear truth and was deeply mournful in her poor soul filled with desire of love and desire of the world and humanity, because life insisted on continuing so cruelly, as in a mad triumphal progress, crushing her memories under its chariot-wheels, clattering through her melancholy with its trumpet-blasts, making her see the paltriness of mankind, the pettiness of its feeling, the littleness of its soul, which is nevertheless the only thing it has....

The duchess locks the twice-precious casket away again. She forgets what is going on about her, what is awaiting her; she gazes, dreams and lives again in the past, with the enjoyment which a woman finds in the past when she loses her youth.

There is a knock at the door, a footman appears and bows:

"Excellency, the cook begs urgently to be allowed to speak to you in person...."

"The cook?..."

She raises her beautiful face, dreaming, half-laughing, with its profile like Cleopatra's, so Egyptian in its delicacy and symmetry, settles herself a little higher on the couch and leans on her hand:

"Let him come in...."

Everything returns to her, reality, the actual day; and she smiles because of it and shrugs her shoulders: such is life.

The footman goes out; the cook enters in his white apron and white cap: he is nervous and, now that his mistress is already frowning her eyebrows because of his disrespectful costume, he begins to stammer:

"Forgive me, excellency...."

And he points with an unhappy face to his apron, his white sleeves....

And he complains that the head gamekeeper has not provided sufficient ortolans. He cannot make his pasty; he dares not take it upon himself, excellency.

She looks at him with her sphinx-like eyes; she has a great inclination to burst out laughing at his comical face, his despairing gestures, his outstretched arms, to laugh and also to cry wildly and loudly.

"What are we to do, excellency, what are we to do?"

The town is too far away; there is no time to send there before dinner and, for the matter of that, they never have anything in the town. Besides, it is really the steward's fault, excellency; the steward should have told her excellency....

"There are larks," she says.

"Those were to go to Lipara to-morrow, excellency, to his excellency the duke!"

The duchess shrugs her shoulders, laughing a little:

"It can't be helped, my friend. His imperial highness the Duke of Xara comes before his excellency, does he not? Make a *chaufroid* of larks."

Yes, that is what he had thought of doing, but he had not ventured to suggest it. Yes, that would do very well, admirably, excellency.

She gives another little laugh and then nods, to say that he can go. The cook, evidently relieved, bows and disappears. She rises, looks at herself in a mirror as she stands erect in her lazily creased folds of pink and salmon-colour and old lace, stretches her arms with a gesture of utter fatigue and rings for her maid, after which she enters her dressing-room. Does she want to laugh again ... or to cry again? She does not know; but she does know that she has to get dressed.... Whatever confront a person, love or ortolan-pasty, that person must dress, must dress and eat and sleep ... and after that the same again: dress ... and eat ... and sleep....

2

Three carriages, with postillions, bring Othomar, Herman and the others along the broad, winding, switchback road to Castel Vaza. It is five o'clock in the afternoon; the weather is mild and sunny, but not warm: a fresh breeze is blowing. The landscape is wide and noble; with each turn of the road come changes in the panorama of snow-clad mountains. The country is luxuriantly beautiful. The little villages through which they drive look prosperous: they are the duke's property. Between Vaza and the castle the land has been spared by the water: the overflowing of the Zanthos has inundated rather the eastern district. It is difficult here to think constantly of that dreadful flood and of the condition of Lipara yonder, which the emperor has proclaimed in state of siege. It is so beautiful here, so full of spring life; and the sunset after a fine, summery day is here devoid of sadness. The chestnut-trees waft their fresh green fans; and the sky is still like mother-of-pearl, though a dust of twilight is beginning to hover over it. A lively conversation is in progress between the princes, Ducardi and Von Fest, who sit in the first carriage: they talk with animation, laugh and are amused because the villagers sometimes, of course, salute them, as visitors to the castle, with a touch of the cap or a kindly nod, but do not know who they are. Prince Herman nods to a handsome young peasant-girl, who stays staring after them open-mouthed, and recalls the delightful big-game hunt last year when he was the duke's guest, together with the emperor and Othomar. They did not see the duchess that time: she was unwell.... General Ducardi tells anecdotes about the war of fifteen years ago.

And they all find some difficulty in fixing their faces in official folds when they drive through the old, escutcheoned gate over the lowered drawbridge into the long carriage-drive and are received by the chamberlain in the inner courtyard of the castle. This is prescribed by etiquette. The duchess must not show herself before the chamberlain, surrounded by the duke's whole household, has bidden the Duke of Xara welcome in the name of his absent master and offered the crown-prince a telegram from Lipara, which the steward hands him on a silver tray. This telegram is from the Duke of Yemena; it says that his service and that of his son, the Marquis of Xardi, about the person of his majesty the emperor, the Duke of Xara's most gracious father, prevent them from being there to receive their beloved crown-prince in their castle, but that they beg his imperial highness to look upon the house as his. The prince reads the telegram and hands it to his aide-de-camp, the Count of Thesbia. Then, conducted by the chamberlain, he ascends the steps and enters the hall.

Notwithstanding that it is still daylight outside, the hall is brilliantly lighted and resembles a forest full of palm-trees and broad-leaved ornamental plants. The duchess steps towards the crown-prince and breaks the line of her graciousness in a deep curtsey. He has seen her bow like this before. But perhaps she is still handsomer in this plain black velvet gown and Venetian lace, cut very low, her splendid bosom exposed, white with the grain of Carrara marble, her statuesque arms bare, a heavy train behind her like a wave of ink; a small ducal coronet of brilliants and emeralds in her hair, which is also black, with a gold-blue raven's glow.

She bids the princes welcome. Othomar offers her his arm. Prince Herman and the equerries follow them up the colossal staircase, through the hedge of flunkeys, who stand motionless with fixed eyes that do not seem to see. Then through a row of lighted rooms and galleries to a great reception-room, glittering with light from the costly rock-crystal chandelier, in which the candle-light coruscates and casts expansive gleams and shimmers over the marble mosaic of the floor and along the decorative mirrors, in their frames of heavy Louis-XV. arabesques, and the paintings by renascence masters on the walls.

A momentary standing reception is held, a miniature court: in their dazzling uniforms—for it was a delightful, though long drive from Vaza and the men had had time to change into their full-dress uniforms in the town—the equerries and aides come, one after the other, to kiss the duchess' hand; except the Gothlandic officers, she knows them all, nearly all intimately; she is able to speak an almost familiar word to each of them, while the gold of her voice melts between her laughing lips and her great, Egyptian eyes look out, strangely dreaming. So she stands for a moment as a most adorable hostess between the two princes, she, a woman, alone among these officers who surround them, in the midst of a cross-fire of compliments and badinage that sparkles around them all. Then the steward appears, while the doors open out and the table is revealed brightly glittering, and bows before his mistress as a sign that she is served. The duchess takes the crown-prince's arm; the gentlemen follow.

The dinner is very lively. They are an intimate circle, people accustomed to meet one another every day. The duchess sees that an easy tone is preserved, one of light familiarity, which restrains itself before the crown-prince, yet gives a suggestion of the somewhat cavalier roughness and *sans-gêne* that is the fashionable tone at court. The Gothlandic officers are evidently not in the secret; Von Fest, a giant of a fellow, looks right and left and smiles. For the rest, the duchess possesses this smart, informal manner in a very strong degree, but moderates herself now, although she does sometimes lean both her shapely elbows on the table. The crown-prince once more has that indescribable stiffness which makes things freeze around him; the ease which he displayed at Altara has again made way for something almost constrained and at the same time haughty; his smiles for the duchess are forced; and the handsome hostess in her heart thinks her illustrious guest an insufferable prig.

Possibly Othomar behaves as he does because of the conversations, which all focus themselves about the duchess and concern the gossip of the Imperial; the inundations are hardly mentioned, hardly either the state of siege in the capital; only a single word now and again recalls them. But for the greater part all this seems to be forgotten here, in these delightful surroundings, at this excellent dinner, under the froth of the soft gold lycilian from the duke's private vineyard. This lycilian is celebrated and they also celebrate it now: even the crown-prince touches glasses with the duchess with a courteous word or two, which he utters very ordinarily, but which they seem to think a most witty compliment, for they all laugh with flattering approbation, with glances of intelligence; and the duchess herself no longer thinks him so insufferable, but beams upon him with her full and radiant laugh. But what has he said? He is astounded at himself and at their laughter. He intended nothing but a commonplace; and....

But he remembers: it is always like that; and he now understands. And he thinks them feeble and turns to Ducardi and Von Fest; he forces the conversation and suddenly begins to talk volubly about the condition of the town of Vaza, which also has suffered greatly. Then about Altara. He gives the duchess a long description of the bursting of the Therezia Dyke. The duchess thinks him a queer boy; for an instant she fancies that he is posing; then she decides that for some reason or other he is a little shy; then she thinks that he has fine, soft eyes, looking up like that under his eyelids, and that he has a pleasant way of telling things. She turns right round to him, forgets the officers around her, asks questions and, with her elbows on the table and a goblet of lycilian in her hand, she listens attentively, hangs on the young imperial lips and feels an emotion. This emotion comes because he is so young and august and has those eyes and that voice. She is attracted by his hands, with their broad, delicate shape, as of an old strength of race that is wearing out; she notices that he looks now and then at his ring. And, becoming serious, she talks of the dreadful times, of all those thousands of poor people without a roof over their heads, without anything.... This is, however, only the second moment that she has thought of those thousands; the first was that short half-hour when the duke's chaplain was asking her for money and how she wished it bestowed.... She remembers that, at the time of this conversation with the chaplain, a cutter from Worth's was waiting for her to try on the very dress which she is now wearing and she thinks that life's accidents are really most interesting. She knows, in her inner consciousness, that this philosophy is as the froth of champagne and she herself laughs at it. Then she again listens attentively to Othomar, who is still telling of the nocturnal watch in St. Therezia's Church. The officers have grown quiet and are listening too. His imperial highness has made himself the centre of conversation and dethroned the duchess. She has noticed this too, thinks it strange of him but nice, above all does not know what she wants of him and is charmed.

3

After dinner a cosy gathering in two small drawing-rooms. One of them contains a billiard-table; and the duchess herself, gracefully pointing her cue, which she holds in her jewelled fingers, plays a game with Prince Herman, Leoni and young Thesbia. Sometimes, in aiming, she hangs over the green table with an incredible suppleness in her heavy lines; and the beautiful Carrara breast heaves the Venetian lace and the black velvet up and down at each rapid movement. In the other room, under a lamp of draped lace, Othomar and General Ducardi and the Gothlandic equerries are attentively engaged in studying on an accurately detailed ordnance-map the route which they are to follow to-morrow on horseback to the inundated villages. The steward and a footman go round with coffee and liqueurs.

When the game of billiards is over, the duchess comes into the next room with her gentlemen, laughing merrily. The prince and his officers look up, politely smiling, from their map, but she, bewitchingly:

"Oh, don't let me disturb you, highness!..."

She takes Dutri's arm for a stroll on the terrace outside. The doors are open, the weather is delicious: it is a little cool. The steward hangs a fur cloak over her bare shoulders. On the long terrace outside she walks with Dutri to and fro, to and fro, constantly passing the open doors and as constantly throwing a glance to the group under the lamp: bent heads and fingers that point with a pencil. Her step is light on the arm of the elegant equerry; her train rustles gaily behind her. She talks vivaciously, asks Dutri:

"How are you enjoying your tour?"

"Bored to death! Nothing and nobody amusing, except the primate's secretary!... Those Gothlanders are bores and so terribly provincial! And it's tiring too, all this toiling about! You see, I look upon it as war and so I manage to carry on; if I were to look upon it as times of peace, I should never pull through. Fortunately our reception has been tolerably decent everywhere. Oh, there is no doubt the crown-prince is making himself popular...."

"A nice boy," she says, interrupting him. "I had hardly seen him for a long time since, when he was studying at Altara; after that I only remember seeing him once or twice at the Imperial, shot up from a child like an asparagus-stalk and yet a mere lad. I remember it still: he flushed when I curtseyed to him. Then again lately, at Myxila's...."

Dutri is very familiar with the duchess: he calls her by her Christian name, he always flirts with her a little, to amuse himself, from swagger, without receiving any further favours; they know each other too well, they have been in each other's confidence too long and she looks upon him more as a *cavaliere servente* for trifling services and little court intrigues than as one for whom she could ever feel any sort of "emotion."

"*Ma chère Alexa*, take care!" says he, wagging his finger at her.

"Why?" she retorts, defiantly.

"As if I did not see...."

She laughs aloud:

"See what you please!" she exclaims, indifferently, with her voice of rough *sans-gêne*, which is in fashion. "No, my dear Dutri, you needn't warn me, I assure you! Why, my dear boy, I have two girls to bring out next year! In two years' time I may be a grandmamma. I have given up that sort of thing. I can't understand that there are women so mad as always to want that. And then it makes you grow old so quickly...."

Dutri roars; he can't restrain himself, he chokes with laughing....

"What are you laughing at?" she asks.

He looks at her, shakes his head, as though to say he knows all about it:

"Really, there's no need for you to play hide-and-seek like that with me, Alexa. I know as well as you do ... that you yourself are one of those mad women!..."

He bursts out laughing again; and this time she joins in:

"I?"

"Get out! You want that as much as you want food and sleep at regular intervals. You would have been dead long ago, if you had not had your periodical 'emotions'. And, as to growing old, you know you hate the very thought of it!"

"Oh no! I do what I can to remain young, because that's a duty which one owes to one's self. But I don't fight against it. And you shall see, when the time comes, that I shall carry my old age very gracefully...."

"As you carry everything."

"Thanks. Look here: when I begin to go grey, I shall put something on my hair that will make me grey entirely and I will powder it, do you see? That's all!"

"A good idea...."

"Dutri...."

He looked at her, understood that she wanted to ask him something. They walked on for an instant silently, in the dark; constantly walking to and fro, they each time passed twice through the light that fell in two wide patches through the doors on to the terrace. The park was full of black shadow and the great vases on the terrace shone vaguely white; above, the sky hung full of stars.

"What did you want to ask me?" asked the equerry.

She waited till they had passed through the light and were again walking in the darkness:

"Do you ever hear of him now?"

"Thesbia had a letter from him the other day, from Paris. Not much news. He's boring himself, I believe, and running through his money. It's the stupidest thing you can do, to run through your money in Paris. I think Paris a played-out hole. Of course it couldn't be anything else. A republic is nothing at all. So primitive and uncivilized. There were republics before the monarchies: Paradise, with Adam and Eve, was a republic of beasts and animals; Adam was president...."

"Don't be an idiot. What did he write?"

"Nothing particular. But what a mad notion of his, to send in his papers as captain of the guards! How did he come to do it? Tell me, what happened between you two?"

They were walking through the light again and she did not answer; then, in the darkness:

"Nothing," she said; and her voice no longer had that affected smartness of brutality and *sans-gêne*, but melted in a plaintive note of melancholy.

"Nothing?" said Dutri. "Then why...?"

"I don't know. We had talked a great deal together and so gradually began to feel that we could no longer make each other happy. I really can't remember the reason, really I can't."

"A question of psychology therefore. This comes of all that sentiment. You're both very foolish. Meddling with psychology when you're in love is very imprudent, because then you start psychologizing on yourselves and cut up your love into little bits, like a tart of which you are afraid you won't be able to get enough to eat. Practise psychology on somebody else, that's better: as I do on you, Alexa."

"Come, don't talk nonsense, Dutri. Don't you know anything more about him?"

"Nothing more, except that he has made himself impossible for our set. And that perhaps through your fault, Alexa, and through your psychology."

She walked silently, leaning on his arm; her mouth trembled, her Egyptian eyes grew moist:

"Oh!" she said; and she suddenly made the equerry stand still, grasped his arm tightly and looked him straight in the face with her moist eyes. "I loved him, I loved him, as I have never loved any one! I ... I still love him! If he were to write me one word, I should forget who I was, my husband, my position, I should go to him, go to him.... Oh, Dutri, do you know what it means, in our artificial existence, in which everything is so false around you, to ... to ... to have really loved any one? And to know that you have that feeling as a sheer truth in your heart? Oh, I tell you, I adore him, I still adore him ... and one word from him, one word...."

"Lucky that he's more sensible than you, Alexa, and will never say that word. Besides, he has no money: what would you do if you were with him? Go on the stage together? What a volcano you are, Alexa, what a volcano!"

He shook his foppish, curly head disapprovingly, adjusted the heavy tassels of his uniform. She took his hand, still serious, not yet relapsing into her tone of persiflage:

"Dutri, when you hear from him, will you promise to tell me about him? I sometimes hunger for news of him...."

She looked at him with such intense, violent longing, with such hunger, that he was startled. He saw in her the woman prepared to do all things for her passion. Then he smiled, flippant as always:

"What silly creatures you all are! Very well, I promise. But let us go in now, for the geographical studies seem to be finished and I am dying for a cup of tea...."

They went indoors. Busying herself at the tea-table, letting her fingers move gracefully over the antique Chinese cups, she straightway asked the crown-prince which road his highness proposed to take, feeling great concern about the inundated villages, the poor peasants, agreeing entirely in all things with the Duke of Xara, bathing in the sympathy which she gathered from his sweet, black, melancholy eyes—eyes from which she felt tempted to kiss all the melancholy away—bathing in his youthful splendour of empire....

Dutri helped her to sugar the tea. He watched her with interest: he knew her fairly well, she retained very little enigma for him; yet she always amused him and he always found in her a fresh subject for study.

4

It was one of the historic apartments of Castel Vaza, an ancient, sombre room in which the emperors of Liparia who had been guests of the dukes of Yemena had always slept on an old, gilt bed of state, raised five steps from the floor, a bed around which the heavy curtains of dark-blue brocade and velvet hung from an imperial crown borne by cherubs. On the walls were portraits of all the emperors and empresses who had rested there: the dukes of Yemena had always been much loved by their sovereigns and the pride of the ducal family was that every Liparian emperor had been at least one night its guest. Historical memories were attached to every piece of furniture, to every ornament, to the gilt basin and the gilt ewer, to everything; and the legends of his house rose one by one in Othomar's mind as he stretched himself out to rest.

He was very weary and yet not sleepy. He felt a leaden stiffness in his joints, as though he had caught cold, and a continuous shiver passed through his whole body, a mysterious quivering of the nerves, as if he were a tense string responding to a touch. The week spent at Altara, the subsequent five days at Vaza, the drives in the environs had tired him out. During the day he could not find a moment's time to yield to this fatigue, but at night, as he lay stretched for rest, it shattered him, without being followed by a healthy sleep.

He was used to his little camp-bed, on which he slept in his austere bedroom at the Imperial, the bed on which he had slept since childhood. The state-beds, at the Episcopal, at Vaza and now here, made him feel strange, laid-out and uncomfortable. His eyes again remained open, following the folds of the tall curtains, seeking to penetrate the shadows which the faint light of a silver lamp drove creeping into the corners. He began to hear a loud buzzing in his ears.

And he thought it curious to be lying here on this bed on which his ancestors had already lain before him. They all peered at him from the eight panels in the walls. What was he? An atom of life, a little stuff of sovereignty, born of them all; one of the last links of their long chain, which wound through the ages and led back to that mysterious, mystical origin, half-sacred, half-legendary, to St. Ladislas himself.... Would that same thing come after him also, a second chain which would wind into the future? Or...? And to what purpose was the ever-returning, endless, eternal renascence of life? What would be the end, the great end?...

Suddenly, like a vision, the night on the Therezia Square recurred to his mind, the thundering salute from the fort, thrice repeated, and the mighty, roaring onslaught of an approaching blackness, resembling a sea. Was it only a humming in his ears, or ... or was it really roaring on again? Did the black future come roaring on, in reply to his question as to the end, the great end, with the same sound of threatening waters which nothing could withstand? It burst through dykes; it dragged with it all that was thrown up as a protection, inexorable, and — with its grim, black, fateful frown and the sombre pleats of its inundations, which resembled a shroud trailing over everything that was doomed—it marched to where they stood, his kin, on their high station of majesty by the grace of God and of St. Ladislas; to where his father sat, on their age-old throne, crowned and sceptred and bearing the orb of empire in his imperial palm; and it did not seem to know that they were divine and sacred and inviolate: it seemed to care for nothing in its rough, sombre, indifferent, unbelieving, roaring profanation; for suddenly, fiercely, it dragged its black waves over them, dragged them with it—his father, his mother, all of them—and they were things that had been, they of the blood imperial, they became a legend in the glory of the new day that rose over the black sea....

His ancestors stared at him and they seemed to him to be spectres, themselves legends, falsities against which tradition would no longer act as a protection. They seemed to him like ghosts, enemies.... He opened wider his burning eyes upon their stiff, trained and robed or harnessed figures, which seemed to step towards him from the eight panels of the walls, in order to stifle him in their midst, to oppress him in a narrow circle of nightmare on his panting breast, with iron knees forcing the breath out of his lungs, with iron hands crushing his head, from which the sweat trickled over his temples.

Then he felt afraid, like a little child that has been told creepy stories, afraid of those ghosts of emperors, afraid of the glimpses of visions which again flashed pictures of the inundations before him: the meadow with the corpses, the men in the punt fishing up the woman. The corpses began suddenly to come to life, to burst out laughing, with slits of mouths and hollow eyes, as though they had been making a fool of him, as though there had been no inundations; and the dusk of the bed-chamber, filled with emperors, pressed down upon him as with atmospheres of nitrogen.

"Andro! Andro!" he cried, in a smothered utterance and then louder, as though in mortal anguish, "Andro! Andro!..."

The door at the end of the room was thrown open; the valet entered, alarmed, in his night-clothes. The reality of his presence broke through the enchantment of the night and exorcized the ghosts back into portraits.

"Highness!..."

"Andro, come here...."

"Highness, what's the matter?... How you frightened me, highness! What is it?... I thought...."

"What, Andro?"

"Nothing, highness. Your voice sounded so terribly hoarse! What's the matter?..."

"I don't know, Andro: I am ill, I think; I can't sleep...."

The man wiped Othomar's clammy forehead with a handkerchief:

"Will your highness have anything to drink? A glass of water?..."

"No, thank you, thank you.... Andro, can you come and sleep in here?"

"If you wish it, highness...."

"Yes, here, at the foot of my bed. I believe I'm not very well, Andro.... Bring your pillow in here."

The man looked at him. He was not much older than his prince. He had waited on him from childhood and worshipped him with the worship of a subject for majesty; he felt wholly bound to him, tied to him; he knew that the prince was not strong, but also that he never complained....

Growing suddenly angry, he turned to go to his room and fetch his pillow:

"No wonder, when they fag and tire you like this!" he cried, unable any longer to restrain his fury. "General Ducardi no doubt thinks that you have the same tough hide as himself!"

Muttering in his moustache, he went away, returned with his pillow and laid it on the step of the bed of state:

"Are you feverish?" he asked.

"No ... yes, perhaps a little. It will pass off, Andro. I ... I am...."

He dared not say it.

"I am a little nervous," he continued; and his eyes went anxiously round the room, where the emperors were once more standing quiet.

"Would you like a doctor fetched from Vaza?"

"No, no, Andro, by no means. What are you thinking of, to make such a disturbance in the middle of the night? Go to sleep now, down there...."

"Will you try to sleep also then, my 'princie'?" he asked, with the endearing diminutive which in his language sounded like a caress.

Othomar nodded with a smile and suffered him to shake up his pillows after the manner of a nurse.

"What a bed!" muttered Andro. "It might be a monument in a cemetery!..."

Then he lay down again, but did not sleep; he stayed awake. And, when Othomar asked, after an interval:

"Are you asleep, Andro?"

"Yes, your highness," he answered, "nearly."

"Is there anything murmuring in the distance? Is it water or ... or is it my fancy?"

The man listened:

"I can hear nothing, highness.... You must be a little feverish."

"Take a chair and come and sit by the head of the bed...."

The man did as he was told.

"And let me feel you near me: give me your hand, so...."

At last Othomar closed his eyes. In his ears the buzzing continued, still continued.... But under the very buzzing, while the lightness in his head lifted like a mist, the Crown-prince of Liparia fell asleep, his clammy hand in the hard hand of his body-servant, who watched his master's restless sleep in the quivering round the mouth, the jerking of the body, until, to quiet him, he softly stroked the throbbing forehead with his other hand, muttering compassionately, with his strange, national voice of caress:

"My poor princie!..."

The dawn rose outside; the daylight seemed to push the window-curtains asunder.

5

The next morning the duchess was to preside at the breakfast-table: she was in the dining-room with all the gentlemen when Othomar entered, as the last, with Dutri. His uniform of blue, white and silver fitted him tightly; and he saluted, smilingly, but a little stiffly, while Herman shook hands with him and the others bowed, the duchess curtseying deeply.

"How pale the prince looks!" Leoni said to Ducardi.

It was true: the prince looked very pale; his eyes were dull, but he bore himself manfully, ate a little fish, trifled with a salmi of game. Yet the prince's fatigue was so evident that Ducardi asked him, softly, across the table:

"Is your highness not feeling well?..."

All eyes were raised to Othomar. He wished to give the lie to their sympathy:

"I'm all right," he replied.

"Did your highness have a bad night?" continued Ducardi.

"Not very good," Othomar was compelled to acknowledge, with a smile.

The conversation continued, the duchess gave it a new turn; but after breakfast, on the point of departure—the horses stood saddled in the courtyard—Ducardi said, bluntly:

"We should do better not to go, highness."

Othomar was astonished, refused to understand.

"You look a little fatigued, highness," added Ducardi, shortly; and, more softly, deprecatingly, "And it's not surprising either, that the last few days have been too much for you. If your highness will permit me, I would recommend you to take a rest to-day."

Already a soft feeling of relaxation overcame the prince; he felt too much delighted at this idea of rest to continue his resistance. Yet his conscience pricked him at the thought of his father: a feeling of shame in case the emperor should hear of his exhaustion, which seemed so clearly evident.

And he absolutely insisted that the expedition should not be abandoned altogether. He yielded to Ducardi in so far as not to go himself and to take repose, provided that they thought he needed it; but he urgently begged Prince Herman and the others to follow the route planned out for that day and to go. And this he said with youthful haughtiness, already relieved at the thought of the day of repose before him—a whole day, unexpectedly!— but above all afraid of allowing his joy to be perceived and therefore sulking a little, as though he wished to go too, as though he thought General Ducardi foolish, with his advice....

The gentlemen went. The duchess herself conducted Othomar to the west wing, pressed him to rest in her own boudoir. Through the windows of the gallery Othomar saw Herman and the others riding away; he followed them for an instant with his eyes, then went on with the duchess and across the courtyard saw a groom lead back to the stables the horse that had been saddled for him, patting its neck. He was still disturbed by mingled emotions: the pleasant anticipation of resting, a little anxiety lest he should betray himself, a certain feeling of shame....

In the boudoir the duchess left him alone. It was quiet there; outside, the lordly fallow-deer grazed peacefully. The repose of the boudoir of a woman of the world, with the rich, silent drapery of silken stuffs, the inviting luxury of soft furniture, the calm brilliancy of ornaments each a costly object of art, surrounded him with a hushed breathlessness, like a haze of muslin, fragrant with an indefinable, gentle emanation, which was that woman's very perfume. The indolence of this present moment suddenly overwhelmed Othomar, a little strangely, and dissolved his thoughts in gentle bewilderment. He felt like a runaway horse that has suddenly been pulled up and stands still.

He sat down for a minute and looked out at the deer. Then he rose, reflected whether he should ring and thought better to look round for himself. On the duchess' little writing-table—Japanese lacquer inlaid with mother-of-pearl landscapes and ivory storks—he found a sheet of paper, a pencil.

And he wrote:

"To HER MAJESTY ELIZABETH
"EMPRESS OF LIPARIA.

"CASTEL VAZA,
"—*April*, 18—.

"Pray do not be alarmed if the newspapers exaggerate and say that I am ill. I was a little fatigued and Ducardi advised me to rest to-day. Herman and the others have gone on; to-morrow I hope myself to lead our second expedition from here. The day after that we go to Lycilia.

"OTHOMAR."

Then he rang and, when the footman appeared:

"My valet, Andro."

In a few moments Andro appeared. "Ask for a horse, Andro," said Othomar, "ride to Vaza and dispatch this telegram as quickly as you can to her majesty the empress...."

Andro went out and the strange, indolent vacancy overcame Othomar once more. The sun shone over the park, the deer gleamed with coats like cigar-coloured satin. The last fortnight passed once more before Othomar's eyes. And it was as though, in the vistas of that very short past, he saw spreading out like one great whole, one vast picture of human distress, the misery which he had beheld and endeavoured to soften. And the great affliction that filled the land made his heart beat full of pity. A slack feeling of melancholy, that there was so much affliction and that he was so impotent, once more rose within him, as it never failed to do when he was alone and able to reflect. Then he felt himself small, insignificant, fit for nothing; and something in his soul fell feebly, helplessly from a factitious height, without energy and without will. Then that something lay there in despair and upon it, heavy with all its sorrow, the whole empire, crushing it with its weight.

Serious strikes had broken out in the eastern quicksilver-mines, beyond the Gigants. He remembered once making a journey there and suffering when he saw the strange, ashy-pale faces of the workmen, who stared at him with great, hollow eyes and who underwent a slow death through their own livelihood, in a poisonous atmosphere. And he knew that what he had then seen was a holiday sight, the most prosperous sight that they were able to show him; that he would never see the black depths of their wretchedness, because he was the crown-prince. And he could do nothing for them and, if they raised their heads still more fiercely than they were doing now, the troops, which had already started for the district, would shoot them down like dogs.

He panted loudly, as though to pant away the weight upon his chest, but it fell back again. The image of his father came before his mind, high, certain, conscious of himself, unwavering, always knowing what to do, confident that majesty was infallible, writing signatures with big, firm letters, curtly: "Oscar." Everything signed like that, "Oscar," was immaculate in its righteousness as fate itself. How different was he, the son! Then did the old race of might and authority begin to yield with him, as with a sudden crack of the spine, an exhaustion of the marrow?

Then he saw his mother, a Roumanian princess, loving her near ones so dearly; womanliness, motherliness personified, in their small circle; to the people, haughty, inaccessible, tactless as he was, unpopular, as he was, too, at least in Lipara and the southern part of the empire. He knew it: beneath that rigid inaccessibility she concealed her terror, terror when she sat in an open carriage, at the theatre, at ceremonial functions, or in church, or even at visits to charitable institutions. This terror had killed within her all her great love for humanity and had morbidly concentrated her soul, which was inclined by nature to take a wider outlook, upon love for that small circle of theirs. And beneath this terror hid her acquiescence, her expectation of the catastrophe, the upheaval in which she and hers were to perish!...

He was their son, the heir to their throne: whence did he derive his impotent hesitation, which his father did not possess, and his love for their people, which his mother no longer possessed? His ancestors he knew only by what history had taught him: in the earlier middle-ages, barbarian, cruel; later, displaying a refined sensuality; one monarch, a weakling, ruled entirely by favourites, a *roi-fainéant*, under whom the empire had fallen a prey to intestinal divisions and foreign greed; afterwards, more civilized, a revival of strength, a reaction of progress after decline, followed by the glory and greatness of the empire to the present day.... To the present day: to him came this inheritance of greatness and glory. How would he handle it, how would he in his turn transmit it to his son?

Then he felt himself so small, so timid that he could have run away somewhither, away from the gaping eyes of his future obligations....

6

The luncheon had all the intimacy of a most charming *tête-à-tête*, served in the small dining-room, with only the steward waiting at table. The duchess enquired very sympathetically how Othomar was; the prince already felt really rested, showed a good appetite, was gay and talkative, praised the cook and the famous lycilian wine. When the duchess after luncheon proposed to him to go for a small excursion in the neighbourhood, he thought it an excellent idea. He himself wished to ride—he knew that the duchess was an excellent horsewoman—but Alexa dissuaded him, laughingly, said that she was afraid of General Ducardi, who had recommended the prince to rest, and thought that a little drive in an open carriage would be less tiring. She had remembered betimes that a riding-habit made her look old and heavy; and she was very glad when the prince gave way.

The weather had remained delightful: a mild sun in a blue sky. The landscape stretched wide, the mountains stood shrill and steep, pointing their ice-laden crests into the ether. The drive had all the charm of an incognito free from etiquette, with the prince, in his undress uniform, seated beside the duchess, in a simple, dark gown of mauve corduroy velvet, in the elegant, light victoria, on which the coachman sat alone, without a footman, setting the two slender bays briskly about. The sun gleamed in patches over the horses' sleek hides and cast its reflections in the varnish of the carriage, in the facets of the cut-glass lamps, on the coachman's tall hat and in the buttons of Othomar's uniform. All this sparkle scintillated with short, bright flashes; and thus, lightly flickering, the carriage glided along the road, through a couple of villages, whose inhabitants saluted their duchess, but did not know who the simple young officer was, sitting beside her. A breeze had dried away the dampness of the preceding days and light clouds of dust blew up from under the quick-rolling wheels.

The duchess talked fluently, of Lipara, the emperor, the empress. She possessed the tact of knowing intuitively what to say and what to speak about, when she was anxious to please. Her voice was a charm. She was sometimes capable of great simplicity and naturalness, generally when she was not thinking of making an impression. Intuitively she assumed towards the prince, to make him like her, that same simplicity which was her nature. It made her seem years younger: the smart brusqueness that was in fashion flattered her much less and made her appear older and even vulgar, whereas now she grew refined in the natural distinction of an ancient race. The little black veil on her hat hid the ugly wrinkles about her eyes, which gleamed through it like stars.

The prince remembered stories told by his equerries—including Dutri—about the duchess; he remembered names mentioned in a whisper. He did not at this minute believe in these slanders, as he considered them to be. Sensible as he was to sympathy, he was won over by hers, which he read in her intuitively; and it made him think well and kindly of her, as he thought of all who liked him.

The carriage had been going between terraces of vineyards, when suddenly, as though by surprise, it drove past a castle, half-visible through some very ancient chestnut-trees.

"What estate is that?" asked the prince. "Who are your neighbours, duchess?"

"No one less than Zanti, highness," replied the duchess: she shivered, but tried to jest. "Balthazar Zanti lives here, with his daughter."

"Zanti! Balthazar Zanti!" cried Othomar, in a tone of astonishment.

He stood up and looked curiously at the castle, which lay hidden behind the chestnut-trees:

"But how is it, duchess, that last year, when I was hunting here with the emperor, with the duke, I never heard of Prince Zanti or that he lived here?"

The duchess laughed:

"Presumably, highness, because the duke's covers lie in the opposite direction"—she made a vague gesture—"and you never drove past this way and because his majesty will never suffer the name of Balthazar Zanti to be uttered in his presence."

"But none of the equerries...."

The duchess laughed still more merrily, looked at the prince, who was also chuckling, and said:

"It is certainly unpardonable of them not to have informed you more fully of the curiosities in the province of Vaza. But ... now that I think of it, highness, it's quite natural. The castle was empty last year: Zanti was travelling about the country, making speeches. You remember, they were afterwards forbidden by law. His name, therefore, had no local significance here at the time...."

The prince was still staring at the castle, which never came fully into view, when the carriage, in a turn of the road, almost touched a little group as it drove past them, against the slope of a vineyard: an old man, a young girl, a dog. The girl was frail, slender, pale, fair-haired, dressed in furs in spite of the sun and retaining beneath them a certain morbid elegance; she sat on the grass, wearing a dark fur toque on her silvery fair hair; her long, white hand, ungloved, soothingly and insistingly patted the curly head of the retriever, which barked at the carriage. Next to her stood a tall, erect old man, looking eccentric in a wide, grey smock-frock: a grey giant, with a heavy beard and sombre eyes, which shone with a dull light from under the brim of a soft felt hat. The dog barked; the girl bowed—she recognized the duchess as a neighbour—without knowing who the prince was; the old man, however, looked straight before him, frowning and making no sign. The carriage rattled past.

"That was Zanti," whispered the duchess.

"Zanti!" repeated the prince. "And how long has he been living here?"

"Only a very short time: I believe the doctors think the air of Vaza good for his daughter."

"Was that young girl his daughter?"

"Yes, highness. I have seen her once before; she appears to be delicate."

"Prince Zanti, is he not?"

"Certainly, highness; but, by his own wish, Zanti quite plain.... Titles are all nonsense in the nineteenth century, highness."

She jested and yet felt a silent shudder, she knew not why. She thought it ominous that Zanti had come to live so near to Castel Vaza. Shivering, she gave a quick side-glance at the prince. She perceived a strange pensiveness drawing over his face like a shadow. Then, to change the conversation and to think no longer of that horrid man:

"You are looking much better, highness, than you did this morning. The air has done you good...."

She suppressed her shiver. The prince, on the other hand, remained strange: a sudden emotion seemed to be stirring within him. When they were back at the castle, in the boudoir, the duchess offered herself to make the prince a cup of tea. He stood looking out of the window at the deer, but, while she busied herself with the crested, gilt array of her tea-table, she saw him turn pale, white as chalk—as he had looked that morning—his eyes dilating strangely:

"What is the matter, highness?" she cried, in alarm, approaching him.

He turned towards her, tried to laugh:

"I beg your pardon, duchess; I am very discourteous ... to behave like this, but ... but that man took me by surprise." He laughed. "I did not know that he was here; and then the air ... that rarefied air...."

He put his hand to his forehead; she saw him grow paler, his blood seemed to be running out of him, he staggered....

"Highness!" she cried.

But Othomar, groping vaguely with his hand for a support, fell up against her; she caught him in her arm, against her bosom, mortally frightened, and saw that he had swooned. A thin sweat stood on his forehead; his eyes closed beneath their weary lids, as though they were dying away; his mouth was open without breathing.

The duchess was violently alarmed; she was mortally frightened lest anything serious should happen to the Duke of Xara, alone with her in the castle; she suddenly felt that the future of Liparia was entrusted to the support of her arms; she already saw the prince lying dead, herself disgraced at the Imperial.... All this flashed across her brain at the first moment. But she looked at him long; and a gentle expression overspread her face: pride, that the Duke of Xara lay there half-fainting on her shoulder, and sudden passion, containing much motherliness and pity, blended into a strange feeling in her soul. She softly smoothed back his hair, wiped his perspiring forehead with her handkerchief.... And the strange sensation became still stranger within her, intenser in its two constituent parts: intenser in pride, intenser in compassionate love, that of a mistress and mother in one. Then, with a smile, she pressed the handkerchief, lightly moistened with the imperial sweat, to her trembling lips. The soft aroma of the moisture seemed to intoxicate her with a fragrance of virile youth.... She thought of the letters and photographs in the silver casket with the turquoises. A deep melancholy, because of life, smarted through her soul; yet more of her memories seemed to fly away like dust. Then, refusing to yield any longer to this melancholy, she bent her head and, serious now, giving herself to the present, which revived her with new happiness, she pressed her lips, trembling still more than before, on Othomar's mouth. For a moment she lingered there; her eyes closed; then she gave her kiss.

They opened their eyes together, looked at each other. Earnestly sombre, almost tragically, she flashed her glance into his. He said nothing, remained gazing at her, still half in her arms. The colour came mantling back to his cheeks. Their eyes imbibed one another. He felt the unknown opening before him, he felt himself being initiated into the world of knowledge which he suspected in her and did not know of himself. But he felt no joy because of it; her eyes continued sombre. Then he merely took her hand, just pressed it in a solitary caress and said, his eyes still gazing into her deep, quiet, dark glances of passion, his features still rigid with surprise:

"I was feeling a little giddy, I fear, just now? Please forgive me, duchess...."

She too continued to look at him, at first sombrely, then in smiling humility. Her pride soared to its climax with one beat of its wings: the mouth of her future emperor was still sealed with her kiss! Her love touched her inner life as a wafting breeze skims over a lake, rippling its surface into utter silver with a single fresh gust and stirring it to its very depths; she worshipped him because of his youthful majesty, which so graciously accepted her kiss without further acknowledgment, because of his imperial candour, his boyish voice, his boyish eyes, the pressure of his hand: the only thing he had given her; and she experienced all this as a very strange, proud pleasure: the delight of assimilating that candid youth, that maiden manhood, as a magic potion that should restore her own youth to her.

7

They dined late that evening, as they had waited for Herman and the others. The conversation at table turned upon the condition of the lowlands, upon the peasants, who had lost their all. The duchess was silent; the conversation did not interest her, but her silence was smiling and tranquil.

That evening Othomar again studied the map with Ducardi, under the lace-covered lamp. The evening had turned cold, the terrace-doors were closed. The duchess did not feel inclined for billiards, but sat talking softly with Dutri in the second drawing-room. She looked superb, serene as a statue, in her dress of old lace, pale-yellow, her white bosom rising evenly with her regular breathing; a single diamond star gleamed in her front hair.

Othomar pointed with the pencil across the map:

"Then we can go like this, along this road.... Look, General Ducardi; look here, Colonel von Fest: this is where I drove this afternoon with the duchess; and here, I believe, is where Zanti lives. Did you know that?"

The officers looked up, looked down at the spot to which the crown-prince pointed, expressed surprise:

"I thought that he lived in the south, in Thracyna," said the young Count of Thesbia.

Othomar repeated what the duchess had told him.

"Zanti!" cried Herman. "Balthazar Zanti? Why, but then it is he!... I was talking this afternoon to a party of peasants; they told me of the new huts which a new landlord was fitting up in the neighbourhood, but they spoke in dialect and I could not understand them clearly; I thought they said Xanti and I never suspected that it could be Balthazar Zanti. So he's the man!"

"Huts?" asked Othomar.

"Yes, a village of huts, it seems; they said he was so rich and so generous and was housing I don't know how many peasants, who had lost all that they possessed."

"I now remember reading in the papers that Zanti had gone to live at Vaza," said Leoni.

"I should like to see those huts: we can take them on our way to-morrow," said Othomar.

General Ducardi compressed his bushy eyebrows:

"You know, highness, that his majesty is anything but enamoured of Zanti and is even thinking of exiling him. It would perhaps be more in accordance with his majesty's views to ignore what Zanti is doing here for the moment."

Othomar, however, was not disposed to yield to the general; a youthful combativeness welled in his breast.

"But, general, to ignore anybody's good work in these times is neither gracious nor politic."

"I am convinced that, if his majesty knew that Zanti was occupying his castle here, he would have specially requested your highness to hold no communication with the man," said Ducardi, with emphasis.

"I am not so sure of that, general," said Othomar, drily. "I believe, on the contrary, that, if his majesty knew that Zanti was doing so much for the victims of the inundations, his majesty would overlook a good deal of his amateur communism."

Ducardi gnawed his moustache with a wry smile:

"Your highness speaks rather light-heartedly of that amateur communism. Zanti's theories and practice are more than mere dilettantism...."

"But, general," rejoined Othomar, gently, "I really do not understand why Zanti's socialism need prevent us at this moment—I repeat, at this particular moment—from appreciating what he is doing, nor why it need interfere with our visiting his huts, considering that we have come to Vaza to inform ourselves of everything that concerns the inundations...."

Ducardi looked at him angrily. He was not accustomed to being contradicted like this by his highness. The others listened. The duchess herself, attracted by the discussion, amid which she heard Othomar's voice ringing with youthful authority, had approached with Dutri, curiously.

"To say the least of it, it could do no harm just to see those huts: I must grant my cousin as much as that, general," said Herman of Gothland, who was beginning to like Othomar.

Von Fest also supported this view, convincingly, roundly, honestly, thought that they could do no less, having regard to the victims whom Zanti had housed. Every one now gave his opinion: Leoni thought it impossible that the crown-prince should visit Vaza and not those huts; it would look as though his highness were afraid of a bugbear like Zanti. The fact that Othomar was contradicting Ducardi gave them all grounds for thwarting the old general, who hitherto had conducted the expedition with a sort of military tyranny which had frequently annoyed them. Even Dutri, who as a rule was rather indifferent, joined forces with them, cynically, his eyes gleaming because Ducardi for once was being put in his place. He winked at the duchess.

And only Siridsen and Thesbia took Ducardi's side, hesitating because the general declared with such conviction that the emperor's will would be different from his son's wish; especially Thesbia:

"I can't understand why the prince insists so," he whispered to the duchess in alarm. "Ducardi's right: you yourself know how the emperor loathes Zanti...."

The duchess shrugged her handsome shoulders with a smile, listening to Othomar, whom she heard defending himself, supported by ejaculations and nods from the others.

"Well," she heard Ducardi answer, drily, "if your highness absolutely insists that we should go to Zanti's, we will go; I only hope that your highness will always remember that I did not agree with you in this matter...."

The Duke of Xara now answered laughingly, was the first to make peace after this victory; and, as to the rest of the route to Lycilia, which they worked out on the map, he agreed with the general in everything, with little flattering intonations of approval and appreciation of his penetrating and practical judgement....

"He may not have the makings of a great commander," whispered Dutri to the duchess, "but he will turn out a first-rate little diplomatist...."

But Ducardi was inwardly very angry. For a moment he thought of ascertaining the emperor's wishes by a secret telegram, but he rejected this idea, as it would make a bad impression at the Imperial if the Duke of Xara were not left free in such an apparent trifle. He therefore only attempted, next morning, once more to dissuade Othomar from the visit, but the prince held firm.

"You seem very much opposed to this expedition, general," said Von Fest. "Isn't it really quite reasonable?"

"You don't know the prejudice his majesty has against that man, colonel," replied the general. "As I have told you before, his majesty is thinking of exiling him and is sure to do so when he hears that he has now shut himself in his castle, doubtless with the object of stirring up the peasantry, as he has already stirred up the workmen in the towns. The man is a dangerous fanatic, colonel: dangerous especially because he has money with which to put his visions into practice. He instigates the lower orders not to fulfil their military duties because it is written: 'Thou shalt not kill.' He looks upon marriage as a useless sacrament; and I have heard that his followers simply come to him and that he marries them himself, with a sort of blessing, which in its turn is based upon a text, I forget which. He is always writing socialistic pamphlets, which are promptly seized and suppressed, and he makes seditious speeches. And the man is even standing for the house of deputies!"

"One who abjures his title a member of the house of deputies!" smiled Von Fest.

"Oh, his doctrine swarms with such inconsistencies!" growled Ducardi. "He will tell you of course that, so long as there is nothing better than the house of deputies, he is content to be a member of it. And the crown-prince wants to take notice of what a man like that does!"

Von Fest shrugged his shoulders:

"Let him be, general. The prince is young. He wants to know and see things. That's a good sign."

"But ... the emperor will never approve of it, colonel!" thundered the general, with an oath.

Again Von Fest shrugged his shoulders:

"Nevertheless I should not dissuade him any longer, general. If the prince wants a thing, let him have it, it will do him good.... And, if he gets blown up by his father afterwards, that will do him good too, by way of reaction."

Ducardi looked him straight in the face:

"What do you think of our prince?" he asked, point-blank.

Von Fest returned the general's glance, smilingly, looking straight into his searching eyes. He was honest by nature and upright, but enough of a courtier to be able to dissimulate when he thought necessary:

"A most charming lad," he replied. "But life—or rather he himself—will have to change him very much if he is to hold his own ... later on."

The officers understood each other. Ducardi heaved a deep sigh:

"Yes, there are difficult times coming," he said, with an oath.

"Yes," answered the Gothlandic colonel, simply.

The princes mounted their horses in the courtyard; they took the same road along which Othomar had driven with the duchess the previous afternoon past Zanti's castle. Leoni had learnt where the huts lay; the mountains began to retreat, the road wound curve after curve beneath the trampling hoofs of the horses. Suddenly the Zanthos spread itself out on the horizon: the wide expanse of flooded water, one great lake under the broad, gleaming, vernal sky.

"That must be they," said Leoni.

His finger pointed to a hamlet of long wooden buildings, evidently newly built, smelling of fresh timber in the morning breeze. As they rode nearer, they saw carpenters and masons; a whole work-yard came into view, full of busy movement, with stacks of red bricks and piles of long planks. Singing was heard, with a pious intonation, as of psalms.

Ducardi, whose custom was always to ride in front, to the left of the crown-prince, deliberately reined in his horse, allowed the others to come up with him; Othomar perceived that he did not wish to act on this occasion. He thought it petty of the general and said to Thesbia:

"Ask if Zanti is here."

The aide-de-camp turned and put the question to a sort of foreman. None of the workpeople had saluted; the equerries doubted whether they had recognized the crown-prince. Yes, Zanti was there. Plain "Zanti." Very well, he would fetch him.

The man went. He was long away. Othomar, waiting with the others on horseback, already began to find his position difficult, lost his tact, assumed his stiff rigidity, talked in forced tones to Herman. He found it difficult to wait when one had never done so hitherto. It made him nervous and he made his horse, which was tugging at the reins with skittish movements of its head, nervous too and was already thinking whether it would not be better to ride on....

But just then Zanti, with the foreman who had called him, approached, slowly, making no effort to hurry. He looked under his hand from a distance at the group of officers on horseback, flashing in the sunlight; stood still; asked the foreman some question or other; looked again.

"The unmannerly fellow!" muttered Thesbia.

The aide-de-camp rode up to him angrily, spoke in a loud voice of his imperial highness the Duke of Xara; the duke wished to see the huts.

"They are not huts," said Zanti, in peevish contradiction.

"What then?" asked the aide, haughtily.

"Dwellings," answered Zanti, curtly.

Thesbia shrugged his shoulders with annoyance. But the crown-prince himself had ridden up and saluted Zanti before the latter had vouchsafed any greeting:

"Will your excellency give us leave to look at what you are doing for the victims of the inundations?" he asked, politely, gently, graciously.

"I'm not an excellency," muttered the grey-beard, "but, if you like to look, you can."

"We should like to," replied Othomar, a little haughtily, "but not unless we have your entire approval. You are the master on your own estate; and, if our visit is unwelcome, we will not force our presence on you."

Zanti looked him in the eyes:

"I repeat, if you like to look round, you can. But there is not much to see. Everything is so simple. We make no secret of what we do. And the estate is not mine: it belongs to all of them."

Othomar dismounted, the others followed; with difficulty Leoni and Thesbia found a couple of boys to hold the horses in return for a tip.

Othomar and Herman had already walked ahead with the old man:

"I hear that you are doing much good work to mitigate the disaster of the inundations," said Othomar.

"The inundation is not a disaster."

"Not a disaster!" asked Herman, surprised. "What then?"

"A just punishment of heaven. And there will be more punishments. We live in sinful times."

The princes exchanged a quick glance; they saw that the conversation would not go very easily.

"But the sinners whom heaven punishes you assist for all that, Mr. Zanti," said Herman. "For all these huts...."

"Are not huts. They are sheds, workshops or temporary dwellings. They will grow into a settlement, if such be God's will ... to enable men to live simply, by their work. Life is so simple, but man has made it so strange and complicated."

"But you take in the peasants who have lost their all through the inundations?" Herman persisted.

"I don't take them. When they feel their sins, they come to me and I save them from destruction."

"And do they not come to you also without feeling their sins, because they feel that they will get food and lodging for nothing?"

"They get no food and lodging for nothing: they have to work here, sir!" said the old man. "And perhaps more than you, who walk about in a uniform.... They are paid, according to the amount of work they do, out of the common fund. They are building here and I build with them. Do you see this tree here and this axe? I was employed in felling down this tree when you came and interrupted me."

"A capital exercise," said Herman. "You look a vigorous man."

"So you say you are forming a settlement here?" asked Othomar.

"Yes, sir. The cities are corrupt; life in the country is purifying. Here they live; farther on lies arable land, which I give them, and pasture-land; I shall buy cattle for them."

"So you are simply trying to recruit farmers here?" asked Herman.

"No, sir!" answered the grey-beard gruffly. "I recruit no farmers; they are not my farmers. They are their own farmers. They work for themselves and I am a simple farmer like them. We are all equal...."

"You are a simple farmer," Prince Herman echoed, "yet you live in a castle."

"No, young man," replied Zanti, "I do not live in a castle; I live *here*; my daughter lives there by herself. She is ill.... She would not be able to stand an alteration in her mode of life, or any deprivation. But she will not live long...."

He glanced up, looked at the Princes alternately, askance, almost anxiously:

"She is my only weakness, I think," he said, in a faint, deprecating voice. "She is my sin; I have called in doctors for her and believe in what they say and prescribe. You see, she would not be able to do it ... to follow me in all things, for she has too much of the past in her poor blood. For her, a castle and comfort are necessities, vital necessities. Therefore I leave her there.... But she will not live long.... And then I shall sell it and divide the money, every penny of it, among them all.... You see, that is my weakness, my sin; I am only human...."

The princes saw him display emotion; his hands trembled. Then he seemed to feel that he had already spoken to them too much and too long of what lay nearest to his heart, his sin. And he pointed to the buildings, explained their uses....

"I have read some of your pamphlets, Mr. Zanti," said the crown-prince. "Do you apply your ideas on matrimony here?"

"I apply nothing," the grey-beard growled, resuming his tone of contradiction. "I leave them free to do as they please. If they wish to get married according to your law, they can; but, if they come to me, I bless them and let them go in peace, for it is written, 'Again I say to you, that if two of you shall consent upon earth, concerning any thing whatsoever they shall ask, it shall be done for them by my father who is in heaven. For where there are two or three gathered together in my name, there am I in the midst of them.'"

"And how do you rule so many followers?" asked Herman.

"I don't rule them, sir!" roared the old man, clenching his fists, his face red with fury. "I am no more than any of them. The father has authority in his own household and the old men give advice, because they have experience: that is all. Life is so simple...."

"As you picture it, but not in reality," objected Herman.

Zanti looked at him angrily, stopped still, to be able to talk with greater ease, and, passionately, violently, exclaimed:

"And do you in reality find it better than I picture it? I do not, sir, and I hope to turn my picture into reality. You and yours once, ages ago, made your picture reality; now it is the turn of us others: your reality has lasted long enough...."

Othomar, haughtily, tried to say something in opposition; the old man, however, suddenly turned to him and, gently though roughly, said, his penetrating, fanatical voice which made Othomar shudder:

"For you, sir, I feel pity! I do not hate you, although you may think I do. I hate nobody. The older I have grown, the less I have learned to hate, the more softness has entered into me. See here: I hear something in your voice and see something in your eyes that ... that attracts me, sir. I tell you this straight out. It is very foolish of me, perhaps, to talk like this to my future emperor. But it is so: something in you attracts me. And I feel pity for you. Do you know why? Because the time will come!"

He suddenly pointed upwards, with a strange impressiveness, and continued:

"The hour will come. Perhaps it is very near. If it does not come in your father's reign, it will come in your reign or your son's. But come it will! And therefore I feel pity for you. For you will not have enough love for your people. Not enough love to say to them, 'I am as all of you and nothing more. I will possess no more than any of you, for I do not want abundance while you suffer need. I will not rule over you, for I am only a human being like yourselves and no more human than you.' Are you more human? If you were more, then you would be entitled to rule, yes, then, then ... See here, young man: you will never have so much love for your people as to do all this, oh, and more still and more! You will govern and possess abundance and wage war. But the time will come! Therefore I have pity for you ... although I oughtn't to!"

Othomar had turned pale; even Herman gave a little shudder. It was more because of the oracular voice of the man who was prophesying the doom of their sovereignty than because of his words. But Herman shook off his shudder and, angrily, haughtily:

"I cannot say that you are polite to your *guests*, Mr. Zanti," he said. "I do not speak of his imperial highness...."

Zanti looked at Othomar:

"Forgive me," he said. "I spoke like that for your sake. Your eyes are like my daughter's. That's why I spoke as I did."

Herman burst out laughing:

"A valid reason, no doubt, Mr. Zanti."

Othomar, however, signed to him to cease his tone of persiflage and also with a glance restrained his equerries, who had listened to Zanti's oracular utterances in speechless indignation: the old man had addressed Othomar almost in a whisper. His last words, however, which resounded with emotion, changed this indignation into bewilderment, calmed their anger, made them regard the prophet as half a madman, whose treason the crown-prince was graciously pleased to excuse. And the officers looked at one another, raised their eyebrows, shrugged their shoulders. Dutri grinned. Othomar asked Zanti coolly whether they had not better proceed.

The settlement was very much in its first stage; yet a few farm-houses were beginning to rise up, chestnut-trees lay felled, hundreds of peasants were busily working.

The group of officers excited great curiosity; the princes had been recognized. On almost every side the people stopped work, followed the uniforms with their eyes.

The princes and their suite felt instinctively that a hostile feeling was passing through Zanti's peasants. When they asked a question here and there about the sufferings experienced, the answer sounded curt and rough, with a reference to the will of God, and was always like an echo of Zanti's own words. Pecuniary assistance seemed uncalled for. And Zanti had really nothing to show. The settlement made a poor impression on Othomar, perhaps because of a sort of mortified sovereignty. He was accustomed always to be approached with respect, as a future majesty; and his sensitiveness was more deeply wounded by Zanti's bluntness, by the surliness of Zanti's peasants, than he himself was willing to admit. He felt that at this spot they saw in him not the crown-prince who loved his people and wanted to learn how to succour them, but the son of a tyrant, who would act as a tyrant also when his turn came. He felt that, though Zanti called himself the apostle of peace, this peace was not in his disciples; and, when he looked into their rough, sullen faces, he saw hatred gleam luridly from deep, hollow eyes, as with sudden lightning-flashes....

The weight of it all fell heavily upon his chest; his impotence pressed with a world of inconsolable misery and unappeasable grief upon his shoulders, as though to bear him to the ground. It was the misery and grief not of one, but of thousands, millions. Vindictive eyes multiplied themselves around him in a ferment of hatred; each one of his people who asked happiness of him, demanding it and not receiving it, seemed to be there, staring at him with those wide eyes....

He felt himself turning giddy with an immense feeling of helplessness. He looked for nothing more, this was the end. And he was not surprised at what happened: the man with the brown, hairy, distorted face, who rushed upon him like a nightmare and laid hold of him, full of hatred. A foul, tobacco-laden breath swept over his face, a coarse knife in a coarse fist flashed towards his throat....

A cry arose. A shot rang out, sharp, determined, with no suspicion of hesitation. The man cursed out a hoarse yell, gnashing his teeth in revolt, and struggled, dying. His brains splashed over Othomar, soiling the prince's uniform. And the man plumped down at his feet on the ground, grown limp at once, with relaxed muscles, still clutching the knife in his hairy fingers. All this had happened in a single instant.

It was Von Fest who had fired the shot from a revolver. The colonel drew up his broad figure, looked around him, still held the revolver raised at a threatening slant. The people stood staring, motionless, perplexed by the sudden reality before their eyes.

Zanti, stupefied, gazed at the corpse; then he said, while the startled officers stood by in fussy confusion around the prince:

"Now go and, if you can, go in peace!..."

Full of bitterness, he pointed to the corpse. He shook his head, with the grey locks under the felt hat; tears sprang to the corners of his eyes.

"Thou shalt not kill!" they heard him mutter. "They seem not to know that yet; nobody knows it yet!..."

A strange, mad look troubled his normally clear, grey eyes; he seemed for a moment not to know what he should do. Then he went to a tree, caught up the axe and, without taking further notice of the princes, began to hew like a lunatic, blow upon blow....

The officers hurried to their horses. Dutri gave a last look back: near the corpse, now surrounded by peasants, he saw a woman standing; she sobbed, her desperate arms flung to heaven, she howled, she shook her fist at the equerry's turned face, screaming.

Othomar had said nothing. He heard the woman howling behind him. He quivered in every nerve. On the road, preparing to mount, Ducardi asked him, agitatedly:

"Shall we return to Castel Vaza, highness?"

The prince looked at the general haughtily. Quickly the thought flashed through him that the general had strongly opposed his coming here. He shook his head.

Then his eyes sought Von Fest: they glanced up at the colonel under their eyelids, deep-black, moist, almost reproachful.

But he held out his hand:

"Thank you, colonel," he said, in a husky voice.

The colonel pressed the hand which the prince offered him:

"Glad to be of service, highness!" he replied, with soldierly brusqueness.

"And now let us go on to the Zanthos," said Othomar, walking up to his horse.

But the old general could master himself no longer. In these last moments he had felt all his passionate love—seated hereditarily, firmly in his blood, of a piece with him, his very soul and all that soul—for the reigning house. His fathers had died for it in battle, without hesitation. And with the mad, wide embrace of his long, powerful old arms, he ran up to Othomar, grateful that he was alive, pressed him as if he would crush him against his breast, until the buttons of his uniform scratched Othomar's cheek, and cried, sobbing, under his trembling moustache:

"My prince, my prince, my prince!..."

8

The attempt on Othomar's life was known at Castel Vaza before the princes returned, from peasants of the duke's, who had told the castle-servants long stories of how the prince had been severely wounded. The duchess had at first refused to believe it; then, in rising anxiety, in the greatest tension and uncertainty, she had walked about the corridors. She had first tried to persuade herself that the people were sure to exaggerate. When she reflected that, in the event of Othomar's being wounded, the princes and the equerries would have returned at once, she became more tranquil and waited patiently.

But the chamberlain, who had been to Vaza, returned in dismay: people were very uneasy in the town, pressing round the doors of the newspaper-offices to read the bulletins, which mentioned the attempt briefly, with the provoking comment that further particulars were not yet to hand. The duchess realized that by this time the bulletin had also been telegraphed to Lipara; and she feared not only that Othomar had met with harm, but that she herself would lose favour with the empress....

When the duchess at last, after long watching from a window in the west corridor, saw the princes and their suite come trotting, very small, along a distant road, she could not restrain herself and went to meet them in the courtyard. But she saw that Othomar was unhurt. The Duke of Xara dismounted, smiled, gave her his hand; she kissed it, curtseying, ardently; her tears fell down upon it. The chamberlain approached, assured Othomar, in the name of all the duke's servants, of their heartfelt gratitude that the Duke of Xara had been spared, by the grace of God and the succour of St. Ladislas.

Ducardi had not been able to telegraph from anywhere before, but he now sent in all haste to Vaza with a message for the emperor, mentioning at the same time that the prince had calmly resumed the expedition immediately after the attempt upon his life. Dinner took place amid a babel of voices; the duchess was greatly excited, asked for the smallest details and almost embraced Von Fest. The crown-prince drank to his preserver and every one paid him tribute.

Afterwards Ducardi advised the crown-prince, in an aside, to retire early to rest. The general spoke in a gentle voice; it seemed as though the thought that he might have lost his crown-prince had made him fonder of him. Herman too pressed Othomar to go to bed.

He himself had grown calm, but a vague feeling of lassitude had come over all his being: he had even drunk Von Fest's health in a strangely weary voice. He now took their advice, withdrew, undressed himself; his soiled uniform, which he had changed before dinner, still hung over a chair; he shuddered to think that he had worn it the whole afternoon:

"Those things!" he said to Andro, who was still quite confused and, nervously weeping, was tidying up. "Burn them, or throw them away, throw them away."

Othomar flung himself in his dressing-gown on a couch in the room adjoining his bedroom. This was also an historical apartment, with tapestry on the walls representing scenes from the history of Lipara: the Emperor Berengar I., triumphantly riding into Jerusalem, with his crusaders holding aloft their white banners; the Empress Xaveria, seated on horseback in her golden armour before the walls of Altara, falling backwards, struck dead by a Turkish arrow....

The prince lay staring at them. A deadly calm seemed to make him feel nothing, care about nothing. In his own mind he reviewed the whole historical period from Berengar to Xaveria. He knew the dates; the scenes passed cloudily before his eyes as though tapestries were being unrolled, kaleidoscopically, with the faded colours of old artwork. He saw himself again, a small boy, in the Imperial, in an austere room, diligently learning his lessons; he saw his masters, relieving one another: languages, history, political economy, international law, strategy; it had all heaped itself upon his young brain, piled itself up, built itself up like a tower. By way of change, his military education—drilling, riding, fencing—conducted by General Ducardi, who praised him or grumbled at him, or growled at the sergeants who instructed him. He had never been able to learn mathematics, had never understood a word of algebra; in many subjects he had always remained weak: natural philosophy and chemistry, for instance. For a time he had taken great pleasure in the study of mineralogy and zoology and botany; and afterwards he had shown some enthusiasm for astronomy. Then came the university and his legal studies....

He remembered his little vanities as a child and as a boy, when in his ninth year he had become a lieutenant in the throne-guards; when later he had received the Garter from the Queen of England and the Black Eagle from the German Emperor and the Golden Fleece from the Queen-regent of Spain. With such minor vanity there had always been mingled a certain dread of possible obligations which the Garter or the Eagle might imply: obligations which hovered vaguely before his eyes, which he dared not define and still less ask about of Ducardi, of his father. Gradually these threatening obligations had become so heavy and now, now they were the weights that bore upon his chest....

The weights.... But he did not stir, feeling strangely calm. Then he thought of Von Fest, of the duchess.... Yesterday, her kiss.... He had lain swooning on her shoulder and she had kissed him and long watched him with passionate looks. And all those stories of the equerries....

Then it came as with a fierce wave foaming over his absolute calmness....

Why had that man hated him, tried to murder him, tried to slay him like a beast?... Pride welled up in him, pride and despair. The man had touched him, soiled him with his breath, him, the crown-prince, the Duke of Xara! He gnashed his teeth with rage. That was a thing which Berengar I. would never have suffered! Off with his head! Off with his head!... Oh, that populace which did not know, which did not feel, which pressed up against him, seething and foaming against the throne, which terrified his mother, however haughtily she might look beyond it into the distance, with her imperial composure!...

How he hated it, hated it, with all the hatred of his house for those who were now free and were yet once its slaves! How he would have them shot down, have them shot down when he came into power!...

He looked at Xaveria: she herself was shot down, the haughty amazon; backwards she fell, wounded by the arrow of a Turkish soldier. And he, that morning, if Von Fest had not....

He threw himself back wildly, buried his face in his hands and sobbed. No, no, oh no! He would not shoot them down, not kill them, not hate them! He was not like that: he might be like that for a moment, but he was not like that! He was fond of his people; he was so grateful when they rejoiced, when he was able to help them. Surely he would never have them shot on! He was only growing excited now. What was there in his soul for all of them, for those millions, of whom he had perhaps seen only a few thousands and knew only a few hundreds, but one great love, which threw out arms to them in every direction, to embrace them? Had he not felt this in that black night on the Therezia Square? Were hatred and violence his? No, oh no! He was soft, perhaps too soft, too irresolute, but he would grow older, he would grow stronger; he would wish to and he would make all of them happy. Oh, if they only cared for him, if they only loved him with their great mass of surging, black, frothing humanity, a sable Milky Way of swarming souls, each soul a spark, like his own; oh, if they only loved him! But they must not hate him, not look at him with those bloodshot eyes of hatred, not aim at his throat with those coarse, hairy fingers, not try to murder him, O God, not try to slay him like a bullock, with a common knife, him, their future sovereign!...

And he felt that they did not belong to him and did not know him and did not understand him and did not love him, all of them, and that they hated him merely out of instinct, because he was born upon the throne!

And his despair because of all this spanned out, immense, a desert of black night, which he felt eternities wide around him; and he sobbed, sobbed, like an inconsolable child, because this was as it was and would become more desperate with each day that brought him nearer to his future as emperor and to their future: the mournful day which would rise upon the destruction of the old world....

Then there came a knock at a little door; and the door was softly opened....

"Who's there?" he asked, startled, feeling the breach of etiquette, not understanding why Andro had not come through the anteroom to announce whoever it might be.

"If your highness permits me...."

He recognized the duchess' soft voice, rose, went to the door:

"Come in, duchess...."

She entered, hesitatingly; she had thrown a long cloak over her bare shoulders to go through the chilly passages of the castle....

"Forgive me, highness, if I intrude ... if I disturb you...."

He smiled, said no, apologized for his costume, feeling surprised and pleased....

She saw that his eyes were swimming with moisture:

"I am indiscreet," she said, "but I couldn't help it; I felt I must find out how you were, highness.... Perhaps I wished to surprise you as well: I don't quite know. Something impelled me: I could not help coming to you. You are my guest and my crown-prince; I longed to see for myself how you were.... Your highness bore up well at dinner, but I felt...."

Her voice flowed on, soft and monotonous, as though with drops of balsam. He asked her to sit down; she did so; he sat down by her side; the dark cloak slipped off and she was magnificent, with her white neck, siren-like in her opalescent, pale-green watered silk. He noticed that she had laid aside the jewels which she had worn at dinner.

"I wanted to come to you quietly, through that door," she resumed, "in order to tell you once more, to tell you alone, how unspeakably thankful I am that your highness' life has been preserved...."

Her voice trembled; her ebony glances grew moist; the light of the great candles in the silver candelabra shimmered over the silk of her dress, played with soft light and slumbering shadow in the modelling of her face, in the curve of her bosom.

He pressed her hand; she retained his:

"Was your highness crying when I came in?" she asked.

His tears were still flowing, a last sob heaved through his body.

"Why?" she asked again. "Or am I indiscreet?..."

He looked at her; at this moment he could have told her everything. And, though he contained himself, yet he gave her the essence of his grief:

"I was sad," he said, "because they seem to hate me. Nothing makes me so sad as their hatred."

She looked at him long, felt his sorrow, understood him with her feminine tact, with her courtier-like swiftness of comprehension, which had ripened in the immediate contact of her sovereigns. She understood him: he was the crown-prince, he must suffer his special princely suffering; he must drink an imperial cup of bitterness to the dregs. She remembered that she herself had suffered, so often and so violently, for love, passionate woman that she was; she understood that his suffering was different from hers, but doubtless more terrible, as it seized him already at so young an age and as it depended not upon his own single soul, but upon the millions of souls of his empire. She too had suffered because she had not been loved; he also suffered like that. And so in one instant she understood him quite entirely, with all her strange woman's heart.

A thrill of compassion welled up in her breast as a yet unknown delight and, like a fervent, gentle oracle, she uttered the words:

"They do not all hate you...."

He recognized her passionate glances of the day before. He remembered her kiss. He looked at her long, still hesitating a little in the presence of the unknown. Then he extended his arms and, with a dull cry of despair, hoarse with hunger for consolation, he called to her in his helplessness:

"Oh, Alexa!..."

She first smiled, with radiant eyes, then flung herself bodily into his young arms, crushing him against her bare breast. She felt like a maid and a mother in one. But, when he clung to her in a wild passion of despair, she felt herself to be nothing but a lover. She knew that he would be her last love. The knowledge made her proudly sad and diabolically happy. Her kisses clattered upon his eyes like hail....

And in their love, that night, they mingled the wormwood of what they both were suffering, each seeking consolation for life's sorrows in the other....

9

"To HIS IMPERIAL HIGHNESS THE DUKE OF XARA,

"LYCILIA.

"THE IMPERIAL,
"LIPARA,
" —*April*, 18—.

"MY DEAR BROTHER,

"I want to tell you before you read it in those tedious papers that our respected father and emperor this morning, on my tenth birthday, dubbed me a knight of St. Ladislas in the knights' hall of the palace. You can understand how proud I feel. I shall not tell you about the ceremony, because you will remember that yourself. I was very much impressed as I walked up to our father between all those tall knights in their blue mantles and knelt before his throne. I wore my new uniform of a lieutenant in the guards. The king-at-arms, the Marquis of Ezzera, held up the rule of the order on a cushion, on which I took the oath. I must have looked rather small with my little mantle: the cross of St. Ladislas was just as big on it, however, as on those of all the others. I felt that they were all looking over my head; and that is not a pleasant feeling when you are the hero of the day. But of course I am the youngest of the knights, so there is no harm in my being a little shorter. The sword our father gave me is also a little smaller than that of the other knights, but the hilt is rather pretty and blazes with precious stones. Still, I think I prefer the chasing on the scabbard of yours, but when I am eighteen—so in eight years from now!—I am to have another sword and of course another mantle too.

"Mamma was terribly alarmed and nervous when she heard of that man who attacked you and she wanted to have you recalled at once, because it did not seem safe where you are; and she simply could not understand that this could not be done. But safe: who is safe nowadays? One's not safe in war either and not even here in the Imperial. One shouldn't think so much of all that safety, that's what I say; but of course mamma is a woman and therefore she thinks differently from what we do. The riots and the martial law also upset her, but I think it rather jolly: everything's military now, you know. That Von Fest is a fine fellow. I should like to shake hands with him and to thank him myself; but, as I can't, I beg you *particularly* to do so for me and *on no account* to forget it. You have heard, no doubt, through General Ducardi, that papa is going to make Von Fest a commander of the Imperial Orb. What a pity that we can't create him a knight of St. Ladislas, but for that of course he would have to be a Liparian and not a Gothlander.

"Now, dear brother, I must finish, because Colonel Fasti is expecting me for my fencing-lesson. Give my *very kindest* regards to Herman and General Ducardi and remember me to the others; and accept for yourself the fond embrace of your affectionate brother,

"BERENGAR,

"Marquis of Thracyna

"(Knight of St. Ladislas)."

CHAPTER III

1

It was after the opening of the new parliament. The sun streamed as though with square patches of molten gold along the white palaces of the town, touching with blue what was shadow in the corners.

Two regiments of grenadiers, red and blue, stood in two double lines, drawn up along the principal streets which led from the Parliament House to the Imperial. The crowd pressed and tossed and cheered; all the windows, open wide, swarmed with heads; people looked on from every balcony. A shot thundered from Fort Wenceslas on the sea; the emperor returned; the grenadiers presented arms in company after company....

The lancers lead the van, blue and white, with streaming pennants at the points of their lances, six squadrons of them. The whole strength of the throne-guards, white, with breastplates of glittering gold flashing in the sunlight above the black satin skins of the stallions, ride halberd on thigh, surrounding the gently swaying state-carriages, scintillating with rich gilding and bright crystal and two of them crowned with the imperial crown, with teams of six and eight plumed greys. The horses foam over their bits, impatient, nervously pawing the ground, prancing because of the slow, ceremonious pace along the blinding, flagged roadway. In the first coach, the master of ceremonies, the Count of Threma; in the second, with the crown and the team of eight—and the roar of the cheering rises from behind the hedge of soldiers—the emperor, his uniform all gold, his robes of scarlet and ermine, his crown upon his head. It is the only time that the people have seen their emperor wear his crown.

And they cheer. But the emperor makes no acknowledgment: through the glass of the coach he looks out, to left and right in turns, at the crowd, with a proud smile of self-consciousness and victory; and his face, full of race, full of force, cold with will, proud with authority, is inaccessible in its smile as that of a Roman emperor on his triumphal entry.

It is a triumphal entry, this return from the Parliament House to his Imperial: a triumph over that which they denied him and upon which he has now laid his heavy hand, showing them all that his mere will can bend them to his word and purpose. And the cheers rise louder and louder from that capricious crowd, restrained like a woman by a ruler whom it now adores for his strength and admires for his imperial might, upon which he leans, as he passes from the Parliament House to his own palace, as though it were a whole army that lived upon his nod; and louder and louder, louder and louder the cheers ring out that sunny afternoon over the marble houses; and the emperor smiles continually, as though his smile meant:

"Cheer away! What else can you do but cheer?..."

In the next coach rides the Duke of Xara, robed, crowned; he stares rigidly over the vociferating crowd with the same glance that his mother reserves for the populace. In the next to that, the new governor-general of the capital, the head of the emperor's military household, the Duke of Mena-Doni, a rougher soldier than the Marquis of Dazzara and a less practised courtier, under whose military fist the white capital, like a beaten slave, crouched low during the martial law proclaimed after a single hour of disturbance that ventured to follow upon the emperor's decision to dissolve the house of deputies. His coarse, sensual mouth smiles with the same smile as that of the emperor, whose rude force he seems to impersonate; and he too seems to say:

"Cheer away, shout hurrah!"

Then the following carriages: the imperial chancellor, Count Myxila; the ministers: seven of them forming part of the twelve who wished to resign, the others chosen from among the most authoritative of the old nobility in the house of peers itself!

Cheer away, shout hurrah!

Behind the coaches of the higher court-officials, the Xara cuirassiers, the crown-prince's own regiment; behind them, a regiment of colonials: Africans, black as polished ebony, with eyes like beads, their thick mouths thrust forwards, clad in the muslin-like snow of their burnouses; behind them, two regiments of hussars on heavy horses, in their long, green, gold-frogged coats and their tall busbies.

Was ever parliament opened thus before, with such a display of military force? And outside the town, on the high parade-grounds, do not the people know that there are troops drawn together from every province, camping there for the manoeuvres, the date of which has been accelerated? And the increased garrisons of the forts, the squadron in the harbour? Do the people themselves feel that they can do nothing else than cheer and is that why they are cheering now, happy once more in their cheering, with Roman docility and southern submission, enamoured of the emperor because of the weight of his crushing fist, loving the crown-prince for the attractive charm of his attitude in the north, or perhaps because they think him interesting after an unsuccessful attempt on his life?

And they seem not to feel that, through the grenadiers presenting arms, they see neither the emperor nor the crown-prince saluting; they cheer away, loving them in spite, perhaps because, of their indifference; they cheer away like madmen....

Slowly the procession wends its way along the interminable main streets. The whole city, despite its marble, trembles with the clatter of the horses' hoofs upon the flagged pavement. Between the front escort and the endless escort in the rear, the state-carriages, with their glittering throne-guards, shimmer like a kind of jewel, small, rare, carefully guarded. The cavalry are at this moment the soul of Lipara, their echoing step its heart-beat; and between the grenadiers and the tall houses the massed and cheering populace seems to have hardly room to breathe.

The procession approaches the Imperial. Along the immense marble fore-court the lancers and cuirassiers range themselves on three sides, before the wings and along the front. Outside them the guards are drawn up in line. The Africans close off the courtyard....

The carriages pull up; and the emperor alights. With the crown-prince by his side, he goes through the vestibule up the stairs. The corridors of the palace swarm with gold-laced uniforms; a packed suite crowds up behind Oscar and Othomar. The master of the robes, with twelve grooms of the bed-chamber, comes towards the emperor, who takes off his crown, as does the crown-prince; their robes are unfastened for them.

They go to the great white hall, white with the Corinthian columns with gilt capitals. The empress and the Princess Thera are there, surrounded by their ladies. It is a great day: in this sun-apotheosis of the opening of parliament the monarchy is triumphing over the threats of the future and deferring that future itself. The empress, in her trailing pale-mauve velvet, steps towards her spouse and curtseys before him ceremoniously. The princess, the mistress of the robes, all the ladies curtsey....

Outside, in front, the square is now filled by the multitude; an excited popular clamour surges up against the immovable palace, as it were the sea against a rock. The doors of the centre balcony are opened. The emperor and the prince will show themselves....

"Only just salute once," whispers the emperor to his son, sternly.

The sun outside rains down gold upon the swarming mass, tinging it with many-changing, chameleon, southern tints between the white, motionless wings of the Imperial, whose caryatids look down placidly. The imperial pair step on the balcony. Hats are thrown up towards them; the yelling bellows with a shout as from a single noisy, vulgar throat and echoes through the open doors against the gilt ceiling and columns of the white hall. The empress is frightened by it, turns pale; her breath catches....

On the balcony the Emperor of Liparia salutes his excited people with a solitary wave of the hand; the Duke of Xara bows his head slightly.

2

There was no more talk of a revision of the constitution and reform of the hereditary house of peers. The constitutional majority of three-fourths which is required in the house of deputies before such a proposal can be taken into consideration, though there at first, no longer existed after the new elections. Oscar, immediately after his return from Altara, had shown them his daring strength. Lipara was surrounded with troops: this was as well, for the manoeuvres, for the King of Syria, who was expected. The forts were strengthened, the fleet lay in the harbour; then came the imperial decree that the house of deputies should simply ... be dissolved. What an outcry, after the promulgation of that decree, in the newspapers and in the streets! For one moment, at night, there was an abortive riot. But the emperor, furious with the Marquis of Dazzara for his delay in taking prompt and energetic measures, had next day affirmed his august dissatisfaction. The marquis was shown that there were moments when the emperor was not to be trifled with; the emperor dismissed him personally, on the spot, and told him he could go. Crushed, his eyes full of despair, the marquis left the Imperial; in the fore-court his carriage crossed that of the Duke of Mena-Doni, lieutenant-general of the hussars; he saw the duke's sensual, Neronic head, covetous with ambition, staring up at the front of the palace. The marquis threw himself back in his carriage, wringing his hands and weeping like a child....

That same morning martial law was proclaimed at Lipara and the Duke of Mena-Doni appointed governor of the capital. With a great military display and a speech of three words the emperor dissolved the house of deputies. The people trembled, beaten off, thrashed, reduced to crouching at the imperial feet. The decree was issued for the general election. Must the people be chastised to make them attached to their emperor? Was it because of the innumerable articles in the newspapers of the northern provinces— Altara, Vaza and Lycilia—which bestowed all their sympathy upon their most charming, charitable crown-prince, indefatigable, omnipresent, mitigating what suffering he could? Was it because of the colossal, fabulous presents of millions contributed from the imperial privy purse to the fund for the victims of the disaster? The result of the elections became known: the new house of deputies contained a bare, impotent majority of constitutionals. What did it profit that the liberal papers shrieked of intrigue and undue pressure? Without and within the city lay the army; each day the emperor showed himself, with by his side the Duke of Mena-Doni....

The emperor invited the old ministry to remain in office, but dismissed those of the ministers who were not absolutely authoritative.

The crisis was at an end. The great spring manoeuvres were to take place on the parade-ground so soon as the King and Queen of Syria arrived at Lipara.

In Othomar there sprang up a vast admiration for his father. He did not love him with the fondness, the intimacy, the still almost childish dependence with which he loved the empress; he had always looked up to him; as a child he had been afraid of him. Now, after the personal courage which he had seen the emperor display, the sovereign power which he had watched him exercise, his majesty rose higher before Othomar's eyes, as it were the statue of a demi-god. He felt himself a lowly mortal beside him, when he thought:

"What should *I* have done, if I had had to act in this case? Should I have dared to take the prompt decision to dissolve the house of deputies and should I not have feared an immediate revolution in every corner of the country? Should I, after the disturbances, have dared to dismiss the Marquis of Dazzara at once, like a lackey, attached as he was to our house and descended from our most glorious nobility? Should I have dared to summon that duke, that swashbuckler, with his cruel face, even before I had dismissed the marquis, so that the one arrived as the other departed?"

And he already saw himself hesitating in imagination, not knowing what would be best, above all not knowing what would be most just; he pictured himself advised by old Count Myxila, at last determined to dissolve the deputies, but not dismissing the marquis, not declaring martial law in Lipara and assembling the troops too late and seeing the revolution burst out at all points simultaneously, with bomb upon bomb....

To do what was most just, this seemed to him the most difficult thing for a sovereign.

But the emperor's monarchic triumph had this result, that, clearly as Othomar saw his own weakness, a reflex of strength and determination was cast upon him from his father himself, by whose side he stood. Moreover, he had not much time for brooding. Each day brought its special duties. Scarcely was he able to allow himself one hour of solitary repose. He was accustomed to this life of constant movement, of constant public appearances, now here, now there, so thoroughly accustomed to it that he did not feel the fatigue which was already exhausting him before his tour in the north and which had now eaten into his nerves and marrow. He gave this fatigue no thought, regarded it perhaps as an organic languor, a transitory symptom, which was bound to pass. And each day brought its own fatigue. Thus he had grown accustomed to rise early, at seven every morning; Lipara then still lay white and peaceful in its rosy slumber of the dawn; he rode out on his thorough-bred Arab, black Emiro, with his favourite collie close behind him, galloping with him, its pointed nose poked out, its shaggy collar sticking up; unaccompanied by equerries, he rode through the park of the Imperial to the Elizabeth Parks, in the afternoon the resort of elegant carriages and horsemen, but in the morning peaceful, wide and deserted, with barely a solitary early rider, who made way respectfully for the prince and took his hat off low. Then he rode along the white quays with their villas and palm-trees, their terraces and aloes; and the incomparable harbour lay before him, always growing an intenser blue beneath the pink morning light, which became cruder. Higher up, the docks, the ships, the hum of industry already audible. Slowly he walked his horse along the harbour; in the porticoes of the villas he sometimes caught a glimpse of a woman's figure, saw her eyes following him through roses and clematis. He loved this ride because of the soft, fresh air, because of his horse, his dog, because of his solitude with these two, because of the long, silent quays, the wide, silent sky, the distant horizon still just enveloped in latest morning mist. The morning breeze blew against his forehead under his uniform cap; thoughts wandered at random through his brain. Then he shook himself free from this voluptuousness, rode back to the town and went to the Xaverius Barracks, occupied by the lancers; to the Wenceslas Barracks occupied by the grenadiers; or to the Berengar Barracks, occupied by the hussars. Here he enquired, investigated, inspected; and here he found his equerries, Dutri and Leoni; he rode back with them to the palace, and repaired to his father's room. This was the hour when Count Myxila came to the emperor and when affairs of state were discussed with the imperial chancellor; lately the crown-prince had assisted at these meetings. Next he visited the empress, who was expecting him: it was generally a most delightful moment, this which they spent confidentially together before lunch, a moment full of charm and intimacy. He sat close by her on a low chair, took her hand, poured out to her the burdens of his heart, communicated to her his anxiety about the future, about himself when later he himself would wear the crown. At such times his eyes peered up through their lashes, with their dark melancholy; his voice was querulous and begged for comfort. And she encouraged him: she told him that nothing happened but what had to happen; that everything was inevitable in the world's great chain of events, joined link by link; that he must wait for what might come, but at the same time do his duty; and that he must not unnerve himself with such endless pondering, which led to nothing. He told her how he feared his own hesitation and how he suspected that his decisions would always come too late; and she, gently laughing, replied that, if he knew his own faults so well, he should train himself to make his mind. He questioned her about justice—the one thing that seemed impossible to him on earth—and she referred him to his own feeling, as a human soul. But yet, intensely sweet as these hours were, he felt that he remained the same under their interchange of words and that, though words had been exchanged, nothing was changed within him. Wherefore he thought himself wicked and was afraid that he did not love his mother enough, with enough conviction. Then he looked at her, saw her smiling, divined beneath her smile the nervous dread which would never again relinquish its grasp of her and felt that she spoke like this only for his sake, to cheer him, and not from conviction. And his thoughts no longer wandered discursively about him, as on his morning ride along the quays: they fell like fine mists one upon the other in his imagination and formed his melancholy.

Lunch was taken privately. After lunch he sat for an hour to Thera, who was painting his portrait. In the afternoon there were always different things to do: exhibitions, charities, institutions of all kinds to be visited, a foundation-stone to be laid, a man-of-war to be launched. Every minute was filled; and each day filled his minutes differently from the day before. Dinner was always a meal of great etiquette and splendour; every day there were numerous guests: diplomatists, high officials, officers. It lasted long; it was an emperor's daily ceremonial banquet. Then in the evening the parties at court, or at the houses of the ambassadors or dignitaries; the theatres and concerts. The prince, however, never stayed late. He then read or worked for a couple of hours in his own room; at twelve o'clock he went to bed.

He was used to this life of monotonous variety, had grown up in it. So soon as he returned from Lycilia to Lipara—the city was then still under martial law—he found it waiting for him busier than ever; the opening of parliament had followed close upon his return. The emperor was pleased with the crown-prince's conduct in the north, perhaps because of the praise which the northern newspapers bestowed upon the Duke of Xara for his ready sympathy, because of his moment of popularity. He wanted to let his son take more and more part in affairs of state and discussed them with him more frequently either alone or in the company of the imperial chancellor. But the stern measures of drastic violence which the Duke of Mena-Doni had taken—he himself at Lipara, his officers at Thracyna: furious charges of hussars against the threatening crowds—these revolted Othomar; he had heard of them with anguish and despair, though he knew that there was nothing to be achieved by gentleness. And with his veneration for the emperor, as for a demi-god of will and force, there was mingled a certain antipathy and grudge, which divided him from his father and made any interchange of thought between them difficult.

Now, after the opening of parliament, the town, the whole country had quieted down; the troops, however, remained on the parade-ground, for the approaching manoeuvres. The arrival of the King and Queen of Syria was fixed. Othomar's days succeeded one another as before. He was entertained at banquets by the officers of the throne-guards and of the other regiments to which he belonged. Yes, this was his hour of popularity. It was already said that his surname one day would be Othomar the Benevolent. It was at this time that he laid the foundation-stone of a great alms-house, to whose establishment the will of an immensely wealthy, childless duke—one of the oldest Liparian families, which had become extinct—had contributed millions.

Othomar's gentleness was in amiable contrast with Oscar's justly exerted but rough force. He himself, however, was inwardly very much astonished at this talk of benevolence: he liked to do good, but did not feel the love of doing good as a leading feature in his character.

After the dinner given to him by the staff-officers, Othomar was to go in the evening with Ducardi, Dutri and Leoni to the Duke of Yemena, to thank the court marshal officially for the hospitality shown him at Castel Vaza. The duke occupied at Lipara a large, new house; his old family-residence was at Altara.

It is nine o'clock; the crown-prince is not yet expected. The duke and duchess, however, are already receiving their guests; the duchess sent out numerous invitations when Othomar announced his visit. The spacious reception-rooms fill up: almost the whole of the diplomatic corps is present, as are some of the ministers and great court-officials with their wives, old Countess Myxila and her daughters and a number of officers. They form the intimate circle of the Imperial. A jaunty familiarity prevails among them, with the *sans-gêne* in vogue.

Near the duchess stands Lady Danbury, the wife of the British first secretary, and the Marquis of Xardi, the duke's son. They are talking busily about the Dazzaras:

"I've seen them," says Lady Danbury. "It's shocking, shocking. They're living at Castel Dazzara, that old ruin in Thracyna, with their five daughters, poor things! The ceilings are falling in. Three crooked old men in livery; and the liveries even older than the servants. And debts, according to what I hear, debts! I was astonished to see how old the marchioness had grown; she has taken it terribly to heart, it seems."

"Grown old?" asks the duchess. "I thought she looked quite young still, last time I saw her...."

She detests Lady Danbury, who is tall, thin and sharp-featured, her appearance rather suggesting that of a graceful adder. And she continues:

"She still looked so well; she is slender, but she has a splendid neck and shoulders.... I really cannot understand how she can have grown so old...."

And, as though brooding over this puzzle, the duchess stares at the lean shoulders of Lady Danbury.

Xardi's eyes glitter; he expects a skirmish.

"They say that the marquis *used* to be one of your intimates, don't they?" the Englishwoman insinuates.

But that hateful "used to be" grates on Xardi's nerves.

"I am very fond of the Dazzaras," says the duchess; "but"—and she laughs mysteriously and meaningly—"he was always an unlucky bird...."

"His excellency the Duke of Mena-Doni," the butler announces.

"The rising sun!" Xardi whispers to Lady Danbury.

Mena-Doni bows before the duchess, who smiles upon him. Lady Danbury, standing by Xardi's side, continues:

"And the lucky bird?"

"Oh no!" says Xardi, with decision. "At least, not altogether...."

They look at each other and laugh:

"Imperial eagles are the finest birds, after all, don't you think?" says Lady Danbury, jestingly.

"What do you know about it?"

"Alas, I am too unimportant to know anything! Before I get so far in my zoological studies...."

"But what have you heard?"

"What everybody hears when Dutri can't hold his tongue."

"What about?"

"About a certain tender parting at Castel Vaza...."

The Marquis of Xardi bursts out laughing. Lady Danbury suddenly clutches his arm:

"I say, Xardi, I know less slender people than the Marchioness of Dazzara who would fall into a decline if they lost the imperial favour. *Et toi?*"

The marquis laughs loudly and:

"Even the crown-princely favour," he whispers, behind Lady Danbury's Watteau fan.

And they chuckle with laughter together.

"His imperial highness the Duke of Xara; their excellencies Count Ducardi, Prince Dutri and the Marquis of Leoni!" are announced, slowly and impressively.

There is a slight movement in the groups. The room divides into two rows; a couple of ladies get entangled in their trains and laugh. Then they all wait.

Othomar appears at the open door; Ducardi, Dutri and Leoni are behind him. The old duke hastens towards the prince; the Marquis of Xardi hurriedly thrusts Lady Danbury's fan into her hand and joins his father.

The old duke is a well-knit, elegant man, full of racial refinement, with a clean-shaven face; he is dressed simply in evening-clothes, with the broad green riband of a commander of the Imperial Orb slanting across his breast and the grand cross of St. Ladislas round his neck.

Othomar wears his full-dress uniform as colonel of the Xara Cuirassiers, silver, red and white; he holds his plumed helmet under his arm; he presses the duke's hand, he addresses him with genial words; but, in the ingenuousness of his youthful soul, he feels bitter remorse gnawing at his conscience now that he speaks of Castel Vaza, now that he listens to the cordial protestations of the duke. Othomar also shakes hands with the Marquis of Xardi.

Then the duchess approaches and greets the crown-prince with her famous curtsey. Lady Danbury envies her her grace and asks herself how it is possible, with those statuesque lines; she cannot deny that the Duchess of Yemena is a splendid woman.... Between the duke and the duchess, the prince walks down the row of bowing guests; the Marquis of Xardi follows with the equerries.

Othomar has seen the duchess once or twice at the Imperial since his return to Lipara, but never alone. They now exchange courteous phrases, with official voices and intonations. The groups form once more, as at an intimate rout.

The duchess walks on with Othomar, till they reach the long conservatory, dimly lighted, dusky-green, with the stately palm-foliage of the tall plants, with the delicate tracery of the bamboos, which exude beads of dew against the square panes. They are silent for a moment, looking at each other; and Othomar feels that his emotions for this woman are nothing more than fleeting moments, cloudlets in his soul. The unknown has opened out to him, but has turned to disillusion. Nevertheless he is thankful to her for what she gave him: the consolation of her passion, while his eyes were still moist with tears. She strengthened him by this consolation and made him discover his manhood. But everything in life is twofold; and his gratitude has a reverse of sin. He sees the duke in the distance holding an animated conversation, underlined with elegant, precise gestures, with Ducardi; and remorse softly pierces his boyish soul.

And next to his gratitude he feels his disillusion. Love! Is this love?... He feels nothing; nothing new has come into his heart. He sees how deliciously beautiful the duchess is in her ivory brocade, her train edged with dark fur, her bodice cut square, a string of pearls round her neck. The half-light drifts past her through the plants, a faery green, with a gentle slumbering and with shadows full of mystery; her face, with its delicate smile, stands out against the background of blurred darkness. He recalls her kiss and the mad embrace of her arms. Yes, it was a blissful enervation, an intoxication of the flesh, an unknown giddiness, a physical comfort. But love: was it love?... And he has to make up his mind: perhaps it is love; and, though he feels something lacking in his soul, he makes up his mind for all that: yes, perhaps that is what it is ... love.

"And when shall I see your highness again?" she whispers.

The question is put crudely and surprises him. But this single second of momentary solitude is so precious to the duchess that she cannot do otherwise. She observes his surprise and adores him for his innocence; and her eyes gaze so beseechingly that he replies:

"To-morrow I am dining with the French ambassador; after that I am going to the opera.... Can I find you here at eleven o'clock?"

He is surprised at the logical sequence of his thoughts, at his question, which sounds so strangely in his ears. But she answers, laughing disconcertedly:

"For God's sake, highness, not here, at eleven o'clock! How could we!... But ... come to ... Dutri's...."

She stammers; she remembers the equerry's luxurious flat and sees herself there again ... with others. And in her confusion she does not perceive that she has wounded him deeply and torn his sensitiveness as though with sharp claws; she fails all the more to perceive this, because he answers, confusedly:

"Very well...."

They return, laughing, with their official, colourless voices; they walk slowly: he, so young in his silver uniform, with the helmet, with its drooping plume, under the natural grace of his rounded arm; she, with her expansive brilliancy, trailing her ivory train, waving her fan of feathers and diamonds to and fro against her Carrara-marble bosom. All eyes are turned in their direction and observe the duchess' triumph....

And Othomar now knows that his "love" will become what is called a *liaison*, such as he has heard of in connection with this one and that, or read of in novels. He had not yet imagined such an arrangement. He does not know how he is to tell Dutri that he has made an assignation with the duchess in his rooms; and, when he thinks of the equerry, something of his innate sovereignty is chipped off as little pieces of marble or alabaster might be from a frail column....

Joining the duke and the general, he talks of the approaching manoeuvres. He now sees the duchess standing at a distance and Mena-Doni bending his Neronic head close to her face. His great antipathy for this man is mingled with jealousy. And, while he smiles and listens to the Duke of Yemena, he feels that he now knows for certain that his love after all *is* love, because jealousy plays a part in it.

3

Next morning, when Othomar rode out alone, he was thinking the whole time of Dutri. The difficulty of broaching the subject to his equerry struck him as unsurmountable. His heart beat when he met Dutri waiting for him in the Xaverius Barracks. But the young officer had the tact to whisper to him, very calmly and courteously, as though it were the simplest matter in the world:

"I was talking with the Duchess of Yemena, highness.... Her excellency told me that your highness wished to speak to her in private and did me the honour.... Will your highness take this key?..."

Othomar mechanically accepted the key. His face remained rigid and serious, but inwardly he felt much annoyed with the duchess and did not understand how and why she could drag Dutri into their secret. The ease and simplicity with which she had evidently done so flashed across him as something alarming. A confusion seemed to whirl through his head, as though the duchess and Dutri had, with one breath, blasted all sorts of firm convictions of his youth. He thought of the old duke. He considered all this wrong. He knew that Dutri was a young profligate; he was in the habit of hearing the whole gazette of court scandal from him, but he had never believed one-half of what Dutri related and had often told the equerry bluntly that he did not like to hear ill spoken of people whom they saw daily, people attached to his house. Now it seemed to him that everything that Dutri had said might be true and that yet worse things might well take place. This key, offered with such simple politeness, with such libertine ease, appeared to him as an object of searing dishonour. He was already ashamed of having put the thing in his pocket....

He went on, however. The key burnt him while he spoke with General Ducardi and, on his return to the Imperial, with his father and Myxila. Before going to visit the empress, who was awaiting him, he locked it away in his writing-table; then slowly, his forehead overshadowed, step by step he went through the long galleries to the empress' apartments. In the anteroom the lady-in-waiting rose, curtseyed, knocked at the door and opened it:

"His highness the Duke of Xara...."

Othomar silently made the sign of the Cross, as though he were entering a church:

"May God and His Mother forgive me!" he murmured between his lips.

Then he entered the empress' room.

She was sitting alone in the large drawing-room, at one of the open windows overlooking the park. She wore a very simple, smooth, dark dress. It struck him how young she looked; and he reflected that she was younger than the duchess. An aureole of delicate purity seemed to quiver around her tall, slender form like an atmosphere of light and gave her a distinction which other women did not possess. She smiled to him; and he came up slowly and kissed her hand.

She had not yet seen him that day; she took his head between her cool, slim hands and kissed him.

He sat down on a low chair by her side. Then she passed her hand over his forehead:

"What's the matter?" she asked.

He looked at her and said there was nothing particular. She suspected nothing further; this was not the first time he brought her a clouded forehead. She stroked it once more:

"I promised papa to have a serious talk with you," she said.

He looked up at her.

"He thought it better that I should talk to you, because it was his idea that I could do so more easily. For the rest, he is very pleased with you, my boy, and rejoices to find that you have such a clear judgement, sometimes, upon various political questions."

This opinion of his father's surprised him.

"And about what did you promise to talk to me?"

"About something very, very important," she said, with a gentle smile. "About your marriage, Othomar."

"My marriage?..."

"Yes, my boy.... You will soon be twenty-two. Papa married much later in life, but he had many brothers. They are dead. Uncle Xaverius is in his monastery. And we—papa and I—are not ever likely to have any more children, Othomar."

She put her arms about him and drew him to her. She whispered:

"We have no one but you, my boy, and our little Berengar. And ... papa therefore thinks that you ought to marry. We want an hereditary prince, a Count of Lycilia...."

His eyes became moist; he laid his head against her:

"Two to become emperor? Berengar, if I should be gone before him: is not that enough, mamma?"

She smilingly shook her head in denial. No, that was not certainty enough for the house of Czyrkiski-Xanantria.

"Mamma," he said, gently, "when sociologists speak of the social question, they deplore that so many children are born among the proletariate and they even hold the poor parents, who have nothing else but their love, responsible for the greater social misery which they cause through those children. Does not this reproach really affect us also? Or do you think an emperor so happy?"

Her brow became overcast.

"You are in one of your gloomy moods, Othomar. For God's sake, my boy, do not give way to them. Do not philosophize so much; accept life as it has been given to you. That is the only way in which to bear it. Do not reflect whether you will be happy, when you are emperor, but accept the fact that you must become emperor in your turn."

"Very well, for myself: but why children, mamma?"

"What sovereign allows his house to die out, Othomar? Do not be foolish. Cling to tradition: that is all in all to us. Don't have such strange ideas upon this question. They are not those of a future—I had almost said—autocrat; they are not those of a monarch. You understand, Othomar, do you not? You must, you must marry...."

Her voice sounded more decided than usual, sounded almost hard.

"And, dearest boy," she continued, "thank the circumstances and marry now, as quickly as possible. Our relations with foreign countries are at this moment such that there are no particular indications as to whom you ought to marry. You can more or less pick and choose. For you are the crown-prince of a great empire, my boy, of one of the greatest empires in Europe...."

He tried to speak; she continued, hurriedly:

"I repeat, you can—very nearly—choose. You don't know how much that means. Appreciate this, appreciate the circumstances. Travel to all the courts of Europe that are worth considering. Use your eyes, make your choice. There are pretty princesses in England, in Austria...."

Othomar closed his eyes an instant, as though exhausted with weariness:

"Later on, mamma," he whispered.

"No, my boy," said the empress, "do not speak of later on, do not put off. Think it over. Think how you will order your journey and whom you will take with you and then talk it over with papa and Myxila. Will you promise?"

He just pressed his head against her and promised, with a weary smile.

"But what's the matter with you, my boy?" she asked. "What is it?"

His eyes grew moist.

"I don't know, mamma. I am so tired sometimes...."

"Aren't you well?"

"Yes, I'm all right, but I am so tired...."

"But why, my child?"

He began to sob softly:

"Tired ... of everything ... mamma."

She looked at him for a long time, shook her head slowly, disapprovingly.

"Forgive me, mamma," he stammered, wiping his eyes. "I shan't give way like this again...."

"You promised me that once before, Othomar dear."

He leant his head against her once more, like a child:

"No, really," he declared, caressingly, "I really will resist it. It is not right of me, mamma. I will employ myself more, I shall grow stronger. I swear to you I shall grow stronger for your sake...."

She again looked long in his eyes, with her pure smile. Utter tenderness went out from her to him; he felt that he would never love any one so much as his mother. Then she took him in her arms and pressed him close against her:

"I accept your promise and I thank you ... my poor boy!" she whispered through her kiss.

At this moment there came a buzz of young voices, as though from birds set free, out of the park, through the open windows. The tripping of many little feet grated on the gravel. A high, shrill, childish voice suddenly rang with furious words from among the others; the others were silent....

The empress started with a shock that was electric. She drew herself up hastily, deadly pale:

"Berengar!" she cried; and her voice died away.

"And I shall tell his majesty what a scoundrel you are and then we'll see! Then we'll see, then we'll see!..."

The empress trembled as she leant out of the window. She saw ten or eleven little boys; they looked perplexed.

"Where is his highness?" she asked.

"His highness is over there, ma'am!" shyly answered a little count, pointing to the back-court, which the empress could not see.

"But what is happening? What a noise to make! Send his highness here at once! Berengar! Berengar!"

His highness, Berengar, was called and came. He passed through the little dukes and counts and looked up at the window through which his mother was leaning. He was a small, sturdily built, vigorous little chap; his face was crimson with indignation, his two small, furious eyes were like two black sparks.

"Berengar, come here!" cried the empress. "What is all this? Why can't you play without quarrelling?"

"I'm not quarrelling, mamma, but ... but I shall tell papa ... and ... and then we'll see! Then we'll ..."

"Berengar, come in here at once, through the palace, at once!" commanded the empress.

Othomar looked out from behind the empress at the group of boys. He saw Berengar speak a word of apology to the biggest little duke and disappear through the back-court.

A minute later, the boy entered the room.

"Berengar," said the empress, "it's very bad manners to make such a noise in the park ... and just behind the palace too."

The boy looked at her with his serious little crimson face:

"Yes, mamma," he assented, gently.

"What happened?"

Berengar's lips began to tremble.

"It was that beastly sentry ..." he began.

"What about the sentry?"

"He ... he didn't present arms to me!"

"Didn't the sentry present arms to you? Why not?"

"I don't know!" cried Berengar, indignantly.

"But surely he always does?"

"Yes, but this time he did not. He did the first time when we passed, but not the second time.... We were playing touch and, when we ran past him the second time, he didn't present arms!"

Othomar began to scream with laughter.

"There's nothing to laugh at!" cried Berengar, angrily. "And I shall tell papa and then you shall see."

"But, Berengar," said the empress, "did you expect the man to present arms to you every time you ran past him while you were playing touch?"

Berengar reflected:

"He might at least have done it the second time. If it had been three, or four, or five times, I could have understood.... But only the second time!... What can the boys have thought of me?"

"Listen, Berengar," said the empress, "whatever happens, it is not at all proper for you to call people names, whoever they may be, nor to make such a noise in the park, right behind the palace. An emperor's son never calls names, not even to a sentry. So now you must go straight to that sentry and tell him you are sorry you lost your temper so."

"Mamma!" cried the child, in consternation.

The empress' face was inflexible:

"I insist, Berengar."

The boy looked at her with the greatest astonishment:

"But am I to say that ... to the sentry, mamma?"

"Yes."

Evidently Berengar at this moment failed to understand the order of the universe; he suspected for an instant that the revolution had broken out:

"But, mamma, I can't do that!"

"You must, Berengar, and at once."

"But, mamma, will papa approve of it?"

"Certainly, Berengar," said Othomar. "Whatever mamma tells you to do papa of course approves of."

The boy looked up at Othomar helplessly; his little face grew long, his sturdy little fists quivered. Then he burst into a fit of desperate sobbing.

"Come, Berengar, go," the empress repeated.

The child was still more dismayed by her severity: that was how he always saw her stare at the crowd, but not at her children. And he threw himself with the small width of his helpless little arms into her skirts, embraced her and sobbed, with great, gulping sobs:

"I can't do it, mamma, I can't do it!"

"You must, Berengar...."

"And ... and ... and I *shan't*, I *shan't!*" the boy screamed, in a sudden fury, stamping his foot.

The empress did nothing but look at him, very long, very long. Her reproachful glance crushed the boy. He sobbed aloud and seemed to forget that his little friends outside would be sure to hear his highness sobbing. He saw that there was nothing to be done, that he must do it. He must! His imperial highness Berengar Marquis of Thracyna, knight of St. Ladislas, must say he was sorry to a sentry and one moreover who denied him, his highness, his rights.

His medieval little childish soul was all upset by it. He understood nothing more. He only saw that he must do as he was told, because his mother looked at him with such a sad expression:

"Othomar!" he sobbed, in his despair. "Othomar! Will ... you ... go with me ... then? But how am I to do it, how am I to do it?"

Othomar smiled to him compassionately and held out his hand to him. The empress nodded to the princes to go.

"How am I to do it? O God, how am I to do it?" she still heard Berengar's voice sobbing desperately in the lobby.

Elizabeth had turned deadly pale. As soon as she was alone, she sank into a chair, with her head flung back. Hélène of Thesbia entered at this moment:

"Madam!" cried the young countess. "What is it?"

The empress put out her hand; Hélène felt that it was icy cold.

"Nothing, Hélène," she replied. "But Berengar frightened me so terribly. I thought ... I thought they were murdering him!"

And in an hysterical fit of spasmodic sobbing she threw herself into the countess' arms.

4

That night, before Othomar left with his equerries to dine at the French ambassador's, he drew Dutri aside:

"I see, prince, that her excellency the duchess confides in you fully," he said, in curt tones. "I do not doubt that her confidence is well placed. But I assure you of this: if it should ever appear that it was misplaced, I shall never—now or at any later period—forget it...."

Dutri looked up strangely; he heard his future emperor address him. Then he pouted like a sulky child and said:

"I cannot say that your highness is very grateful for the hospitality which I have offered you...."

Othomar smiled painfully and gave him his hand....

"Or that it is kind of your highness to threaten me to-day with your displeasure," Dutri continued.

"I know you, Dutri," the prince said in his ear. "I know your tongue. That's my only reason for warning you.... And now, for God's sake, say no more about this, for it ... it all gives me pain...."

Dutri was silent, thought him a child and a prince in one. He shrugged his shoulders silently at Othomar's incomparable innocence, but he shuddered when he thought of a possible disgrace. He had no fortune; his position with the crown-prince was his life, his ambition, his all, for now and for later, when the prince should be emperor!... How pleased he had been at first that Alexa had told him everything, that he knew a secret of his prince, who never seemed to have any secrets! A vague pleasure that this secret would give him a power over his future emperor had already flitted through his head, full of frivolous calculations. And now the prince was threatening him and that power was frustrated at its very inception! And Dutri was now almost sorry that he had learned this secret; he even feared that the emperor might come to hear of it, that he would be visited with the father's displeasure even before the son's....

"If only Alexa had not dragged me into it!" he complained to himself, with his shallow fickleness of thought.

But, although Dutri was silent and even contradicted the rumour, the crown-prince's *liaison* was discussed, possibly only because of Alexa's triumphant glances whenever Othomar addressed a word to her at a reception, at a ball. Nevertheless, Dutri's contradiction introduced a certain confusion—for he was known as a ready blabber—and people did not know what to think or what to believe.

But Othomar did not feel happy in his love. The fierce passion of this woman with her fiery glances, who overpowered him one moment with her kisses and the next crept before him like a slave and crouched at his feet in humility before her future sovereign, at first astonished him and, in one or two of his fits of despair, carried him away, but in the long run aroused in him a feeling of disinclination and opposition. In the young equerry's scented flat where they met—it was as dainty as any young girl's sitting-room and padded like a jewel-case—he sometimes felt a wish to repulse this woman, for all that she loved him with her strange soul and did not feign her love; he felt a wish to kick her, to beat her. His temperament was not fit for so animal a passion. She seemed to harry his nerves. She revolted him at times. And yet ... one single word from him and she mastered her fierceness, sank down humbly by his side, softly stroked his hand, his head; and he could not doubt that she adored him, perhaps a little because he was the crown-prince, but also greatly for himself.

And so April came; already it was almost summer; the King and Queen of Syria were expected. They had been first to the sultan and afterwards to the court of Athens. From Liparia they were to go on to the northern states of Europe. On the day of their arrival, Lipara fluttered with flags; the southern sun, already potent, rained down gold upon the white city; the harbour rippled a brilliant blue. A hum of people—tanned faces, many peasants from Thracyna still clad in their parti-coloured national dress—swarmed and crowded upon the quays. On the azure of the water, as on liquid metal, the ironclads, which were to welcome the king and queen and serve as their escort, steamed out to the mouth of the harbour. There, on the *Xaveria*, with their suite of admirals and rear-admirals, were the two princes, Othomar and Berengar, and their brother-in-law, the Archduke of Carinthia. Innumerable small boats glided rapidly over the sea, like water-spiders.

A shot from Fort Wenceslas, tearing the vivid ether, announced the moment at which the little fleet met the Syrian yacht and the oriental potentates left her for the *Xaveria*. From the villas on the quays, from the little boats full of sight-seers, every glass was directed towards the blue horizon, tremulous with light, on which the ships were still visibly shimmering. Half an hour later there rose, as though coming from the Imperial, the cheers of the multitude, surging louder and louder towards the harbour. Through the rows of the grenadiers, who lined the streets from the palace to the pavilion where the august visitors were to land, came the landaus, driven by postillions, in which their majesties sat. These were followed by the carriages of the two sisters, the Archduchess of Carinthia and Thera, and of the suite.

The fleet, with the Syrian yacht in its centre, had steamed back into the harbour. Across the guard-of-honour formed by the throne-guards, through the purple draperies and the flags, the crowd were able to see something of the meeting of the sovereigns in the pavilion. They shouted their hurrahs; and then the procession drove to the Imperial, the emperor with the King of Syria in the first carriage, the empress with the queen in the next; after these, the landaus with the princes and princesses and the suite.

A series of festivals and displays followed. After the tragedies of the inundations and the parliamentary crisis, a mood of gaiety blew over the capital, as it glittered in the sun, and lasted till late in the lighted rooms and parks of the Imperial. This gaiety was because of the eastern queen. The King of Syria may have had a few drops of the blood of Solomon still flowing through his veins. But the queen was not of royal descent. She was the daughter of a Syrian magnate and her mother's name was not mentioned in the *Almanach de Gotha*. That mother was doubtless a favourite of dubious noble descent, but nobody knew who she had been exactly. A *demi-mondaine* from Paris or Vienna, who had stranded in the east and made her fortune in the harem of some great Syrian? A half-European, half-Egyptian dancer from a Cairene or Alexandrian dancing-house? Whoever she was, her lucky daughter, the Queen of Syria, showed an unmistakable mixture of blood, something at once eastern and European. Next to the true Semitic type of the king, who possessed a certain nervous dignity in his half-European, half-oriental uniform glittering with diamonds, the queen, short, fat, chubby, pale-brown, had the exuberant smiles, the restless movements, the turning head and rolling eyes of a woman of colour. Her very first appearance, as she sat in the carriage, next to the delicate figure of the Empress Elizabeth, in a gaudy travelling-dress and a hat with great feathers, bowing and laughing on every side with profuse amiability, had affected the Liparians, accustomed to the calm haughtiness of their own rulers, with an apparently inextinguishable gaiety. The Queen of Syria became the universal topic of conversation; and every conversation referring to her was accented with a smile of wickedness. Withal she seemed so entirely good-natured that it was impossible to say a word against her; and people were only amused about her. They remembered that the Syrians had subscribed fabulous sums at the time of the inundations. And the merriment that blew over Lipara was a southern merriment, free from malice and vented in sheer jolly laughter and delight, because the Liparians had never seen so droll a queen.

The great manoeuvres took place on the parade-ground. The king accompanied the emperor and the princes on horseback, with a bevy of European and oriental aides-de-camp. Their consorts with their suite watched the march-past from landaus. Berengar marched bravely with his company of grenadiers, in which he was a lieutenant, as well as he could march with his short little legs, and stiffened his small features, so as not to betray the difficulty it cost him to keep pace with his men's long step. The hussars astonished the Syrian monarch by their unity with their horses, when in wild career they threw themselves half off and in still more rapid rushes picked up a flag from the ground, swung themselves up again with a yell and waved the bunting. The Africans executed their showy fantasias, brandished their spears, which flashed like loosened sheaves of sunbeams, and came fluttering on in clouds of white burnouses and dust, amid which their negro heads clustered darkly in endless black patches and their eyes glistened.

In addition there was a military tournament, followed by garden-parties, races, regattas, popular games and fireworks. Lipara was one city of pleasure. Every day it was traversed by royal processions, the array of uniforms glittered like live gold, the imperial landaus rattled in the sun, with the spokes of their wheels flashing through the light dust which flew up from the flagged pavements of the town. Most brilliant of all, like drops of white flame, were the diamonds which the Syrian pair wore even in the streets. At night, when the sun ceased shining, there shone over the white town, vague with evening light, and over its violet harbour, festoons of salamanders and gaudy bridges of fire, factitiously bright beneath the silent silver glances of the stars; rockets fell hissing into the water, on which the boats showed black, and left behind them a faint, oppressive savour of gunpowder in the night.

In the great hall of pillars the ceremonial banquets followed one after the other, with a display of gold plate of incredible value. The Queen of Syria wore her curious, theatrical costumes, her broad bosom always crossed by the blue ribbon of an order covered with badges; her hair was dressed with tall plumes, hung with small diamonds. She talked with great vivacity, thankful for the kindness of her Liparian friends, for the enjoyment and for the cheering. Her profuse gestures enlivened everybody, introduced an element of fun into the stately Liparian etiquette. Elizabeth herself could not but laugh at them. The queen played her royal part with the self-possession of a bad but good-natured actress. She spoke to everybody, spread amiable little atoms of her small, chubby, brown majesty over one and all. Next her sat the king, looking dignified and wise as Solomon. The emperor praised him for a sensible, broad-minded sovereign: the king had already paid many visits to Europe. The Syrian aide-de-camps were dignified too, calm and composed, a little stiff in their ways, adapting themselves to western manners; the queen's ladies-in-waiting wore the trains of their Paris or London dresses a little strangely, but still looked slender in them, brown and attractive, with their curly little heads and long, almond-shaped eyes: still they would have been prettier in draped gold-gauze.

The Syrians stayed twelve days before going on to Italy. It was the last evening but one: in the Imperial a suite of fourteen rooms had been lighted up around the great ballroom for a ball. Three thousand invitations had been sent out. In the fore-court and in the neighbouring main-streets stood the grenadiers.

The ballroom was at the back of the palace; the tall, balconied windows were open and looked across their balustrades upon the shadows of the park of plane-trees. The band resounded from the groups of palms in the gallery. The imperial quadrille had been formed in the centre of the room: the emperor with the queen, the king and the empress, the Archduke of Carinthia and Thera, Othomar with the archduchess. The other official quadrilles formed their figures around them. Hundreds of guests looked on.

From the coruscating rock-crystal of the chandeliers, the electric light flowed in white patches out of the high dome, glided along the inlaid-marble walls and porphyry pillars of the ballroom and poured in millions of scintillations on the smooth facets of the jewels, on the gold of the uniforms and court-dresses, on the shimmering white brocades of the trains; for white was prescribed: all the ladies were in white; and the snow of the velvets, the lily glow of the satins were silver-shrill. One blinding whirl of refulgence passed through the immense room with its changing glamours. For the light never stood still, continually changed its brightest spot, turned the ball into one glittering kaleidoscope. The light gilded each bit of gold-lace, was caught in every brilliant, hung in every pearl. The music seemed to be one with that light; the brass resounded like gold.

The Duchess of Yemena stood among a group of diplomatists and equerries; she rose monumental in her beauty, which was statuesque and splendid in this wayward illumination. She seemed supernaturally tall, thanks to the heavy Watteau plait which trailed from her back in white brocade. She wore her tiara of emeralds and brilliants; and the same green stones sparkled in a great jewelled spray that blossomed over her bodice.

The emperor came up to her; she drooped in her famous curtsey and Oscar jested with her for a moment. When the emperor had passed on, she saw the crown-prince approach. She curtseyed again; he bowed smilingly and offered her his arm. Slowly they went through the ballroom.

"I have something important to say to you," he whispered, in a conversational tone.

He could not move away with her; they would be missed. So they continued to walk through the rooms.

"It is so long since I saw you ... alone!" she whispered, reproachfully, in the same voice. "And what did ... what did your highness wish to say to me?"

They spoke cautiously, with the smile of cool conversation on their lips, deadening the sound of their voices, casting indifferent glances around them, to see whether they could be overheard.

"Something ... that I have long wanted to tell you.... A decision I have to take...."

The words came crumbling in fragments from his lips and not sounding with their true accent, from caution. She perceived that he was about to tell her some great piece of news. She trembled without knowing why.... He himself did not know whether what he was doing was cruel or not: he did not know this woman well enough for that. But he did know that he had purposely chosen this difficult moment for his interview, because he was uncertain how she would bear it ... how she would bear it in a *tête-à-tête*, when she would be able to give way to her passion. Here he knew how she would bear it: smilingly, as a woman of the world, although it turned to anguish for her. Perhaps after all he was cruel.... But it was too late now: he must go through with it.

She looked up at him, moving the feathers of her fan. He continued:

"A decision.... When our Syrian guests have left ... I ... I am going on a journey...."

"Where to, highness?"

"To ... to different European courts...."

She asked nothing more; her smile died away; then she smiled again, like an automaton. She asked nothing more, because she well knew what it meant when a crown-prince went on a journey to different European courts. That meant a bridal progress. And she merely said, in a voice that could not but sound plaintively:

"So soon?..."

So soon!... Was her imperial romance to last so short a time? She had indeed known that this might be the end of it, for she knew him to be too pure to retain her by the side of a young consort. Also she had pictured an end like this after a year, two years perhaps, she withdrawing herself, and she had pictured to herself that she would do so without any feeling of spite against her young future empress. But now! So soon! Barely a few weeks! So short a time as that no romance of her life had ever lasted! She felt an aching melancholy; a mist hazed over her eyes; and the lights of the ballroom shimmered before her as if through water. She constantly forgot to smile, but, so soon as she remembered, she smiled again:

"So soon?..."

"It must be...."

Yes, it must be, it could not be otherwise. For her, this was the end of her life. She felt no despair because of this ending; only a smarting sorrow. It was the end. After this imperial romance there would be no other. Oh no, never more! She would sacrifice her youth to it; she would launch her stepdaughters into society. She would be grateful that she had lived and would now grow old. But old: she was still so young, she still felt herself so young! She now first perceived how she loved her crown-prince. And she would have liked to be elsewhere, far from the brilliant ball, to embrace him once more alone, for the last time.... Oh, this sorrow because everything must end, as though nothing were more than a fleeting perfume!...

"I am trusting you, duchess," he now said. "I hope you will say nothing about this journey. You understand, it is all still a secret; no choice has been made yet ... it has been discussed with no one except their majesties and Myxila. I can trust you, can't I?"

She smilingly nodded yes.

"But I wanted to tell you at once," he continued.

She smiled again. At this moment a strange storm seemed to burst ... behind the palace, under the palace, where? Right through the blare of the music and the blaze of the light, a crash of thunder shook and rolled. It was as though the palace had been struck by lightning, for immediately afterwards, through the open windows, there came from one of the back-wings of the palace a rattling clatter of stones, which seemed tossed into the air, of great rafters, which fell noisily and roughly, of shivers of glass, which seemed to be splintering shrilly on every side....

The music was suddenly silenced. The uniforms, the court-trains rushed to the open balconies, which overlooked the park; but the night was dark, the park was hushed. A last couple of rafters seemed to be still falling, with a last crash of stones....

In the bright glare of the electric light, faces turned deathly pale, like the faces of corpses. Eyes stared at one another in terror. The duchess half-sank against Othomar when she saw Elizabeth tear past her with wild, vacant eyes and out at a door, her long, white velvet train trailing madly after her, round the corner. The mistress of the robes followed her; so did Hélène of Thesbia. The emperor appeared to give the chamberlains some hurried orders; then he also left the ballroom, accompanied by a few officers.

Shortly afterwards the music again burst forth from the balcony in the gallery. Many equerries and aides-de-camp were seen bowing to their partners, the ladies trembling as they rose. The ball proceeded; the uniforms and trains glittered as before in the windings of the waltz. But the smiles seemed to have been obliterated from the dancers' features and their pallid faces turned the ball into a dance of death.

Leoni, shivering, bowed before Othomar:

"A dynamite explosion, low down in the cellars of the western back-wing. The anterooms of his majesty's private apartments are destroyed. His majesty requests your highness to make every effort to continue the ball. All officers and court-ladies are commanded to dance."

The duchess clutched Othomar's arm, almost fainting. The rumour spread around them. The equerries dragged their partners along half-swooning. Two were seen carried away in a dead faint. The Queen of Syria stood vacantly beside the Archduke of Carinthia, who put his arm round her heavy waist to dance. She did not yet seem able to make up her mind.

Othomar passed his arm round the duchess:

"O God, I can't do it!" she stammered. "For God's sake, highness, don't ask me!...."

"We must," he said. "His majesty wishes it...."

"His majesty wishes...." she repeated.

Her legs trembled beneath her as though with electric thrills. Then she let him take her and they danced.

Every one danced.

The empress had rushed up the stairs and along the galleries to the bedroom-floor. She did not see that two ladies were following her; she thrust back a door:

"Berengar!" she screamed.

The young prince's bedroom was lighted. The boy had half-risen, in his little shirt, from his camp-bed. His valet and a chambermaid stood in dismay in the middle of the room.

"Berengar!" the empress gasped out, rejoicing when she saw him unharmed.

She threw her arms around him, pressed him to her bosom.

"Oh, mamma, you're hurting me!" cried the boy, indignantly.

Her jewels had brought a drop of blood from his little bare chest. She now embraced him more gently, with nervous sobs that choked in her throat. A spray of diamond ostrich-feathers fell to the ground; the maid picked them up with awkward fingers.

"Mamma, are they blowing up the palace?"

"No, Berengar, no, it's nothing...."

"Mamma, I want to go and look! I must see what's happening!"

"Berengar...."

The door had been left open; the emperor entered, calmly. The ladies stood in the corridor, waiting for the empress....

"Papa, may I go with you and look?"

"No, Berengar, there's nothing to see. Go to sleep...."

Then he offered his arm to Elizabeth:

"Madam," he said, tranquilly.

She threw him an imploring glance. He continued to hold out his arm to her. Then she kissed the boy once more, soothed him to sleep:

"Wait a moment," she stammered to Oscar.

She went to the glass; the maid, with her clumsy fingers, fastened the jewelled spray to the edge of the low-cut bodice, spread out the square train.

"I'm ready," the empress said to Oscar, in a lifeless voice.

She took his arm; the emperor just pressed her hand; and they nodded once more to Berengar and went.

Arm-in-arm the imperial pair appeared for the second time at the ball. The empress was pale but smiling. She was magnificent, delicate with dainty majesty in the trailing white velvet, upon which, on the bodice and over the front of the skirt, flickered sprays of diamond ostrich-feathers, formed into fleurs-de-lys. An empress' crown of brilliants crowned her small, round head.

It was two o'clock. Generally the sovereigns were accustomed to stay till one o'clock at the court balls. The Queen of Syria, however, in her exuberant love of life, had begged them to stay longer. They had consented. Had they left at one o'clock, the explosion would have taken place at the moment when Oscar would probably just have entered his apartments. They had first talked of the anterooms only: but it would now appear that great damage had also been done to the emperor's own room.

Supper began. They supped in a large hall; from every table rose a palm-tree and the hall was thus turned into a forest of palms. The floor was strewn with gold sand, which powdered the trains as their wearers walked upon it. Electric light shone through the long leaves like moonlight. In this moonlight the faces remained deadly white, like patches of chalk, above the glittering crystal and all the gold plate. The music clattered with great cymbal-strokes of brass.

5

"To HER MAJESTY THE QUEEN OF GOTHLAND.

"IMPERIAL,

"LIPARA,

" —*May*, 18—.

"MY DEAREST SISTER,

"At last I can find time to write to you. The excitement of the visit of our good Syrians is over and Lipara has calmed down. But my reflections are nothing but sadness. And this is why, Olga.

"I fear that Othomar is much more ill than the doctors perceive. He has become thinner and looks very bad. He never complains much, but yet he told me lately that he often felt tired. The doctors think that he needs a rest and recommend a long sea-voyage. His journey through Europe, about which I wrote to you in my last, will have to be postponed. And now I want to ask you a favour.

"I know that Herman is soon going to take a long voyage on the *Viking* to India, Japan and America; and it would be my fondest wish at this moment that Othomar might accompany him. When the doctors advised a sea-voyage, I discussed the matter to Oscar, but we came to no decision. My boy, you must know, Olga, has no friend of his own age; and this made me so sad and we did not know how nor with whom to send him on this voyage in a way which would be pleasant for him and which would not involve a solitary banishment from our home-circle. He is on excellent terms with his equerries, but yet that is not what I should desire: a cordial, mutual, confidential friendship with some one of his own age with whom he could spend a certain time, solely with a view to enjoyment and relaxation.

"I know quite well that it is to some extent my boy's fault and due to his innate diffidence and reticence. Nevertheless he has qualities for which he could easily be loved, if they were known, if he allowed them to appear. Don't you agree, Olga? You are fond of him too: it is not only my own blind mother's love that finds my son lovable and sympathetic? And that is why I should be so very glad if Herman would take him with him and learn to know him better: who knows whether they would not then come to love each other! Othomar has already told me that, on their journey through the north of Liparia, they were drawn much closer together than they had thought they would be; but it was a busy time: every moment was filled with duties and business and they had no time to talk together and get to know each other. And yet, at such a difficult period of united labour, two young men can learn to know each other even without talking. At any rate, they have already become more friendly. At one time, Olga, they used to dislike each other, to my bitter sorrow; they would even not meet; even outwardly there was nothing but coolness between them: oh, how unhappy all this used to make me, when I saw our boys so hostile to each other and remembered how *we* used to be, Olga, when we were girls together in our beautiful old castle near Bucharest! How we lived bound up in each other! Olga, Olga, how terribly long ago that all is! Our parents are dead, our brothers dispersed, the castle is deserted and we are separated: when do we see each other? Scarcely now and then, for a couple of days at a time, when we meet somewhere for a wedding of relations; and then these are always restless days, when we can see next to nothing of each other. Then, sometimes, not even every year, a fortnight either in Gothland or here. You sometimes reproach me that I, who am so fond of Gothland, come to you so seldom, but it is always for the same reason: Othomar does not care to leave Liparia and I can't leave my husband. I can be strong when I am at his side, but alone I am so weak, Olga. That anything might happen to *him* which I should not share increases my dread unbearably. I felt that again quite lately, when I was with Thera at Altara: our visit was announced and binding; and, however unwilling I was to leave Oscar, I was obliged to go, was I not? It was just at that trying period; Lipara was under martial law. But Oscar wished me to go and I went. Oh, how I suffered at that time!

"But I am becoming used to my fears, I do not complain and I accept life as it comes; I only hope that my boy will also learn to accept it thus. Perhaps he will learn. Indeed it is not so easy for him, for he will have to do more than his mother, who, as a woman, can be much more passive; and it is easier to learn to acquiesce passively than actively. But the Saints will surely give him strength later to bear his lot and his crown; this I rely upon. And yet, O Olga, it makes me so immensely sad that we are sovereigns! But let me not continue in this strain: it weakens one, it is not right, it is not right....

"There is also a secret reason why I should like to get Othomar away from Lipara, though it always grieves me so much to part from my darling. There seems after all to be some truth in those rumours about the Duchess of Yemena: Oscar asked Myxila about it and he could not deny it and even said that it was generally known. I do my best not to take it too much to heart, Olga, but I think it a terrible thing. O God, let me not think or write about it any more; otherwise it will go whirling so in my poor head! What can my son see in a woman who is older than his own mother! What a terrible world, this is, Olga, in which these things take place; and how can there be such women, whom you and I will never understand! For, after all, temperament is not everything: every woman has her own heart; and in that we ought all to see one another; but it would seem that we can't. In my sadness about this, I prefer to assume that the woman loves my boy and therefore deceives her husband. Oh, it is so wicked also of my boy: why need he be like this, he who is otherwise so good! I just assume that she loves him. Not long ago we had my last drawing-room, the function with which, as you know, our winter-season ends; and, when she came up to me and bowed before me and pressed her lips to my hand, she must have felt my disapproval and my sadness radiating from my fingers, for she rose out of her curtsey with a desperate look of anguish in her eyes and a sort of sob in her throat! I stared at her coldly, but all the same I pitied her, Olga, for, when a woman of our world is so little able to control herself at a ceremonial moment, in the presence of her empress, her soul must have sustained a severe shock: do you not think so too?

"We are now quiet. In a week we are going to our summer-quarters in Xara, at Castel Xaveria; the weather is already very hot here. I should so much like to have your answer before we leave and to know how Herman takes my request. I know that he is very fond of me and will doubtless gladly grant it and that he will try to like Othomar for my sake; and let me hasten to add that it is also *Othomar's* dearest wish that he should travel with Herman. The sea-voyage did not attract him in the least at first, because he knew of no one to take with him and he said he preferred to go with us to Castel Xaveria; but, when I mentioned Herman, he joined in my plan entirely.

"Olga, what will the summer bring us, peace or not? I dare not hope. The winter has been horrible; our northern provinces have not yet recovered from the disasters. The misery there is irretrievable. There is an epidemic of typhoid and there have been many cases of cholera. The strikes in the east are now over, but I am so afraid of that rough, violent repression. Oh, if everything could only be done with gentleness! That attempt on Othomar's life and the explosion at the last ball have also made me so ill. How I should love to see you and take you in my arms: can you not come to Castel Xaveria and spend the summer with us? It would give me such intense, such intense pleasure!

"Kiss Siegfried and the children for me. And answer me soon, will you not? I embrace you fervently.

"Your affectionate sister,

"ELIZABETH."

CHAPTER IV

1

August, on the Baltic. The grey billows curl against the rocks with high, rounded crests of thick foam. The sky above is one wide cupola, through which drift great mountain-ranges of grey-white clouds. They come up slowly, filling the firmament with their changing, shadowy masses, like chains of rocks and Alps floating on the air, and slowly drift away again. The sea has a narrow beach, with many crumbling cliffs; quite close at hand loom sombre green pine-woods. With the gloom of the pine-woods for a background, as it were half out of the cliffs rises old Altseeborgen. It is a weather-beaten castle, at which the writhing waves seem to gnaw; its three tall, uneven towers soar round and massive into the sky. The broad road to the castle slants up from the woods terrace-wise and leads to the esplanade at the back, where the main entrance is. Round the castle the wide granite terraces are cut into stairs, with their rugged balustrades, whose freestone is worn away by the salt air. These terraces enjoy a more extensive view of the sea as they rise higher, higher; and, seen from the topmost terrace, the sea lies against the beach, to right and left, in one great, strangely mobile expanse, a living element. Across the sea the south-winds blow upon the castle; the pine-woods shelter it to some extent from the northernly gales.

From the tallest tower an imposing standard flaps gaily in the air: two yellow stripes and a white stripe between, with the dark patch of the crenellated fortress which forms the arms of Gothland. It floats there on the sunless morning like a smile in the sky; it swells and falls limp again and then again lets itself be blown high up by the wind, which comes swinging lustily over the water.

A young man and a girl are walking on the beach; they talk, smile, look at each other. She is taller than he, with a very fair complexion; under her little sailor-hat a few of her auburn tresses, tangled by the wind, blow across her face; she keeps on smoothing them away. She wears a simple blue serge skirt and a white blouse, with a broad leather belt around her waist. Her dainty little feet, in their black-silk stockings and yellow-leather shoes, are constantly uncovered by the wind. She carelessly swings a pair of gloves in her hand.

The young man wears a light check summer suit and a straw hat. He is short and slender; his black eyes have a look of gentle melancholy. He appears to be telling the girl by his side a tale of travel; she listens, with her smile.

Round about them, in spite of the wind, the atmosphere is full of peace. Walking along the beach, they go by the castle, pass round behind it and look up. From one of the windows somebody gaily waves a hand and calls out something. They try to hear, with their hands to their ears, but they shrug their shoulders: the wind has blown the words away. They wave their hands again and walk on.

They do not go far, however, always along the beach. Yonder lies the fishing-village, lie a couple of small villas, almost cottages. One of them seems just to have been taken by a large family, for the holiday-month no doubt; a hum of voices issues from it, children chase one another along the beach; a tiny girl, in running, bumps against the young man.

"Hullo there!" he says, pleasantly, with a laugh.

Laughing they walk on.

The children run along. A fisherman comes with his nets, grins cheerily and mutters a greeting. A fat lady in the verandah has been watching the young people inquisitively; she sees the fisherman touch his cap and beckons to him:

"Who are that lady and gentleman?"

The fisherman points cheerily to Altseeborgen:

"From the castle."

"But who are they?" asks the lady, alarmed.

"Well, the gentleman is the Prince of Liparia and the young lady is an Austrian princess," says the fisherman, as if it could not well be anybody else.

The lady looks in dismay after the princely pair and then in despair at her running children. The young couple are just turning back in their walk; they are now laughing even more gaily than before and are hastening a little towards the castle, as though they had delayed too long. The lady, still pale, does not dare to offer excuses, but makes a low bow; she receives a pleasant greeting in return.

2

The royal family of Gothland were in the habit of spending the whole summer at Altseeborgen. The beach was particularly well-suited for laying out a watering-place around the fishing-village, but King Siegfried would never hear of this: the beach and the village were royal domains; a few modest villas were all that he had granted permission to build. Generally these were visited in the summer by two or three middle-class families with their children. Altseeborgen should never become a modern bathing-place, however excellent the fashionable world might consider it as a means of summer display, lying as it did in the immediate neighbourhood of the royal castle.

But the Gothlandic family made a point of guarding the freedom of their summer lives. They lived there for four months, without palace-etiquette, in the greatest simplicity. They formed a numerous family; and there were always many visitors. The king attended to state-affairs in homely fashion at the castle. His grandchildren would run into his room while he was discussing important business with the prime minister, who came down to Altseeborgen on certain days. He just patted their flaxen curls and sent them away to play, with a caress. Staying at the castle were the Crown-prince Gunther and the Crown-princess Sofie, a German princess—Duke and Duchess of Wendeholm—with their four children, a girl and three boys. Next to the duke came Prince Herman; next to him Princess Wanda, twenty years of age; next to her, the younger princes, Olaf and Christofel. In addition there were always two old princesses, sisters of the king, widows of German princes. From all the courts of Europe, which were as one great family, different members came from time to time to stay, bringing with them their respective *nuances* of a different nationality, something exotic in voice and manner, so far as all this was not merged in their cosmopolitanism.

Othomar had been three months at sea with Herman; they had touched shore in India, China, Japan and America. They had travelled incognito, so as to escape all official receptions, and Othomar had borne no other title than that of Prince Czykirski. The voyage had done Othomar much good: he was even feeling so well that he had written to the Empress Elizabeth that he would like to stay some time longer in the family-circle at Altseeborgen, but that he would afterwards undertake his long-contemplated journey to the European courts.

Their easy life in each other's company had done much to bring the cousins closer together. Herman had learnt to see in Othomar, beneath his stiffness and lack of ease, a young crown-prince who was afraid of his future, but who possessed much reasonableness and was willing to learn to acquiesce in life and to fortify himself for his coming yoke of empire. He understood Othomar and felt sorry for him. He himself took a vital pleasure in life: merely to breathe was an enjoyment; his existence as a second son, with only his naval duties, which he loved by heredity, as a descendant of the old sea-kings might well love them, opened before him a prospect of nothing but continued, cloudless freedom from care; that he was a king's son gave him nothing but satisfaction and delight; and he appreciated his high estate with jovial pleasure, skimming the cream from a chalice out of which Othomar in due time would drink gall and wormwood. If at first he compared Othomar with his brother, the Duke of Wendeholm—a crown-prince too, of Gothland he—Herman now compared them no longer; his judgement had become more reasonable: he understood that no comparison was possible. Liparia was a tremendous, almost despotic empire; the people, especially in the south, always very fickle, always kept in check by force, on account of their childish uncertainty as to what, in their capriciousness, they would do next. The Gothlanders, on the other hand, calmly liberal in temperament, devoid of noisy vehemence, ranged themselves peacefully, with their long-established, ample constitution, round King Siegfried, whom they called the father of his country. That Gunther was not afraid of having to wear the crown one day, was this a reason why Othomar should be without his fear? Did Othomar not possess the gentler qualities, which are valued in the narrow circle of intimate surroundings and arouse esteem among a few sympathetic natures, rather than that fiercer brilliancy of character, which makes its possessor stand out in clear relief in high places and awakens admiration in the multitude? Was this boy, with his soul full of scruples, his nostalgia after justice, his yearning for love, his easily wounded sensitiveness, was he the son of his ancestors, the descendant of Berengar the Strong, Wenceslas the Cruel, son of the warlike Xaveria, or was he not rather the child of his gentle mother alone?

It was not in Herman's way to reflect much and long on all this, but it came to him suddenly, abruptly, like a new view that is opened out in a brighter light. And what had been antipathy in him became compassion, friendship and astonishment at the disposition of the universe, which knew not what else to do with a soul like Othomar's but to crush it beneath a crown.

The simple family-life at Altseeborgen worked on Othomar like a cure. He felt himself reviving amid natural surroundings, his humanity developing wide and untrammelled. Accustomed as he was to the ceremonial life of the Imperial, with its court-etiquette strictly maintained by the Emperor Oscar, he was at first surprised, but soon delighted by the almost homely simplicity of his Gothlandic relations. In former years, it is true, he had paid an occasional brief visit to Altseeborgen, but had never stayed long enough to be able to count himself, as now, quite one of themselves.

Othomar was at this moment the only visitor from abroad, except the Archduchess Valérie, a niece of the Emperor of Austria. Did the young people suspect anything, or not? Were their names coupled together by the younger princes and princesses? Not so, to all outward seeming: only once or twice had Princess Sofie or Princess Wanda found it necessary to hush her young brothers with a glance. And yet it was with a serious intention that the Queen of Gothland, in concert with the Emperor of Liparia and Valérie's parents—the Archduke Albrecht and the Archduchess of Eudoxie, who lived at Sigismundingen Castle—had brought the young people together. The Emperor Oscar would certainly have preferred one of the young Russian grand-duchesses, a niece of the Czar, for his daughter-in-law; but the difference in religion remained an insurmountable obstacle; and the emperor, despite his preference, had no objection to the Austrian alliance.

Perhaps Othomar and Valérie divined this intention, but the secret caused no constraint between them; they were both so accustomed to hearing the names of well-known princes or princesses connected with theirs and even to seeing them mentioned in the papers: announcements of betrothals which were immediately contradicted; they had even jested together about the number of times that public opinion had married them to this one or to that, each time to somebody else; sometimes even the news came as a surprise to themselves, which they found in the newspapers and laughed at. They paid no heed therefore to the rare mischievous remarks of Prince Olaf or Prince Christofel, sturdy lads of seventeen and fifteen, who thought it great fun to tease. And all this time Queen Olga, so sensible and reasonable, brought not the least influence to bear upon them. She had invited them together, but she did nothing more. Perhaps she observed silently how they behaved towards each other and wrote just one letter on the subject to her sister, but she kept quite outside the meshes which were weaving between their two crowned lives. Yet it was difficult for her to stand aloof. She was fond of Valérie and thought that this marriage would be in every way good. But added to that came urgent letters from Sigismundingen and even from Vienna, where they wished for nothing more eagerly than to see the young archduchess Duchess of Xara. For this, apart from the natural inclination of the Austrian court to set store by a renewed alliance with Liparia, there were other reasons of a more intimate character.

3

The sun had appeared through the clouds in the afternoon and made the grey of the sky and the water turn blue with the hazy blueness of a northern summer. The sea glowed and put on scales of gold; the weather-beaten castle stood blistering its broad granite pile in the sun, as an old man does his back. The striped canvas awning was lowered on the top terrace, which led into the great hall through three glass doors. Rugs lay scattered over the ground. Princess Sofie and the Archduchess Valérie sat in great wickerwork chairs, painting in water-colours. From the hall sounded, monotonously, the soft exercises of Princess Elizabeth, the crown-princess' eldest daughter, who was practising. Princess Wanda sat on the ground, romping a trifle boisterously with her youngest two nephews, Erik and Karl. On a long wicker chair lay Prince Herman, with both legs up; next to him was a little table heaped with newspapers and periodicals, some of which had fallen to the ground; a great tumbler of sherry-cobbler stood on the wicker ledge of his chair; the blue smoke rose from a cigarette between his fingers.

Sofie and Valérie compared their sketches and laughed. They looked at the sky, which was bisected by the awning: the clouds, woolly white, surged one above the other; the sea was dazzling with its golden scales, like a giant cuirass.

"What are you two painting there?" asked Herman, who was turning the pages of an illustrated paper.

"Clouds," replied Valérie, "nothing but clouds. I have persuaded Sofie to make studies of clouds with me. Presently, if you're not too lazy, you must come and look at my album." She gave a little laugh. "It contains nothing but clouds!"

"By Jove!" drawled Herman. "How very odd!..."

"Yes," said Sofie, dreamily, "clouds are very nice, but you never know how to catch them: they change every instant."

"Erik," said Herman, "just ask Aunt Valérie to lend me her album."

"No, no," cried Wanda, "go and fetch it yourself, lazybones!..."

But Erik wanted to go; and there came a great struggle. Wanda hugged the little fellow tight in her arms; Karl joined in: there was a general romp and Wanda, laughing, fell sideways to the ground.

"But, Wanda!" said Sofie, reprovingly.

Valérie stood up and went to Herman:

"With all this, you're not seeing my clouds, you lazy boy. I suppose I must take pity on you. Look...."

Herman now suddenly drew himself up and took the album:

"How funny!" he said. "Yellow and white and violet and pink. All sunsets!"

"And sunrises. I dare say I see more of them than you do!"

"The things you see in clouds, Valérie! It's astonishing. How one person differs from another! I should never take it into my head to go and sketch clouds. You ought to come for a cruise with me one day; then you could make whole collections of clouds."

"Why didn't you propose that earlier?" said Valérie, jestingly. "Then I might have joined you and Xara."

"But where is Othomar?" said Herman.

Valérie said that she did not know....

Herman sipped his sherry-cobbler. Wanda wanted a taste, but Herman refused and told her to ring for a glass for herself. Wanda insisted; he seized her by the wrists.

"But Wanda!" Sofie repeated, reprovingly, languidly, drawing her hand over her forehead and laying down her brush.

Wanda laughed gaily:

"But Wanda!" she mimicked.

And they all laughed at Sofie, including Sofie herself:

"Did I speak like that?" she asked, with her languid voice. "I don't know: I get so sleepy here, so lazy...."

They were all making fun of Sofie, when voices sounded from the hall, shrill, old voices. It was the two dowagers, with Othomar; the old ladies were talking in a courtly, mincing way to the young prince, who brought them chairs. The aunts had had a siesta after lunch; they now made their reappearance, with tapestrywork in large reticules. All greeted them with great respect, beneath which lurked a spark of mischief.

"*Pardon, lieber Herzog,*" murmured old Princess Elsa, the older of the two, "I would rather have that little chair...."

Princess Marianne also wanted a small, straight chair; the old ladies thanked Othomar with an obeisance for his gallantry, sat down stiffly and began their embroidery: great coats-of-arms for chair-backs. They were very stately, with clear-cut but wrinkled faces, grey *tours* and black lace caps; they wore crackling watered-silk gowns, of old-fashioned cut. Now and then they exchanged a quick, sharp word, with a sudden crackling movement of their sharp cockatoo-profiles; they gazed thoughtfully for a moment out to sea, as though they were bound to see something important arriving out of the distance; then they resumed their work. Their old-fashioned, stately, tight-laced, shrivelled figures formed a strange contrast with the easiness of the young people in their simple serge summer suits: they made Princess Wanda's tangled hair and rumpled blouse look perfectly disreputable.

A third old lady came sailing up; she seemed as though she were related to the two dowagers, but was actually Countess von Altenburg, who used to be mistress of the household to Princess Elsa. Behind her were two footmen, carrying trays with coffee and pastry, the old princesses' *goûter*. The countess made a stately curtsey before the young princes.

"The territory is occupied," whispered Herman to Valérie.

They had all sat down again and among themselves were teasing Othomar with his three Fates, as they called them, unheard by the aunts or the countess, who was rather deaf. A noisy babel of tongues ensued: the aunts spoke German and screamed, to make themselves heard, something about the calmness of the sea into the poor old ears of the countess, who poured out the coffee and nodded that she understood. The younger princes talked English for the most part; Herman sometimes spoke a word or two of Liparian to Othomar; and the children, who had gone to play on a lower terrace, chattered noisily in Gothlandic and French indifferently.

The footmen had brought out afternoon tea and placed it before Princess Sofie, when a lady-in-waiting appeared. She bowed to the young crown-princess and said, in Gothlandic:

"Her majesty requests your royal highness to come to her in the small drawing-room."

"Mamma has sent for me," said Princess Sofie, in English, rising from her chair. "Wanda, will you pour out the tea? Children, will you go upstairs and get dressed? Wanda, tell them again, will you?"

The crown-princess went through the hall, a great, round, dome-shaped apartment, full of stags' antlers, elks' heads, hunting-trophies, and then up a staircase. In the queen's anteroom the footman opened the door for her. Queen Olga was sitting alone; she was some years older than her sister, the Empress of Liparia, taller and more heavily built; her features, however, had much in common with Elizabeth's, but were more filled out.

"Sofie," she at once began, in German, "I have had a letter from Sigismundingen...."

The Duchess of Wendeholm had sat down:

"Anything to do with Valérie?" she asked, in alarm.

"Yes," the queen said, with a reflective glance. "Poor child!..."

"But what is it, Mamma?"

"There, read for yourself...."

The queen handed the letter to her daughter-in-law, who read it hurriedly. The letter was from the Archduchess Eudoxie, Valérie's mother, written with a feverish, excited hand, and said, in phrases which tried to seem indifferent but which betrayed a great satisfaction, that Prince Leopold of Lohe-Obkowitz was at Nice with Estelle Desvaux, the well-known actress, that he was proposing to resign his titular rights in favour of his younger brother and that he would then marry his mistress. The letter requested the queen or the crown-princess to tell this to Valérie, in the hope that it would not prove too great a shock to her. Further, the letter ended with violent attacks upon Prince Leopold, who had caused such a scandal, but at the same time with manifest expressions of delight that now perhaps Valérie would no longer dream of becoming the lady of a domain measuring six yards square! The archduke added a postscript to say that this was not a vague report but a certainty and that Prince Leopold himself had told it to their own relations at Nice, who had written to Sigismundingen.

"Has Valérie ever spoken to you about Prince Lohe?" asked the queen.

"Only once in a way, mamma," replied the Duchess of Wendeholm, handing back the letter. "But we all know well enough that this news will be a great blow to her. Is she not in the least prepared for it?"

"Probably not: you see, we had none of us heard or read anything about it! Shall I tell her? Poor child!..."

"Shall I do so, mamma? As I told you, Valérie *has* spoken to me...."

"Very well, you do it...."

The duchess reflected, looked at the clock:

"It is so late now: I'll tell her after dinner; we are none of us dressed yet.... What do you think?"

"Very well then, after dinner...."

The crown-princess went out: it was time to hurry and dress. At seven o'clock a loud, long bell sounded. They assembled in the hall; the dining-room looked out with its large bow-windows upon the pine-forest. It was a long table: King Siegfried, a hale old sovereign with a full, grey beard; Queen Olga; the Crown-prince Gunther, tall, fair, two-and-thirty; Princess Sofie and her children; Othomar, sitting between his aunt and Valérie; Herman and Wanda; Olaf and Christofel; the two dowagers with Countess von Altenburg; equerries, ladies-in-waiting, chamberlains, Princess Elizabeth's governess, the little princes' tutors....

The conversation was cheerful and unconstrained. The ladies wore simple evening-frocks; the king was in dress-clothes, the younger princes and equerries in dinner-jackets. The young princesses wore light summer dresses of white serge or pink *mousseline-de-laine*; they had stuck a flower or two from the conservatory into their waist-bands.

Valérie talked merrily; Herman once more teased her about her cloud-sketches, but Othomar said that he admired them very much. Queen Olga and Princess Sofie exchanged a glance and were quieter than the others. The king also looked very thoughtfully at the young people. After dinner the family dispersed; the crown-prince and Herman went for a row on the sea, with the younger princes and the children, in two boats. Wanda and Valérie, their arms wound around each other's waists, strolled up and down along the front-terrace; the awning was already drawn up for the night. The sea was still blue, the sky pearl-grey and no longer so bright; above the horizon the sun still burnt ragged rents in the widely scattered clouds.

The girls strolled about, laughed, looked at the two little boats on the sea and waved to them. Very far away, a steamer passed, finely outlined, with a dirty little ribbon of smoke. The young princes shouted, "Hurrah! Hurrah!" and hoisted their little flag.

"Do look at those papers of Herman's!" said Valérie. "Aunt Olga hates that untidiness...."

She pointed to all the magazines and newspapers which the servants had forgotten to clear away. They lay over the long wicker chair, on the table and on the ground.

"Shall I ring to have them cleared away?" asked Wanda.

"Oh, never mind!" said Valérie.

She herself picked up one or two papers, folded them, put them together; Wanda again waved to the boats with her handkerchief.

"My God!" she suddenly heard Valérie murmur, faintly.

She looked round: the young archduchess had turned pale and sunk into a chair. She had dropped the papers again; one of them she held tight, crushing it convulsively; she looked down at it with eyes vacant with terror:

"It's not true," she stammered. "They always lie.... They lie!"

"What is it, Valérie?" cried Wanda, frightened.

At this moment the Duchess of Wendeholm came out through the hall:

"Valérie!" she called.

The girl did not hear. The duchess came nearer:

"Valérie!" she repeated. "Could I talk to you for a moment, alone?"

The archduchess raised her pale little face. She seemed not to hear, not to understand.

"My God!" whispered the duchess to Wanda. "Does she know?"

"What?" asked Wanda.

But a footman also came through the hall; he carried a silver tray with letters. There were a couple of letters for the duchess; he presented them to her first; then one to Valérie. In spite of her blurred eyes, the archduchess seemed to see the letter; she snatched at it greedily. The man withdrew.

"O ... God!..." she stammered at last.

She pulled the letter from the envelope, half-tearing it in her eagerness, and read with crazy eyes. Sofie and Wanda looked at her in dismay.

"O ... God!" screamed the archduchess in agony. "It's true ... it's true ... it's true! ... Oh!..."

She rose, trembling, looked about her with wild eyes and threw herself madly into the duchess' arms. A loud sob burst from her throat, as though a pistol-shot had gone through her heart.

"He writes it to me himself!" she cried out. "Himself! It's true what the paper says.... Oh!..."

And she broke down, with her head on Sofie's shoulder. Sofie led her back into the hall; Valérie allowed herself to be dragged along like a child. Wanda followed, crying, wringing her hands, without knowing why. From the boats, which were now very far away, the young princes waved once more; little Princess Elizabeth even tried to call out something; she could not understand why Wanda and Valérie were such muffs as not to wave back.

The sun sank on the horizon; the glowing clouds were all masked in little frothy, gold-rose mists with shining edges; but evening fell, the sky grew dark: one by one the little pink clouds melted away; still one last cloud, as though with two wings formed of the last rays of the setting sun, flickered up softly, as if to fly, and then suddenly sank, with broken wings, into the violet dusk. The first stars twinkled, brightly visible.

4

Next morning, very early, at half-past five, the Archduchess Valérie climbed down the terraces of Altseeborgen. She had merely told her maid that she would be back in time for breakfast, which the family took together. Resolutely, as though impulsively, she descended terrace after terrace. She met nobody but a couple of servants and sentries. She walked along the bottom terrace to the sea; there was a little square harbour, cut out of the granite, where the rowing- and sailing-boats lay moored in a boat-house. She chose a long, narrow gig and unhooked it from its iron chain. She took her seat adroitly and grasped the sculls: a few short strokes took her clear of the little harbour and out to sea.

A south-westerly wind was blowing over the sea. The water was strangely grey, as though it were mirroring in its oval the uncertain sky above: a dull-white sky in which hung dirty shreds of clouds blown asunder. The horizon was not visible; light mists floated over it, blotting out the division between sea and sky with smeared tints. The wind blew up strongly.

Valérie removed her little sailor-hat; and her hair blew across her face. She had intended to row to the fishing-village, but she at once felt that it was beyond her strength to work up against the wind. So she let herself go with the wind. For a moment she thought of the weather, the wind, the sky; then she cast aside all thought. She pulled sturdily at the sculls.

Though the sea was comparatively calm, the boat was constantly swinging over the smooth back of a wave and then sinking down again. Splashes of spray flew up. When Valérie, after a little while, looked round, she was a trifle startled to see Altseeborgen receding so far from her. She hesitated once more, but soon let herself go again....

On leaving the castle, she had had no thought, only an impulse to act. Now, with her very action, thought rose up again within her, as though roused from its lethargy by the wind. Valérie's eyes stared before her, wide and burning, without tears.

It was true, it was real. This was the wheel continually revolving in her thoughts. It was true, it was real. It was in the papers which Herman had been skimming through for hours; Sofie had told her; his own letter informed her of it.

She no longer had that letter, it was destroyed. But every word was still branded on her imagination.

It was his letter, written in his own words, in his style. How she had once worshipped his every word! But these words, were they indeed his? Did he write like that? Could she picture to herself that he would ever speak thus to her?

He would not like to make her unhappy by loving her against the wish of her parents, her imperial relations. It was true, of course, that he was not her equal in birth. His house was of old nobility, but nothing more. She was of the blood royal and imperial. He was grateful to her for stooping to him and wishing to raise him to her level. But it was not right to do this. The traditions of mankind should be inviolate: it was not right, especially for them, the great ones of the earth, to act against tradition. They should be grateful for the love which had brought happiness to their souls, but they must not expect more. It was not the wish of Vienna that they should love each other. Would he ever be able to make her entirely happy, would she, if they were married and retired with their love to a foreign country, never look back with yearning and feel homesick for the splendour from which he had dragged her down? For, if they married, he would be still less her equal than he was before, thanks to his emperor's disfavour. No, no, it could not be. They must part. They were not born for each other. For a short moment they had shared the glorious illusion that they were indeed born for each other; that was all. He would be grateful to her for that memory all his life long.

With a breaking heart he took leave of her: farewell, farewell! It was all over: his proud career, his life, his all. He begged her to forgive him. He knew that he was too weak to love her against the will of his sovereign. And for that he begged her to forgive him. She would hear a woman's name mentioned in connection with his own: for this also he begged her pardon. He did not love that woman, but she was willing to console him in his grief....

The wind had suddenly increased in violence, with heavy, regular blasts. The sky was dark overhead. The waves rolled more wildly against the boat and swung it up on their backs as it were on the backs of sleek sea-monsters. The spray had wetted Valérie. She looked round. Altseeborgen lay very far away, scarcely within sight; she could just see the flag defined against the sky like a tiny ribbon.

"I must be mad," she thought. "Where am I going to?... I must turn back...."

But it was difficult to bring the boat round. Each time the wind beat it off again and drove it farther. Despair came upon Valérie, body and soul, moral and physical despair.

"Well, let it be," she thought.

She let the sculls drop, drifted farther away, away. And why not? Why should she not let herself drift away? Without him, without him ... she could not live! Her happiness was ruined; what was life without happiness? For she wanted happiness, it was essential to her....

She sat half-huddled in the boat. The sculls flapped against the sides. A wave broke over her. Her eyes stared burning before her, into the distance.

A second wave broke; her feet were wet through. She slowly drew herself up, looked at the angry sea, at the lowering sky. Then she grasped the sculls again, with a sigh of pain:

"Come on!" she thought.

She rose higher and sank lower. But with a frantic effort she made the boat turn:

"It *shall!*" she bit out between her teeth. She kept the boat's head to the wind and began to row. It *shall*. She wrinkled her forehead, gnashed her jaws, grated her teeth together. She felt her muscles straining. And she rowed on, up against the wind. With her whole body she struggled up against the stiff breeze. It *shall*. It *must*. And she grew accustomed to the exertion; she rowed on mechanically. So much accustomed did she grow to it that she began to sob as she rowed....

O God, how she had loved him, with all her soul! Why? Could she tell? Oh, if he had only been a little stronger, she would have been so too! What mattered to them the disfavour of her uncle the emperor, so long as they loved each other? What the fury of their parents, so long as they loved each other? What did they care for all Europe, so long as they cared for each other? Nothing, nothing at all.... If he had only dared to grasp happiness for them, when it fluttered before them, as it flutters only once before mortal men! But he had not dared, he felt himself too weak to risk that grasp, he acknowledged it himself.... And now ... now it was over, over, over....

As she sobbed she rowed on. Her arms seemed to swell, to burst asunder. A few thick drops of rain fell. What was she really rowing on for? The sea meant death, release from life, oblivion, the extinction of scorching pain. Then why did she row on?

"O God, I don't know!" she answered herself aloud. "But I must! I must!..."

And with successive jerks of her strong imperial body she worked herself back, towards life....

But at Altseeborgen they were in great alarm. It was three hours since Valérie had left the castle. The maid was unable to say more than that her highness had assured her she would be back to breakfast. The sentries had seen her go down the terraces, but had paid no further heed to the direction which her highness had taken. They thought it was towards the woods, but they were not sure....

Every minute the alarm increased; no suspicion was uttered, but they all read it in one another's eyes. King Siegfried ordered that they should themselves set out and search quietly, so as to attract no attention among the household and the people of the village. There could be no question of her having lost her way: the pine-woods were not extensive and Valérie knew Altseeborgen well. And there was nothing besides the woods, the beach and the village.

The king and the crown-prince themselves went into the woods, with an equerry. Herman and his younger brother Olaf went into the village, to the left; Othomar and Christofel along the sea, to the right. The queen remained behind with the princesses, in palpitating uncertainty. For all their efforts to bear up and to eat their breakfasts, a sort of rumour had already spread through the castle.

Othomar had gone with Christofel along the rocky shore; the rain began to come down, in hard, thick drops.

"What are we really looking for here?" asked Othomar, helplessly.

"Perhaps she has thrown herself into the sea!" answered the young prince.

And for the first time of his life, he felt afraid of those depths, which meant death. Unconsciously they went on, on, on....

"Let's go back," said Othomar.

Nevertheless they continued to go on; they could not give in....

Then a scream sounded over the water: they started, but at first saw nothing.

"Did you hear?" asked Christofel, turning pale, thinking of ghostly legends of the sea.

"A sea-mew, I expect," said Othomar, listening, however.

The scream was repeated.

"There, don't you see something?" asked Christofel, pointing.

He pointed to a long streak that came surging over the water.

Othomar shook his head:

"No, that's impossible!" he said. "It's a fisher-lad."

"No, no, it's a rowing-boat!" cried Christofel.

They said nothing more, they ran along. The streak became plainer: a gig; the scream rang out again, piercingly.

"My God!... Valérie!" shouted Othomar.

She called back a few words; he only partly understood them. She was rowing not far from the shore towards the castle. Othomar took off his coat, his shoes, his socks, turned up his trousers, his shirt-sleeves.

"Take those with you," he cried to Christofel, "and go back to the castle, tell them...."

He ran on his bare feet over the rocks and into the sea, flung himself into the water, swam out to the boat. It was very difficult for him to climb into the little gig without capsizing it. It lurched madly to right and left; however, with a single, quick, light movement, Othomar managed to jump in.

"I give up...." said Valérie, faintly.

She let go the sculls; he seized them and rowed on. For an instant she fell against him, but then sat up straight, so as not to hamper him.

<h1 style="text-align:center">5</h1>

The young archduchess did not appear at luncheon; she was asleep. Not long before dinner—it was raining and the queen was taking tea in the hall with the princesses, the aunts, the children—she appeared. She looked rather pale; her face was a little drawn, her eyes strangely wide and burning. She was wearing a simple summer costume of some soft, pale-lilac material, with two white ribbons tied round her waist; the colour went well with her strange hair, which now looked brown and then again seemed auburn. The queen held out her hand to Valérie, shook her head and said:

"You naughty girl! How you frightened us!"

Valérie kissed the queen on the forehead:

"Forgive me, aunt. The wind was so strong, I could hardly make way against it. I oughtn't to have gone. But I felt a need ... for movement."

The queen looked at her anxiously:

"How are you feeling now?"

"Oh, very well, aunt! Rather stiff; and a little headache. It's nothing. Only my hands are terribly blistered: just look...."

And she laughed.

The old aunts asked for copious details of what had happened: it was difficult to make them understand. Wanda sat down between the two of them, told them the story; their sharp cockatoo-profiles kept on wagging up and down at Wanda, in astonishment. The aunts pressed their hands to their hearts and looked at Valérie with terror in their eyes; she smiled to them pleasantly. When Countess von Altenburg appeared, the aunts took the old mistress of the household between them and in their turn told her the story, screeching it into the countess' poor old ears. King Siegfried entered; he went up to Valérie, who rose, took her head in his hands, looked at her and shook his grey head; nevertheless he smiled. Then he looked at his sisters; he was always amused at them; they were still in the middle of their story to the countess and kept on taking the words out of each other's mouths.

"Come, it was not so dreadful as all that!" said the king, interrupting them. "It's very nice to go rowing like that, once in a way, and an excellent remedy for a sick-headache. You ought to try it, Elsa, when you have one of yours."

The old princess looked at him with a sugary smile; she never knew whether her brother meant a remark of this kind or not. She shook her stately head slowly from side to side:

"No, *lieber Siegfried*, that is more than we can do. *Unsere liebe Erzherzogin* is still a young thing!..."

Othomar, Gunther and Herman entered: they had been playing billiards; the young princes followed them. Valérie gave a little shiver, rose and went up to Othomar:

"I thank you, Xara," she said. "I thank you a thousand, thousand times!"

"But what for?" replied Othomar, simply. "I did no more than row you a bit of the way back. There was no danger. For, if you had been too tired to go on rowing, you could always have jumped into the sea and swum ashore. You're a strong swimmer. You would only have lost the boat."

She looked at him:

"That's true," she said. "But I never thought of it. I was ... bewildered perhaps. I should not have done that; I had a fixed idea that I had to row back. If I hadn't been able to keep on rowing, I should certainly.... Don't refuse my thanks, I beg of you: accept them."

She put out her hand; he pressed it. He looked up at her with quiet surprise and failed to understand her. He did not doubt but that she had that morning left the castle with the intention of committing suicide. Had she felt remorse on the water, or had she not dared? Did she want to live on and did she therefore turn back? Was she so shallow that she had already recovered from the great grief which had crushed her the night before? Did she realize that life rolls with indifferent chariot-wheels over everything, whether joy or pain, that is part of ourselves and that it is best to care for nothing and also to feel nothing? What of all this applied to her? He was unable to fathom it. And once more he saw himself standing perplexed before the question of love! What was this feeling worth, if it weighed so little in a woman's heart? How much did it weigh with him for Alexa? What was it then?... Or was it something ... something quite different?

At dinner Valérie talked as usual and he continued not to understand her. It irritated him, his want of penetration of the human heart: how could he develop it? A future ruler ought to be able to see things at a glance....

And suddenly, perhaps merely because of his desire for human knowledge, the thought arose within him that she was concealing her emotions, that perhaps she was still suffering intensely, but that she was pretending and bearing up: was she not a princess of the blood? They all learnt that, they of the blood, to pretend, to bear up! It was bred in their bones. He looked at her askance, as he sat next to her: she was quietly talking across him to the queen. He did not know whether he had guessed right and he still hesitated between the two thoughts: was she bearing up, or was she shallow? But, yet he was happy at being able to hesitate about her and to refute that first suspicion of shallowness by his second thought. He was happy in this, not solely because of Valérie, that she should be better than he had thought at first; he was happy especially for the general conclusion which he was able to draw: that a person is mostly better, thinks more deeply, cherishes nobler feelings than he allows to appear in the everyday commonplaces of life, which compel him to occupy himself with momentary trifles and phrases. A delicate satisfaction took possession of him that he had thought this out so, a contentment that he had discovered something beautiful in life: a beautiful secret. Everybody knew it perhaps, but nobody let it be perceived. Oh yes, people were good; the world was good, in its essence! Only a strange mystery compelled it to seem different, a strange tyranny of the universal order of things.

He glanced around the long table. Every face wore a look of kindness and sympathy. He was attached to his uncle so calm, gentle and strong, with the seeming dogged silence of his Norse character, with his tranquil smile and now and then a little gleam of fun, aimed especially at the old aunts, but also at the children and even at the equerries, the ladies-in-waiting. He knew that his uncle was a thinker, a philosopher; he would have liked to have a long discussion with him on points of philosophy. He was fond also of his aunt, a first-rate queen: what a lot she did for her country, what a number of charities she called into existence; a first-rate mother: how sensibly she performed her difficult task, the bringing up of royal children! She was more beloved in her country than was his mother, whom yet he adored, in hers; she had more tact, less fear, less haughtiness also towards the crowd. It should perhaps have been the other way about: his mother queen here, her sister empress yonder....

And the crown-prince, with his simple manliness; Herman, with his joviality; the younger brothers, with their vigorous, boyish chaff: how fond he was of them! Sofie, Wanda, the children: how he liked them all! He even liked the aunts and the devoted old mistress of the household. Oh, the world was good, people were good! And Valérie was not indifferent, but suffered in quiet silence, as a princess of the blood must suffer, with unclouded eyes and a smile!

After dinner Queen Olga took Othomar's arm:

"Come with me for a moment," she said.

The rain had ceased; a footman opened the French windows. Behind the dining-room lay a long terrace looking upon the woods. The queen put her arm in Othomar's and began to walk up and down with him:

"And so you are going to leave us?" she asked.

He looked at her with a smile:

"You know I am, aunt; with much regret. I shall often long for Altseeborgen, for all of you. I feel so much at home in your circle. But yet I am anxious to see mamma again: it's nearly four months since I saw her last."

"And are you feeling better?"

"How could I but feel better, aunt? The voyage with Herman made me ever so much stronger; and living here with you has been a delightful after-cure. A delightful holiday."

"But your holiday will soon be over. Will you now be able to play your part again?"

He smiled, while his sad eyes expressed calm resignation:

"Certainly, aunt. Life can't be always holidays. I should think I had had my fill of them, doing nothing for six weeks except lie on the sand, or in the woods, or in that most comfortable wicker chair of Herman's!"

"Have you done nothing besides?" she said, playfully.

"How do you mean?"

"Saved Valérie's life, for instance?"

He gave a slight movement of gentle impatience: "But, aunt, I didn't really. I suppose the papers will go and say I did, but there was really no saving in the matter. Valérie knows how to swim and she was close to the shore."

"I've had a letter from papa, Othomar."

"From papa?"

"Yes.... Have you never thought of ... Valérie?"

He reflected for a second:

"Perhaps," he laughed.

"Do you feel no affection for her?"

"Certainly, aunt.... I thought papa preferred the Grand-duchess Xenia?"

The queen shrugged her shoulders:

"There's the question of her religion, you know. And papa would be just as glad of an Austrian alliance.... How do you propose to make the journey? And when do you start?"

"Ducardi and the others will be here this week. Towards the end of the week. First to Copenhagen, London, Brussels, Berlin and then to Vienna."

"And to Sigismundingen."

"Yes, Sigismundingen, if papa wishes."

"But what do you wish, Othomar?"

He looked at her gently, smiling, shrugged his shoulders:

"But, aunt, what wish have I in the matter?"

"Could you grow fond of Valérie?"

"I think so, aunt; I think she is very sweet and very capable and thorough."

"Yes, that she certainly is, Othomar! Would you not speak to her before you go?"

"Aunt...."

"Why shouldn't you?"

"Aunt, I can't do that. I am only staying a few days longer, and ..."

"Well?"

"Valérie has had a great sorrow. She cannot but still be suffering under it. Think, aunt, it was yesterday. Good God, yesterday!... And to-day she was so calm, so natural.... But it must be so, mustn't it? She must still be suffering very severely. She went on the sea this morning, in this weather: we don't know, do we, aunt, but we all think the same thing! Perhaps we are quite mistaken. Things are often different from what they seem. But, however that may be, she is certainly in distress. And so I can't ask her, now...."

"It's a pity, as you're here together. A thing of this sort is often settled at a distance. If it was arranged here, you would perhaps not need to make the journey."

"But, aunt, papa was so bent upon it!"

"That's true; but then nothing was yet decided."

"No, aunt, let me make the journey. For in any case it's impossible to arrange things here. If papa himself asked me, I should tell him ... that it was impossible."

"Papa does ask you, Othomar, in his letter to me."

He seized her hands:

"Aunt, in that case, write to him and say that it's impossible, at this moment ... oh, impossible, impossible! Let us spare her, aunt. If she becomes my wife, she will still become so while she loves another. Will that not be terrible enough for her, when it is decided months hence? Therefore let us spare her now. You feel that too, as a woman, don't you? There are no affairs of state that make it necessary for my marriage to take place in such a hurry."

"Yet papa wishes you to marry as soon as possible. He wants a grandson...."

He made no reply; a look of suffering passed over his face. The queen perceived it:

"But you're right," she replied, giving way. "It would be too cruel. Valérie, I may tell you, is bearing up wonderfully. That's how a future Empress of Liparia ought to be...."

He still made no reply and walked silently beside her; her arm lay in his; she felt his arm tremble:

"Come," she said, gently, "let us go in; walking up and down like this is fatiguing...."

6

Ducardi, Dutri, Leoni and Thesbia arrived at Altseeborgen; they were to accompany Othomar on his official journey through Europe.

It was one of the last days, in the morning, when Othomar was walking with Herman towards the woods. The sun was shining, the woods were fragrant, the foot slid over the smooth pine-needles. The princes sat down on the ground, near a great pool of water; around them rose the straight pine-trunks, with their knotty peaks of side-branches; the sky faded into the distance with blue chinks showing between the projecting foliage of needles.

Herman leant against a tree-trunk; Othomar stretched himself flat on his back, with his hands beneath his head:

"It will soon be over now," he said, softly.

Herman made no reply, but mechanically swept the pine-needles together with his hand. Nor did Othomar speak again; he swallowed his last moments of relaxation and repose in careful draughts, each draught a pure joy that would never return. In the woods a stillness reigned as of death, as though the earth were uninhabited; the melancholy of things that are coming to an end hung about the trees.

Suddenly Othomar took Herman's hand and pressed it:

"Thank you," he said.

"What for?" asked Herman.

"For the pleasure we have had together. Mamma was right: I did not know you, Herman...."

"Nor I you, dear fellow."

"It has been a pleasant time. How delightfully we travelled together, like two tourists! How grand and glorious India was, don't you think? And Japan, how curious! I never cared much for hunting; but, when I was with you, I understood it and felt the excitement of it: I shall never forget our tiger-hunt! The eyes of the brute, the danger facing you: it's invigorating. At a moment like that, you feel yourself becoming primitive, like the first man. The look of one of those tigers drives away a lot of your hesitation. That's another danger, which mamma is always so afraid of: oh, how enervating it is; it eats up all your energy!... And the nights on the Indian Ocean, on board our *Viking*. That great wide circle around you, all those stars over your head. How often we sat looking at them, with our legs on the bulwarks!... Perhaps it's a mistake to sit dreaming so long, but it rests one so, it rests one so! I shall never forget it, never...."

"Well, old chap, we must do it again."

"No, one never does anything again. What's done is done. Nothing returns, not a single moment of our lives. Later on it is always different...."

He looked round about him, as though some one might be listening; then he whispered:

"Herman, I have something to tell you."

"What is it?"

"Something to confide to you. But first tell me: that time with the tiger, you didn't think me a great coward, did you?"

"No, certainly not!"

"Well, I'm a coward for all that. I'm frightened, always frightened. The doctors don't know it, because I never tell them. But I always am...."

"But of what, my dear chap?"

"Of something inside myself. Look here, Herman, I'm so afraid ... that I shall not be able to stick it out. That at a given moment of my life I shall be too weak. That suddenly I shall not be able to act and then, then ..."

He shuddered; they look at each other.

"It won't do," he continued, mechanically, as though strengthened by Herman's glance. "I shall fight against it, against that dread of mine.... Do you believe in presentiments?"

"Yes, inversely: mine always turn out the opposite!"

"Then I hope that my presentiment won't come true either."

"But what is it?"

"That within the year ... one of us ... at Lipara ... will be dead."

Herman stared at him fixedly. For all his manliness and his muscular strength, there lay deep down within him a certain heritage of the superstition that comes murmuring from the sea as with voices of distant prophecy, a superstition lulled by the beautiful legends of their Gothlandic sea, which, syren-like, sings strange, mystic fairy-tales. Perhaps he had never until this moment felt that some of it flowed in his rich blood; and he tried to shake it off as nonsense:

"But Othomar, do be rational!" he said.

"I can do nothing to prevent it, Herman. I don't think about it, but I feel little sharp stings, like thoughts suddenly springing up. And lately ... oh, lately, it has been worse; it has become a dream, a nightmare! I was walking through the shopping-streets of Lipara and from all the shops came black people and they measured out bales of black crape, with yard-measures, till the streets were filled with it and the crape lay in the town as though in clouds and surged over the town like a mass of black muslin. It made everything dark: the sun could not shine through it and everything lay in shadow. The people did not seem to recognize me and, when I asked what all that crape was for, they whispered in my ears, 'Hush, hush, it's ... it's for the Imperial!' ... O Herman, then I woke and I was damp with perspiration and it was as though I still heard it echoing after me: 'For the Imperial, it's for the Imperial!'"

Herman got up; he was a little nervous:

"Come," said he, "shall we go?... Dreams: don't pay any attention to dreams, Othomar!"

Othomar also rose:

"No, I oughtn't to pay attention to them," he repeated, in a strange tone. "I never used to."

"Othomar," Herman began, decidedly, as though he wished to say something.

"Don't talk to me for a minute; let me be for a moment," Othomar interrupted, quickly, anxiously.

They walked through the woods in silence. Othomar looked about him, strangely, looked at the ground. Herman compressed his lips tightly and puckered up his forehead: he was annoyed. But he said nothing. In a few minutes Othomar's strange glances grew calmer and quieted down into their usual gentle melancholy.

Then he gave a little sigh, as if he were catching his breath:

"Don't be angry," he said, putting his arm through Herman's.

His voice had resumed its usual tone.

"Perhaps it's as well that I have told you; now perhaps it will leave me. So don't be angry, Herman.... I promise you I shan't talk like that again and I shall do my best also not to think like that any more. But, when I have anything on my mind, I must tell it to somebody. And surely that's much better than for ever keeping silent about it! And then, you see, soon I shall have no more time to think of such things: to-morrow we shall be at Copenhagen and then life will resume its normal course. How can I have talked so queerly? How did I take it into my head? Even I can't remember. It seems very silly now, even to myself."

He gave a little laugh and then, earnestly:

"After all, I'm glad that we have had a talk by ourselves, that I have been able to thank you. We're friends now, aren't we?"

"Yes, of course we're friends," replied Herman, laughing in the midst of his annoyance. "But all the same I shall never know you thoroughly!"

"Don't say that just because of a single presentiment, which I think foolish myself. What else is there in me that's puzzling?..."

"No, there's nothing else!" Herman assented. "You're a good chap. I don't know how it has come about, but I like you very much...."

They left the woods; the sea lay before them. Like life itself, it lay before them, with all the mystery of its depths, wherein a multiple soul seemed to move, rounding wave upon wave. Nameless and innumerable were its changes of colour, its moods of incessant movement; and it spewed a foam of passion on its fiercely towering crests. But this passion was merely its superficial manifestation, the exuberance of its endless vitality: from its depths there murmured, in the inimitable melodies of its millions of voices, the mystery of its soul, as it were a glory which the sky above alone knew.

7

"TO HIS IMPERIAL HIGHNESS THE DUKE OF XARA,
"OSBORNE HOUSE, ISLE OF WIGHT.

"IMPERIAL,
"LIPARA,
" —*September*, 18—.

"DEAR SON,

"It was a great pleasure to receive your letter, telling us of the cordial welcome which you met with first at Copenhagen and now in England. We must however express our surprise at what Aunt Olga wrote to us and our regret that you did not act according to our wishes; the Emperor of Austria and the Archduke Albrecht express the same regret in their letters to us. We presume that we did not express ourselves definitely enough in our letter to Aunt Olga: otherwise we cannot imagine why she did not urge you more strongly to ask the Archduchess Valérie for an interview and to speak to her of the important matter which we all at this moment have so much at heart. You would then have been able to announce your engagement *sous cachet* at the courts which you are now visiting; and the betrothal could have been celebrated, at the conclusion of journey, at Sigismundingen. Whereas now you have probably placed yourself in a false position towards our friends Their Majesties of Denmark and of England, as all the newspapers are speaking of a possible betrothal to the Archduchess Valérie and the press is already so kind as to discuss the *pros* and *cons* of this alliance in a loud voice. Your journey, however, would have had to take place *in any case*, as it had already been so long announced—your illness intervened to postpone it—and as it is therefore nothing more than an act of courtesy towards our friends.

"Once again, your neglect to act in accordance with our wishes causes us great regret. We perceive in you, Othomar, a certain tendency towards *bourgeois* hypersensitiveness, which we hope you will learn to master with all the strength you possess. Few of us have in this life escaped a sorrow such as Prince von Lohe-Obkowitz has caused your future bride, but it remains an entirely personal and subordinate feeling and should not be allowed to interfere *in the least* with affairs of such great political importance as the marriage of a future emperor of Liparia. The archduchess will doubtless, when she is older, learn to look at this in the same light; and we hope that she will very soon realize that her affection for Prince Lohe could never have brought her happiness, as it would have caused a rupture with his imperial majesty her uncle and with all her relations.

"Master yourself, Othomar, we ask and urge. You sometimes have ideas and entertain proposals which are not those of a ruler. We have noticed this more than once or twice: among other occasions, when you visited Zanti at Vaza. We did not like to reproach you with this at the time, as we were otherwise very well pleased with you. Your dearest wish will no doubt be that we shall always remain so.

"We hope therefore to see you three weeks hence at Sigismundingen, where the Archduchess Valérie will by then have returned from Altseeborgen to meet you and where we shall also meet the Emperor of Austria.

"It is our fervent hope that the long voyage with Herman will have done you much good and that your wedding will take place at Altara *as soon as possible*. This glad prospect affords us a pleasant diversion from our difficulties with the army bill, which is encountering such stubborn opposition in the house of deputies, though we hope for all that to succeed in carrying it, as it is essential that our army should be increased.

"We cordially embrace you.

"OSCAR."

CHAPTER V

1

It was after the state banquet in the castle at Sigismundingen, where the imperial families of Liparia and Austria were assembled to celebrate the betrothal of the Duke of Xara and the Archduchess Valérie. It was in September: the day had been sultry and in the evening the oppressive heat still hung brooding in the air.

Dinner was just over and the imperial procession returned through a long corridor to the reception-rooms. All the balcony-windows of the brightly-lighted gallery stood open; beneath, as in an abyss of river landscape, flowed the Danube, rolling against the rocks, while above it towered the castle with its innumerable little pointed turrets. The mountain-tops were defined in a sombre, violet amphitheatre against the paler sky, which was incessantly lit with electric flashes, as of noiseless lightning. The wood stood gloomy and black, shadowy, sloping up with the peaked tops of its fir-trees against the mountains; in the distance lay small houses, huddled in the dusk of the evening, like some straggling hamlet, with here and there a yellow light.

The Emperor of Liparia gave his arm to the mother of the bride, the Archduchess Eudoxie; then followed the Emperor of Austria with the Empress of Liparia, the Archduke Albrecht with the Empress of Austria, Othomar with Valérie....

Valérie, lightly pressing Othomar's arm, withdrew with him from the procession:

"It was so warm in the dining-room; you will excuse me," she said to Othomar's sister, the Archduchess of Carinthia, who was following with one of her Austrian cousins.

Valérie's smile requested the archduchess to go on. The others followed: the august guests, the equerries, the ladies-in-waiting; they smiled to the betrothed imperial couple, who stood in one of the open window-recesses to let them pass.

They remained alone in the gallery, before the open window:

"I need air," said Valérie, with a sigh.

He made no reply. They stood together in silence, gazing at the evening landscape. He was wearing the uhlan uniform of the Austrian regiment which he commanded; and a new order glittered amongst the others on his breast: the Golden Fleece of Austria. She seemed to have grown older than she was at Altseeborgen, in her pink-silk evening-dress, with wide, puffed sleeves of very pale-green velvet, a tight-curled border of white ostrich-feathers edging the low-cut bodice and the train.

"Shall I leave you alone for a little, Valérie?" he asked, gently.

She shook her head, smiling sadly. Her bosom seemed to heave with uncontrollable emotion.

"Why, Othomar?" she asked. "I am lonely enough at nights, with my thoughts. Leave me alone with them as little as you can...."

She suddenly held out her hand to him:

"Will you forgive your future empress her broken heart?" she asked, suddenly, with a great sob.

And her pale, shrunken face turned full towards him, with two eyes like those of a stricken doe. An irrepressible feeling of pity caused something to well up unexpectedly in his soul; he squeezed her hand and turned away, so as not to weep.

He looked out of the window. Some of the pointed towers, visible from here, rose with an air of sombre romance against the sky, which was luminous with electricity. Below them, romantically, murmured the Danube. The mountains were like the landscape in a ballad. But no ballad, no romance echoed between their two hearts. The prose of the inevitable necessity was the only harmony that united them. But this harmony also united them in reality, brought them together, made them understand each other, feel and live at one with each other. They were now for a minute alone and their eyes frankly sought the depths of each other's souls. There was no need for pretence between these two: each saw the other's sorrow lying shivering and naked in the other's heart.

It was not the riotous passion of despair that they beheld. They saw a gentle, tremulous sadness; they looked at it with wide, staring eyes of anguish, as children look who think they see a ghost. For them that ghost issued from life itself: life itself became for them a ghostly existence. They themselves were spectres, though they know that they were tangible, with bodies. What were they?

Dream-beings, with crowns; they lived and bowed and acted and smiled as in a dream, because of their crowns. They did not exist: a vagueness did indeed suggest in their dream-brains that something might exist, in other laws of nature than those of their sphere, but in their sphere they did not exist....

His hand was toying mechanically with some papers that lay near him, on the mirror-bracket between two of the window-recesses; they were illustrated periodicals, doubtless left there by some chamberlain. He took one up, to while their sad silence, and opened it. The first thing that he saw was their own portraits:

"Look," he said.

He showed them to her. They now turned over the pages together, saw the portraits also of their parents, a drawing of the castle, a corner of Sigismundingen Park. Then together they read the announcement of their engagement. They were first each described separately: he, an accomplished prince, doing a great deal of good, very popular in his own country and cordially loved by the Emperor of Austria; she, every inch a princess, born to be the empress of a great empire, with likewise her special accomplishments. The eyes of all Europe were fixed upon them at the moment. For their marriage would not only be an imperial alliance of great political importance, but would also tie a knot of real harmony: their marriage was a love-match. There had been attempts to make it seem otherwise, but this was not correct. In Gothland, in the home circle at Altseeborgen, the young couple had learnt to know each other well; their love had sprung like an idyll from the sea and the Duke of Xara had once even saved the archduchess' life, when she had ventured out too far, in stormy weather, in a rowing-boat. Their love was like a novel with a happy ending. The Emperor Oscar would rather have seen the Grand-duchess Xenia crown-princess of Liparia and attached great value to an alliance with Russia, but he had yielded before his son's love.... And the article ended by saying that the wedding would take place in October in the old palace at Altara.

They read it together, with their mournful faces, their wide, fixed eyes, which still smarted with staring into each other's souls. Not a single remark came from their lips after reading the article; they only just smiled their two heartrending smiles; then they laid the paper down again. And she asked, with that strange calm with which this betrothed pair were trying to get to know each other:

"Othomar ... do you care for nobody?"

A flush suffused his cheeks. Did she know of Alexa?

"I did once think that I ... that I was in love," he confessed; "but I do not believe that it was really love. I now believe that I do not possess the capacity to concentrate my whole soul upon a feeling for one other soul alone; I should not know how to find it, that one soul, and I should fear to make a mistake, or to deceive myself.... No, I do not believe that I shall ever know that exclusive feeling. I rather feel within me a great, wide, general love, an immense compassion, for our people. It is strange of me perhaps...."

He said it almost shyly, as though it were something abnormal, that general love, of which he ought to be ashamed before her.

"A great love," he explained once more, when she continued to look at him in silence; and he made an embracing gesture with his arms, "for our people...."

"Do you really feel that?" she asked, in surprise.

"Yes...."

A sort of vista opened out before her, as though an horizon of light were dawning right at the end of her dark melancholy; but that horizon was so far, so very far away....

"But, Othomar," she said, "that is very good. It is very beautiful to feel like that!"

He shrugged his shoulders:

"Beautiful? How do you mean? I cannot but feel it when I see all the misery that exists ... among our people, the lower orders, the very lowest especially. If they were all happy and enjoying abundance, there would be no need for me to feel it. So what is there beautiful about it?"

She gave a little laugh:

"I can't argue against that, it's too deep for me. I can't say that I have ever thought over those social questions; they have always existed as they are and ... and I have not thought about them. But I can feel, with my feminine instinct, that it is beautiful of you to feel like that, Othomar."

She took his hand and pressed it; her face lit up with a smile. Then she looked, pensively, into the dark landscape beneath them and she shivered.

"It's turning chilly," he said. "We had better go in, Valérie; you'll catch cold here."

She just felt at her bare neck:

"Presently," she said.

They glanced down, at the murmuring Danube. A mist began to rise from the river and filled the valley as it were with light strips of muslin.

"Come," he urged.

"Look," she said. "How deep that is, is it not?"

He looked down:

"Yes," he replied.

"Don't you feel giddy?" she asked.

He looked at her anxiously:

"No, not giddy; at least, not at once...."

"Othomar," she said, in a whisper, "I once sat here for a whole evening. I kept on looking down; it was darker than now and I saw nothing but blackness and it kept on roaring through those black depths. It was the evening after our engagement was decided. I felt such pain, I suffered so! I thought that I had won a victory over myself, but they left me no peace and the only use of my victory was to give me strength to do battle again. The news that I was to be your wife came as unexpectedly ... as my great sorrow came! Then I felt so weak because it overwhelmed me so, because they left me no peace. Oh, they were so cruel, they did not leave me a moment to recover my breath! I had to go on again, on! Then I felt weak. I thought that I should never overcome my weakness. I sat here for hours, looking at the Danube. It made me giddy.... At last I thought that I had made up my mind ... to throw myself down.... I already saw myself floating away, there, there, down there, right round the castle.... Why did I not do it? I believe because of ... of him, Othomar. I loved him, I love him *now*, though I ought to have more pride. I would not punish him by committing suicide. He is so weak. I know him: it would have haunted him all his life long!... Then ... then, Othomar, I ran away and I prayed! I no longer knew what to do!"

She hid her face full of anguish in her hands, with a great sob. His eyes had filled with tears; he saw how she trembled. He threw a terrified side-glance at the deep stream below, which roared as though calling....

"Valérie," he stammered, in alarm; "for God's sake let us go in. It's too cold here and ... and...."

She looked at him anxiously too, with haggard eyes:

"Yes, let us go, Othomar!" she whispered. "I am getting frightened here: we have that in our family; there is still so much romance flowing in our veins...."

She took his arm; they went indoors together. But, before entering the suite of anterooms that led to the reception-rooms, she detained him for yet a moment:

"I don't know whether we shall see each other alone again before you return to Lipara. And I still wanted to thank you for something...."

"For what?" he asked.

"For ... something that Aunt Olga told me. For ... sparing me at Altseeborgen. Thank you, Othomar, thank you...."

She put her arm around his neck and gave him a kiss. He kissed her in return.

And they exchanged their first caress.

2

The next day the imperial family of Liparia travelled back from Sigismundingen to Lipara. The reception at the central station was most hearty; the town was covered with bunting; in the evening there were popular rejoicings. The officers of the various army-corps gave the crown-prince banquets in honour of his betrothal. The Archduchess Valérie's portraits were exposed in the windows of all the picture-shops; the papers contained long articles full of jubilation.

It was a few hours before the dinner given by the officers of the throne-guards to their imperial colonel when Othomar was, as it were suddenly, overcome by a strange sensation. He was in his writing-room, felt rather giddy and had to sit down. The giddiness was slight, but lasted a long time; for a long time the room seemed to be slowly trying to turn round him and not to succeed; and this gave a painful impression of resistance on the part of its lifeless furniture. One of Othomar's hands rested on his thigh, the other on the ruff of the collie which had laid its head upon his knee. He remained sitting, bending forward.

When the giddiness had passed, he retained a strange lightness in his head, as though something had been taken out of it. He leant back cautiously; the collie, half-asleep, dreamily opened its eyes and then dozed off again, its head upon Othomar's knee, under his hand. An irresistible fatigue crept up Othomar's limbs, as though they were sinking in soft mud. It surprised him greatly, this feeling; and, looking sideways at the clock, without moving his head, lest he should bring on the giddiness again, he calculated that he had an hour and a half before dinner. This prospective interval relieved him and he remained sitting, as though calculating his fatigue: whether it would pass, whether it would leave his body.

It lasted a long time, so long indeed that he doubted whether he would be able to go. When three-quarters of an hour had passed, he pressed the bell which stood near him on the table. Andro entered.

"Andro...." he began, without continuing.

"Does your highness wish to dress? Everything is put out...."

Othomar just patted the dog's head, as it still lay dozing motionless against his knee.

"Is your highness unwell?"

"A little giddy, Andro; it is passing off already."

"But is your highness right in going? Had I not better send for Prince Dutri?"

Othomar shook his head decidedly and rose:

"No, I'm late as it is, Andro. Come, help me with my things...."

And he entered his dressing-room.

He appeared at the dinner, but made excuses to the officers for his evident languor. He just joined in the toasts by raising his glass, with a smile. It struck them all that he looked very ill, emaciated, hollow-eyed and white as chalk in his white-and-gold uniform. Immediately after dinner he returned to the Imperial, without accompanying them to the Imperial Jockey Club, the club of the *jeunesse dorée*.

He slept heavily; a misty dream hovered through his night. The man who had tried to murder him at Zanti's grinned at him with clenched fists; then the scene changed to the Gothlandic sea and he rowed Valérie along, but, however hard he rowed, the three towers of the castle always drew farther away, unapproachable....

When he awoke, it was already past eight. He reflected that it was too late for his usual morning ride and remained lying where he was. He rang for Andro:

"Why didn't you wake me at seven o'clock?"

"Your highness was sleeping so soundly, I dared not; your highness was not well yesterday...."

"And so you just let me sleep? Very well.... Send word to her majesty ... that I am not well."

The man looked at him anxiously:

"What is the matter with your highness?"

"I don't know, Andro ... I am a little tired. Where's Djalo?"

"Here, highness...."

The collie ran in noisily, put its great paws on the camp-bed, wriggled its haunches wildly to and fro as it wagged its tail....

Then, suddenly, it lay down quietly beside the bed.

The empress sent back to say that she would come at once; she was not yet dressed.... With calm, open eyes Othomar lay waiting for her.

She entered at last, a little agitated with anxiety. She questioned him, but learnt nothing from his vague, smiling replies. She laid her hand on his forehead, felt his pulse and could not make up her mind whether he had any fever. There was typhoid about: she was afraid of it....

The physicians-in-ordinary were called and relieved her mind: there was no fever. The prince seemed generally tired; he had doubtless over-exerted himself lately. He must rest....

The emperor was astonished: the prince had just been resting and had stayed on for weeks at Altseeborgen. What had been the use of it then!

The rumour ran through the palace, the town, the country, through Europe, that the Duke of Xara was keeping his room because of a slight indisposition. The physicians issued a simple and very reassuring bulletin.

However, in the afternoon Othomar got up and even dressed himself, but not in uniform. He had had some lunch in his bedroom and now went to Princess Thera's apartments. She sat drawing; with her was a lady-in-waiting, the young Marchioness of Ezzera.

The princess was surprised to see her brother:

"What! Is that you? I thought you were in bed!..."

"No, I'm a little better...."

He bowed to the marchioness, who had risen and curtseyed.

"Won't you go on with the portrait?" asked Othomar.

Thera looked at him:

"You're looking so pale, poor boy. Perhaps I'd better not. It tires you so, that sitting, doesn't it?"

"Yes, sometimes, a little...."

They were now standing before the portrait; the marchioness had retired, as she always did when the brother and sister were together. The painting was half-covered with a silk cloth, which Thera pulled aside: it was already a young head full of expression, in which life began to gleam behind the black, melancholy eyes, and painted with broad, firm brushwork, with much reflection of outside light, which fell upon one side of the face and brought it into relief, throwing it forward out of the shadow in the background.

"Is it almost finished?" asked Othomar.

"Yes, but you've kept me waiting awfully long for the final touches: just think, you've been away for four months. I haven't been able to work at it all that time. But, you know ... you've changed. If only I shan't have to leave it like this. It's no longer like you...."

"It'll begin to be like me again, when I'm looking a little better!" answered Othomar.

But the princess became rather nervous; she suddenly drew the silk cloth over it again....

Othomar did not appear at dinner; he went to bed early. The next day the doctors found him very listless. He was up but not dressed; he lay in his dressing-gown on the sofa in his room, with the collie at his feet. He complained to the empress that he had such a queer feeling in his head, as though it were about to open and pour out all its contents.

For days this condition remained unchanged: a total listlessness, a total loss of appetite, a visible exhaustion.... The empress sat by his side as he lay on his sofa staring through the open windows into the green depths of the park of plane-trees. The birds chirped outside; sometimes Berengar's small, shrill voice sounded among them, as he played with a couple of his little friends. The empress read aloud, but it tired Othomar, it made his head ache....

After a long conversation between the three doctors and the emperor and empress, Professor Barzia was summoned from Altara for a consultation: the professor was a nerve-specialist of European fame.

In the emperor's room the emperor, the empress and Count Myxila sat waiting for the result of the examination and the subsequent consultation. It lasted long. They did not speak while they waited: the empress sat staring before her with her quiet expression of acquiescence; the emperor walked irritably to and fro. The old chancellor, with his stern, proud face and bald head, stood pensively near the window.

Then the doctors were announced. They appeared, Professor Barzia leading the way, the others following. The empress fancied that she read the worst on the professor's pale, rigid features; one of the physicians, however, nodded his big, kind head compassionately from behind his colleague, to reassure her.

"Well?" asked the emperor.

"We have carefully examined his imperial highness, sir," the professor began. "The prince is quite free from organic disease, though his constitution is generally delicate."

"What's wrong with him then?" asked Oscar.

"The prince's nervous system seems to us, sir, to have undergone an alarming strain."

"His nerves? But he's never nervous, he's always calm," exclaimed the emperor, stubbornly.

"All the more reason, sir, to appreciate the prince's self-restraint. His highness has evidently kept himself going for a long time; and the effort has been too much for him at last. He is calm now, as your majesty says. But his calmness does not alter the fact that his nerves are completely run down. His highness has clearly been overtaxing his strength."

"And in what way?" asked the emperor, haughtily.

"That, sir, would no doubt be better known to those at court than to me, who come fresh from my study and my hospitals. Your majesty will be able to answer that question yourself. I can only give you a few indications. His highness told me that he remembered sometimes feeling those fits of giddiness and exhaustion even before the great floods in the north. That was in March. It is now September. I imagine that his highness has been leading a very active life in the meantime?"

The emperor made movements with his eyebrows as if he could not understand: tremulous motions of his powerful head, with its fleece of silvering hair.

"The journey to the north may in fact have affected his highness, professor," the empress began.

She was sitting haughtily upright, in her plain dark dress. Her face was expressionless, her eyes were cold. She spoke in a matter-of-fact tone, as though she were not a mother.

"His highness is very sensitive to impressions," she continued, "and he received a good many at Altara that were likely to shock him."

The professor made a slight movement of the head:

"I remember, ma'am, seeing his highness at the identification of the corpses in the fields," he said. "His highness *was* very much affected...."

"But to what does all this tend?" asked the emperor, still recalcitrant.

"It tends to this, sir, that his highness has presumably allowed himself no rest since that time...."

"His highness has allowed himself months of rest!" exclaimed the emperor.

"Will your majesty permit us to cast our eyes backwards for a moment? After the very fatiguing journey in the north, the prince returned straight to conditions of political excitement—Lipara was then under martial law—and afterwards came the bustle of a festival time, when the King and Queen of Syria were here...."

The emperor shrugged his shoulders.

"After that, the prince, acting on the advice of my respected colleagues, went on a sea-voyage to restore his health. No doubt his highness then enjoyed some days of rest; but the great hunting-trips in which he took part with Prince Herman were beyond a doubt too much for his highness' strength. Now, quite recently, his highness has been betrothed: this may have caused him some excitement. I am casually mentioning a few of the main facts, sir. I know nothing of the prince's inner life: if I knew something of that, it would certainly make many things much easier for me. But this is certain: his highness has from day to day led a too highly agitated existence, whatever the agitations may have been, great or small. That his highness did not collapse earlier is no doubt due to an uncommon power of self-control, of which I believe the prince himself to be unconscious, and an uncommon sense of duty, which is also quite spontaneous in his highness. These are high qualities, sir, in a future ruler...."

A faint flush dyed the empress' cheeks; a milder expression suffused the coldness of her features.

"And what is your advice, professor?" she asked.

"That his highness should take an indefinite rest, ma'am."

"His highness' marriage was fixed for next month," remarked the empress, in an enquiring tone.

Professor Barzia's face became quite white and rigid.

"It would be simply inexcusable, if his highness' marriage were to take place next month," he said, with his even, oracular voice.

"Postponed, then?" asked the emperor, with suppressed rage.

"Without doubt, sir," replied the professor, with cool determination.

"My dear professor," the emperor growled between his teeth, with a pretence of geniality, "you speak of rest and of rest and of rest. Good God, I tell you, the prince has *had* rest, months and months of it!... Do I ever rest so long? Life is movement; and government is movement. We can't allow ourselves to rest. Why should a young man like the prince be always resting? I never remember resting like that, when I was crown-prince! He may not be as strong as I am, but yet he is of our race! Excitement, you say!

Good God, what excitement? Political excitement? That fell to *my* share, not the prince's! And I had no need of rest after it. And has a prince to go and rest when he gets engaged to be married? Really, professor, this is carrying hygiene beyond all limits!"

"Sir, your majesty has done me the honour to ask my opinion of the prince's condition. I have given that opinion to the best of my knowledge."

"It's rest, then?"

"Undoubtedly, sir."

"But how long do you want him to rest?"

"I am not able to fix a date, sir."

"How long do you want his marriage postponed?"

"Indefinitely, sir."

The emperor paced the room; something unusual passed over his powerful features, a look of anguish....

"That's impossible," he muttered, curtly.

All were silent.

"It's impossible," he, repeated, dully.

"Then his highness will marry, sir," said Barzia.

The emperor stood still:

"What do you mean?" he asked, gruffly.

"That nothing can prevail with your majesty in this most important matter ... except your own sense of what is right and reasonable."

The emperor's breath came in short gasps between his full, sensual lips; his veins swelled thick on his low, Roman forehead; his strong fists were clenched. No one had ever seen Oscar like this before; nor had any one ever dared so to address him....

"Explain yourself more clearly," he thundered into the professor's rigid face.

Barzia did not move a muscle:

"If his highness is married next month ... it means his death."

The empress remained sitting stiff and upright, but she turned very pale, shuddered and closed her eyes as though she felt giddy.

"His death?" echoed the emperor, in consternation.

"Or worse," rejoined Barzia.

"Worse?"

"The extinction of your majesty's posterity."

The emperor rapped out a furious oath and struck his fist on the huge writing-table. The bronze ornaments on it rang. Myxila drew a step nearer:

"Sir," he said, "there is nothing lost. If I understand Professor Barzia, his highness' illness is only temporary and is curable."

"Certainly, excellency," replied Barzia. "So long as it is not forced to become incurable and chronic."

Oscar bit his lips convulsively. His glittering eyes stood out small and cruel. It struck Myxila how much, at this moment, he resembled a portrait of Wenceslas the Cruel.

"Professor," he hissed, "we thank you. Stay at Lipara till to-morrow, so as to observe his highness once more."

"I will obey your majesty's commands," said Barzia.

He bowed, the physicians bowed; they withdrew. Left alone with the empress and the imperial chancellor, Oscar no longer restrained his rage. Like a beast foaming at the mouth, he walked fiercely up and down with heavy steps, gurgling as though the breath refused to come through his constricted throat:

"Oh!" he gnashed between his teeth, bursting out at last. "That boy, that boy!... He's not even fit to get married! His duchess: he was able to get married to her! And that boy, oh, that boy is to succeed me, *me!*..."

A furious laugh of contempt grated from between his large, white teeth, with biting irony.

The empress rose:

"Count Myxila," she said, trembling, "may I beg your excellency to come with me?"

She turned to leave the room. Myxila, hesitating, was already following her to the door.

"What for?" roared the emperor. "What's the reason of that? I have something more to say to Myxila."

The empress gave the emperor a look as cold as ice:

"It is my express wish, sir, that Count Myxila should go with me," she said, in the same trembling voice. "I think your majesty needs solitude. Your majesty is saying things which a father must not even think and which a sovereign must certainly not say in the presence of a subject, not even in that of one of his highest subjects...."

The emperor tried to interrupt her.

"Your majesty," continued the empress, with a haughty tremor, cutting the words from him with her icy-cold, trembling voice as though with a knife, "is saying these things of the future Emperor of Lipara ... and I wish *no* subject, not even Count Myxila, to hear such things; and, moreover, your majesty is saying these things of *my son*: therefore I do not wish to hear them myself, sir! Excellency, I request you once more to come with me."

"Go then!" shouted the emperor, like a madman. "Go, both of you: yes, leave me alone, leave me alone!"

He walked furiously up and down, flung the chairs one against the other, roared like an angry caged lion. He took a bronze statue from a bracket in front of a tall mirror that rose to the ceiling in gilt arabesques:

"There then!" he lashed out, while his passion seemed to seethe mistily in his bewildered brain, to shoot red lightning-flashes from his bloodshot eyes, to drive him mad because of his impotence against the senseless fate and logic of circumstance.

Like an athlete he brandished the heavy statue through the air; like a child he hurled it at the great mirror, which fell clattering in a flicker of shreds.

The empress and Myxila had left the room.

3

The ordinary court-life continued; the empress' first drawing-room took place. The reception-rooms leading to the great presence-chamber were lit up, though it was day-time; the ladies entered, handed their cards to the grand chamberlain, signed their names and waited until their titles were called out by the masters of ceremonies. They stood in low-necked dresses; the long white veils fell in misty folds of gauze from the feathers and jewelled tiaras. It was the first display of the new costumes of the season, the fashion which had sprung into life and now moved and had its being; but the crowded rooms seemed but the antechambers of that display and the upgathered trains gave an impression of preparation for the solemn second, the momentary appearance before her majesty.

The Duchess of Yemena was waiting, her train also thrown over her arm, with the two marchionesses her stepdaughters, whom she was about to present to the empress, when she saw Dutri, bowing, apologizing, twisting through the expectant ladies, to make way for himself through the crowded room:

"Dutri," she beckoned, as he did not seem to perceive her.

He reached her after some difficulty, bowed, paid his compliments to the little marchionesses. They stood with stiff little faces, frightened, round eyes and tight-closed mouths; and the lines of their girlish figures displayed the shyness of novices. With an awkward grace, they kept arranging their heavy court-trains over their arms. They just smiled at Dutri's words; then they looked stiff again, compared the other ladies' dresses with their own.

"Dutri," whispered the duchess, "how is the prince?"

"Just the same," the equerry whispered in reply. "Terribly melancholy...."

"Dutri," she murmured, sinking her voice still lower, "would there be no chance for me to see him?"

Dutri started in dismay:

"How do you mean, Alexa? When?"

"Presently, after the drawing-room...."

"But that is impossible, Alexa! The prince sees no one but their majesties and the princess; he talks to nobody, not even to his chamberlains, not even to us...."

"Dutri," she insisted, with her hand on his arm, "do your best. Help me. Ask for an interview for me. If you help me ... I will help you too...."

He looked at her expectantly.

"What do you think of Hélène?" she asked.

"I think Eleonore prettier," he smiled.

"Well, come to us oftener, to my special days; we never see anything of you. I will prepare the duke...."

She dangled the rich match before his eyes: he blinked them, as he continued to look at her and smile.

"But then you must help me!" she continued, with a gentle threat.

"I will do my best, Alexa, but I can promise nothing," he just had time to reply. "Wait for me after the drawing-room, in one of the other rooms," he whispered, accompanying her for a few steps.

All this time the titles were being cried, ceremoniously, slowly; the ladies moved on, dropped their trains, blossomed out.

"Her excellency the Duchess of Yemena, Countess of Vaza; their excellencies the Marchionesses of Yemena...."

The duchess moved on, the girls followed her, crimson, with beating hearts. They passed through a long gallery, dropping their trains; at the door of the presence-room, before they entered, stood flunkeys who spread out the heavy court-mantles.

"Her excellency the Duchess of ..."

The titles rang out for the second time, this time through the presence-chamber and with a sound of greater reverence, because they echoed in the listening ears of welcoming majesty.

The duchess and the marchionesses entered. Between the wide hangings of dark-blue velvet, on which glittered the cross of St. Ladislas, and under the canopy supported by gilt pillars, sat the empress, like an idol, glittering in the shadow in her watered-silver brocade, the ermine imperial mantle falling in heavy folds to her feet, a small diadem sparkling upon her head. To the right of the throne, on a low stool, sat the Princess Thera, on the left stood the mistress of the robes, the Countess of Threma; round about, on either side, a crowd of ladies-in-waiting, court-officials, equerries, maids of honour, grooms of the bed-chamber....

The duchess made her curtsey, approached the throne and with great reverence, as though with diffident lips, touched the jewelled finger-tips, which the empress held out like a live relic. Then the duchess took two steps backwards; the marchionesses, one after the other, followed her example, surprising everybody by the attractive freshness of their first court-movements, in which the touch of awkwardness became a charm. Then the bows, in a long ritual of withdrawal, backwards. They disappeared through other doors, found themselves in a long gallery, entered other reception-rooms, where people stood waiting for their carriages. And the two girls looked at each other, seeking each other's impressions, still crimson with the excitement in their vain little hearts and strangely surprised at the incomprehensible briefness of this first and all-important moment of their lives as grown-up people, as ladies accompanying their mamma to the Imperial, where they would thenceforth lead their existence. For how many months beforehand they had thought and dreamed of this moment; now, suddenly, with surprising quickness, it was over....

The duchess chucked Hélène under the chin, put Eleonore's veil straight, said that they had curtseyed beautifully, that she had herself even noticed how pleased the Countess of Threma had been with them. Then she chatted busily with the other ladies, introduced the little marchionesses, promised visits. Then she turned to a flunkey:

"Go and see where my carriage is and tell it to leave the rank and drive up last. Here...."

She gave him a gold coin; the flunkey disappeared. A nervous impatience seized the duchess; she looked out anxiously for Dutri. At last her eyes caught sight of him; he came up with his fatuous fussiness:

"Alexa, it's impossible...."

"Have you asked the prince?"

"No, not yet; there's the question, to begin with, whether he'll see *me*. But then ... how am I to take you to him? There are always servants hanging about in the doorways, to say nothing of the guards and halberdiers; in the anterooms you run up against a chamberlain at any moment. Really, it is impossible."

She grew angry:

"Begin by asking him. We'll see later how we're to get to him."

Dutri made graceful gestures of despair:

"But, Alexa, can't you really understand ... that it is impossible?..."

She made no reply, not wishing to reflect, her head filled with her stubborn fixed idea to see the prince, to insist on seeing him. And, suddenly, turning to him:

"Very well, if you don't care to do anything for me, you needn't think I shall help you in *any* way."

Her nervous, angry voice sounded louder than her first whispered words: the two girls heard her.

"Alexa," he besought her, gently.

"No, no," she resisted, curtly.

He thought of his debts and of Eleonore:

"I'll try," he whispered, in despair.

She promptly rewarded him with a smile; he went, hurried away again, with his eternal air of fussy importance, because of his young imperial master, who was so sadly ill. In the anteroom he found the chamberlain on duty:

"Would the prince be willing to see me?"

The chamberlain shrugged his shoulders:

"I'll ask," he said.

He speedily returned: the prince had sent word that Dutri could come in.

Dutri entered. Othomar lay on a couch covered with tiger-skins, in front of his writing-table. He had grown thinner; his eyes were hollow, his complexion was wan; his neck protruded frail and wasted from the loose turn-down collar of his silk shirt, over which he wore a velvet jacket. In his hand he held an open book. Djalo, the collie, lay on the floor.

Dutri the voluble began to press his request in rapid sentences following close upon one another's heels....

"The duchess?" repeated Othomar, faintly. "No, no...."

Dutri galloped on, simulated melancholy, employed words of gentle, insinuating sadness. Othomar's face assumed an expression which was strange to it and quite new: it was as though the melancholy of his features were crystallizing into a stubborn obstinacy, a silent doggedness.

"No," he said once more, while his voice, too, sounded dogged and obstinate. "Make my apologies to the duchess, Dutri. And where ... where would she wish to see me?"

"I did not fail to point out this difficulty to her excellency; but perhaps, if your highness would be so gracious ... one might nevertheless...."

Othomar closed his eyes and threw his head back; his hand fell loosely upon the collie's head. He made no further reply and his lips were tightly compressed.

Dutri still hesitated: what could he do, what should he tell Alexa?...

But the door opened and the empress entered. The drawing-room was over; she had put off her robes and the crown, but she still wore her stiff, heavy dress of silver brocade. She looked coldly at Dutri and bowed her head slightly, as a sign for him to go: the equerry beat a confused retreat, without his usual tact.

Othomar half-rose from his couch:

"Mamma!..."

She sat down beside him, stroked his forehead with her hand:

"How do you feel?"

He smiled and blinked with his eyes, without replying.

"What was Dutri doing here?"

"He wanted ... Oh, mamma, never mind, don't ask me!... How beautiful you look! May I, too, kiss your hand?"

Winningly, jestingly he took her hand and kissed it. She took his book from his fingers, read the treasonable title:

"Are you reading again, Othomar?... You know you mustn't read so much. And why all these strange books?..."

On the table lay Lassalle, Marx, works by Russian nihilists, a pamphlet by Bakounine, pamphlets by Zanti.... The little work which he was reading was by a well-known Liparian anarchist and entitled, *Injustice by the Grace of God;* it overthrew everything: religion and the state; it addressed itself directly to the crowned tyrants in power; it addressed itself directly to Oscar.

"Is it to get back your health, Othomar, that you read this sort of thing?" she asked, in a tone of pained reproach.

"But, mamma, I must see what it is that they want...."

"And what do they want?"

He looked pensively before him:

"I don't know what they want, I can't understand them. They employ very long sentences, the same sentences over and over again, with the same words over and over again. I can just make out that they disapprove of everything that exists and want something different. But yet sometimes...."

"Sometimes what?"

"Sometimes they say terrible things, terrible because they sound so true, mamma. When they speak of God and prove that He does not exist, when they describe our whole system of government as a monstrosity and reject all authority, including our own.... They sometimes speak like children who have suddenly learnt to talk and to judge; and then sometimes they suddenly speak clearly; and then very primitive thoughts arise in me: if God exists, why is there any injustice and misery; and our authority: on what right is that founded? O God, mamma, what right have we to reign over others, over millions? Tell me—but argue from the beginning: don't argue backwards; don't begin with us: begin with our first rulers, our usurpers— what right had they? And does ours merely spring from theirs? Oh, these problems, these simple problems: who can solve them, my God, who can solve them?...."

Elizabeth suddenly turned pale. She stared at him as though he had gone mad:

"Who gives you these books?" she asked, harshly, hoarsely, anxiously.

"Dutri, Leoni; Andro has also fetched me some."

"They're mad!" exclaimed the empress, rising. "Why do you ask for them?"

"I want to know, mamma...."

"Othomar," she cried, "will you do what I ask?"

"Yes, mamma," he replied, gently, "but sit down again and ... and don't be angry. And ... and don't say 'Othomar.' And ... and go and change your dress: oh, I can't see you in that dress; you are so far from me; your voice doesn't reach me and I daren't kiss you: you are not my mother, you are the empress! Mamma, O mamma!...."

Majesty | 153

His voice appealed to her. A powerful emotion awoke in her.

"O my boy!" she cried, with a half-sob breaking in her throat.

"Yes, yes, call me that.... Mamma, let's be quick and find each other again, let us not lose each other. What is your request?"

"Give me all those books."

"I will give them to you; they make me no happier, when all is said!"

"But then why are you unhappy, my boy, my boy?"

"Mamma, look at the world, look at our people, see how they suffer, see how they are oppressed! What shall I ever be able to do for them! I shall always be powerless, in spite of all our power! Oh, it grows so dark in front of me, I can see nothing more, I have no hope; only Utopians have any hope left, but I ... I no longer hope, for I can do nothing, nothing!... O my God, mamma, the whole country is falling upon me and crushing me and I can do nothing, nothing!... I shall have to reign and I shall not be able to, mamma. What am I? A poor sickly boy: how can I become emperor? I don't know why it is, mamma, nor what it comes from, but I don't feel like a future emperor, I feel like a feeble child! I feel like your child, your boy, and nothing more...."

He seemed about to throw himself into her arms, but on the contrary he flung himself backwards, as though he were frightened by her brilliant attire; his head dropped nervelessly on his chest, his arms fell loosely down. She saw his movement: her first feeling was one of regret that she had come to him in court-dress, longing as she did to see him, not allowing herself the time to change. But this regret passed through her as a transient emotion, for it was followed by an intense dizziness, as though a yawning abyss opened at her feet, as though the earth retreated and black nothingness gaped before her. A despair as of utter impotence enveloped her soul. Vaguely she stretched out her arms and threw them round his neck, as though she were groping in the dark, with wandering eyes:

"My boy, don't talk like that any more, because ... when you talk like that, you take away my strength too!" she whispered, in alarm. "For how can it be helped? You must, we all must...."

"Forgive me, mamma, but I ... I shall not be able to. Oh, I see it clearly now! I am not excited, I am calm. I see it, I prophesy it, it can never be...."

"But papa is still so young and so strong, my boy; and, when you grow older...."

"The older I grow, the more impossible it will be, mamma. I was always frightened of it as a child, but I never realized it so desperately as now. No, mamma, it cannot be. Now that I am ill, I have plenty of time to reflect; and I now see before me what the end of all our trouble is bound to be...."

His eyes gazed at the floor in despair; she still half-clung to him, helplessly; a menacing shiver seemed to float through the room.

"Mamma...."

She made no response.

"I must tell you of my resolve...."

"What resolve?..."

"Will you tell it to papa?"

"What, what, Othomar ... my boy?"

"That I can't marry ... Valérie, because...."

"Later, later: you needn't marry yet...."

"No, mamma, I never can, because I...."

She looked at him beseechingly, enquiringly.

"Because I want to abdicate ... my rights ... in favour of ... Berengar...."

She made no reply; feebly she drooped against him, not knowing how to console and cheer him, and softly and plaintively began to sob. It was as though her soul was being flooded with anguish, slowly but persistently, until it brimmed over. She reproached herself with it all. He was her child: the future Emperor of Liparia had derived this weakness from her. And the manifestation of this agonizing mystery of heredity before her despairing eyes deprived her of all her strength, of all her courage, of all her power of acquiescence and resignation.

"Mamma," he repeated.

She sobbed on.

"Don't be so disconsolate.... Berengar will be better than I.... You'll tell papa, won't you?... Or no, never mind, if it costs you too great an effort: I'll tell him myself...."

She started up nervously from her despair:

"O my God, no! Othomar, no! Don't talk to him about it: he is so passionate, he would ... he would murder you! Promise me that you will not talk to him about it! *I* will tell him—O my God!—*I* will tell him...."

But a tremor of hope revived within her.

"But, Othomar, I ask you, why do you do this? You are ill now, but you will get better and then ... then you will think differently!"

He gazed out before him: his presentiment quivered through him; he saw his dream again: the streets of Lipara filled with crape, right up to the sky, where it veiled the sunlight. And over his features there passed again that new air of hardness, of dogged obstinacy which made him unrecognizable; he shook his head slowly from side to side, from side to side:

"No, mamma, I shall never think differently. Believe me, it will be better so."

When she saw him like that, her new hope collapsed again and she sobbed once more. Sobbing, she rose; amid her sorrow yawned a void; she was losing something: her son.

"Are you going?" he asked.

She nodded yes, sobbing.

"Do you forgive me?"

She nodded yes again. Then she gave him a smile, a smile full of despair; lacking the strength to kiss him, she went out, still sobbing.

He remained alone and rose from his couch. He stood in the middle of the room; his eyes stared at the collie:

"Why need I give her pain!" he thought.

Everything in his soul hurt him.

"Why did I go on that voyage with Herman?" he asked himself again. "It was in those first days of rest that I began to think so much. And yet Professor Barzia says, 'Rest!' ... What does he know about me? What does one person know about another?... Djalo!" he cried.

The collie ran up, wriggling, joyfully.

"Djalo, what is right? How ought the world to be? Must there be kings and emperors, Djalo, or had we better all disappear?"

The dog looked at him, wagging its tail violently; suddenly it jumped up and licked his face.

"And why, Djalo, need one man always make the other unhappy? Why need princes make their people unhappy? Will life always remain the same, for ages and ages?..."

Othomar sank into a heap on the couch; his hand fell on the dog, which licked it passionately.

"Oh!" he sobbed. "My people, my people!..."

At this moment the last carriages were driving away in the fore-court of the Imperial; the staring crowd, behind the grenadiers, peeped curiously at the pretty ladies glistening through the glass of the state-coaches. The Duchess of Yemena's carriage came last of all.

4

A spirit of gloom seemed to haunt the ringing marble halls of the Imperial, a dim melancholy to stifle the cadences of the voices and their echoes and to hang from the tall ceilings as it had been a heavy web of atmosphere. It was autumn; the first parties were to take place; the first court-ball was given. But it seemed to be given because there was no help for it: it was a slow, official, tedious function. The more intimate circles of the Imperial, those of the Duchess of Yemena and the diplomatic body, regretted the more select assemblies in the smaller rooms of the empress. They looked upon those great balls as necessary inflictions. The empress' smaller dances, however, were always favoured as most charming entertainments. But the empress had decided that they should not take place, because of the illness of the crown-prince. At this first great ball their majesties appeared only for a brief moment, to take part in the imperial quadrille....

Grey ashes fell over the glittering mood of imperial festivity which so short a time ago had been the usual atmosphere of the palace. The dinners, once the glories of day after day, were shortened; only the most necessary invitations were given. The emperor himself maintained a constant mood of sullenness: the army bill for the augmentation of the active forces was still attacked in principle in the house of deputies; and the emperor was resolved at all costs to uphold his minister of war. Moreover, thanks to the dash of childishness that showed through all his energy, he had not recovered from his disappointment at the postponement of the Duke of Xara's marriage. He seemed in a continual state of irritation because his Liparian world would not go as he wanted it to go.

Neither the empress nor the prince himself thought it a favourable moment to communicate the mournful resolution to the emperor. But for this very reason the empress began silently to cherish fresh hope. Nothing had been said yet: the humiliating secret existed only between her son and herself. Humiliating, because what public reason could he allege for resigning the succession? What pretext would sound plausible enough to conceal the true motive of weakness and impotence? And yet he was her child and Oscar's! It seemed to the empress unfeasible to communicate Othomar's wish to his father and to tell the emperor that his own son had no capacity for government. Oh, what sacrifice would she not be prepared to make, if only she could spare her child this humiliation! But was he really so powerless to master himself and to draw himself up, proudly, under the weight of what was as yet no more than a prince's coronet? Had she but known how to counteract his discouragement; but she had merely sobbed, merely given way before his despair; in vain had she sought in his soul the secret spring that should cause him to rise from the impotence into which the languor of his reflections had made him sink.... And yet she felt that there must be a secret spring, because she instinctively divined its presence in the souls of all her equals: it was the mystery of their sovereignty, the reason why they were sovereigns, the reason of their prerogative. She possessed the adorable, child-like faith that in them, the crowned heads, there exists a common essence of distinction which raises them above the crowd: that single drop of sacred blood in their veins, that single atom of inherited divinity, which sheds lustre through their souls. She believed in their high exclusive right of majesty. Because she believed in that even as she believed in her sinfulness as a human being and in the absolution of her confessor, the Archbishop of Lipara, she could never for one instant doubt their right divine as rulers. Whatever people might think, or write, or want different, theirs was the right: of this she was certain, as certain as of the Trinity. That Othomar had doubted the existence of God had struck her as impious, but it had not shattered her so much as his disbelief in their right. Was he alone then lacking in that essence of distinction, that sacred golden drop of blood, that divine atom? And, if he lacked it, if he, the crown-prince, lacked majesty, was this monstrous lack her fault, the fault of the mother who bore him?

The suspicion of this guilt crushed her; and before she even dared to speak to Othomar she humbled herself before the archbishop. The prelate, alarmed at these portents in the mysterious melancholy of the Imperial, had scarcely known how to comfort her. After that, she remained prostrate for hours before her crucifix. She prayed with all her soul, prayed for light for herself and for her son, prayed for strength and that the spark might descend upon Othomar. When she had prayed thus, so long and with such conviction, there came over her, like an afflatus of the Holy Ghost, a sense of peace. She became herself again, she awaited events, regained her credulous fatalism, her conviction that nothing happens but what must happen and is right. What was wrong did not happen. If it were fated that Othomar must receive that spark, that would be right; if it were fated that he must abdicate, that would be right too, O God, right with a strange, inscrutable rightness!...

Because the days had passed without her having yet spoken to the emperor, she hoped anew; she hoped that Othomar would be his old self again and no longer seek his own degradation. But it was as though she hoped in spite of everything; for, each time that she now saw Othomar, she found him duller and more exhausted, more helpless beneath the certainty of his weakness. Professor Barzia, who treated the prince personally and twice a day gave him his cold-water douche in the palace, seemed to be least uneasy about Othomar's physical weakness. The prince was not robust, but the professor divined in his delicate constitution the presence of the element that had sprung from the first rough, sensual strength of the Czyrkiski race: the Slavonic element, which had become enervated through its Latin admixtures, but had lingered on; a secret toughness, an indestructible factor of unsuspected firmness, which lay deep down, like a foundation, and upon which much seemed to be built that was very slender and fragile. What had once been rude strength the professor believed he had discovered in a certain toughness; what had been cruelty and lust, in a certain enervation, which had hitherto been held in check by self-restraint and a spontaneous sense of duty, but which now suddenly revealed itself in this excessive lassitude. Barzia distinctly perceived in Othomar the scion of his ancestors; and he considered that, though the rich physical vigour of the original sovereign blood had become refined, as if it were now flowing more thinly through feebler veins, yet that blood was not so impoverished that the delicacy of this future emperor need be ascribed to racial exhaustion. Possibly Barzia's sudden affection for the prince tinged this physiological diagnosis with excessive optimism; at any rate, the professor had not the least fear of this fragility, or even of this nervous weakness. What he did fear was lest those mental qualities which had so suddenly endeared the prince to him should not be able to maintain themselves during this period of fatigue and exhaustion. Spontaneous, unreflected, uncalculated he knew those virtues to be in the prince, as it were a treasure unknown to himself: would they be lost, now, in these mournful days, or would they remain, perhaps develop, become more and more refined, make up to Othomar in moral strength for what he lacked in physical strength and in this way cure him? For the professor knew it: these qualities alone could effect a cure....

Othomar himself thought neither of his virtues nor of his blood: he thought of his future and thought of it with an hourly-increasing dread. When the empress asked Barzia whether this rest would be good for the prince and whether distraction would not be better, the professor declared that the prince had had plenty of distraction lately. He must first get over his fatigue, get over it entirely; it mattered less with what the prince kept his brain occupied for the moment....

But Barzia did not mean this altogether and would doubtless have been very far from meaning it at all, had he known of what the prince was thinking, or been fully able to judge his utter lack of mental elasticity.

And the days passed by. Othomar did not mention his resolution to the empress again, desiring to give her as little pain as possible; neither did the empress allude to it: she hoped on.

But in Othomar's meditations it revolved incessantly, like a wheel: he was able to do nothing for his people and yet he loved them; he did not know how to govern them, he would abdicate his rights and his title of crown-prince: Berengar should become Duke of Xara....

The small prince came and paid his brother a short visit every morning; he always wore his little uniform, looking like a sturdy little general in miniature, and Othomar watched him with a smile.

Was there no wish to rule in the boy's medieval little brain, was there no jealousy in his passionate little heart? Othomar remembered the history of Liparia, in the cruel times of their early middle-ages, that terrible drama — they still showed at St. Ladislas the chamber where it had been enacted — that second son stabbing his elder brother in his lust for the crown and hurling the corpse from an oriel window into the Zanthos, which flowed beneath the fortress. What had the boy inherited of this rivalry? And, though this rivalry had been wholly refined into less salient feelings, would not an immense happiness enter Berengar's small princely soul if he were to learn that he might be crown-prince now and that one day he would be ... emperor? But what would the boy think of him, Othomar, for giving away all this magnificence of his own free will? Would he despise him, while yet feeling grateful to him, or would he cherish mistrust, suspecting a lurking mystery behind all this greatness, which Othomar cast from him?...

At such times Othomar would draw the little fellow to him with silent compassion, but would take pleasure in feeling the firm muscles of his sturdy little arms and listening to his short, crisp little speeches. Then Berengar rode away and Djalo was allowed to run with him through the park: in an hour he would bring the dog back to Othomar and talk with great importance of his lessons, which were just beginning.

And, when Berengar had gone, Othomar lay thinking about him in his long hours of reverie, already looked upon his brother as actually crown-prince, erased his own name from the list of future sovereigns, thought of what he would do when he was cured and had shaken off the last remnant of his purple, remembered his uncle Xaverius, who was the abbot of a monastery, and pictured himself studying, compiling works on history and sociology....

5

These were autumn days. The sunny blue of the sky was often clouded with grey; in the morning the winds blew from the north, blew over the sea till it became the colour of steel; then the sun broke through and shone very warmly for a couple of hours, with an occasional cold blast, suddenly and treacherously rushing round the corners of the streets; then, at four or half-past four o'clock, the sun was extinguished and the pale sky was left exhaling its icy chillness on the open harbour, between the white palaces, in the streets and squares.

It was a treacherous time of year: the empress and Berengar had caught cold driving in an open carriage; they both kept their rooms and Othomar in his turn went to visit them; the empress was coughing, the little prince had a temperature; there was never so much illness about as now, the doctors declared. And a melancholy continued to brood through the halls of the Imperial, through the whole town, where the imperial family were no longer seen at the opera and at parties. Never had the daily dinners at the Imperial been so short, with so few guests; and it made an insurmountably sad impression not to see the empress seated next to the emperor, delicate, distinguished, august, but in her stead the Princess Thera, who seemed quite incapable of bringing a smile to Oscar's grim and peevish features.

Othomar did not even know that those about the empress were anxious on her behalf: she always received him with all the cheerfulness that she could muster, in spite of the pain on her chest; the doctors told him nothing, no one gave him the bulletins, every one tried to spare him; and besides there was really less anxiety in the Imperial than in the town and throughout the country. But the little prince received Othomar with less meekness than did the empress; and every day there were silent rages, sulking displays against the doctors for keeping him in bed.

Once, when the crown-prince came to see Berengar, the doctors were with him; the fever had increased, but the little prince wanted to get out of bed; he was naughty, used ugly names, had even struck the good-natured, big-headed doctor and pummelled him with his little clenched fist.

"As soon as you're better, Berengar," said Othomar, after first reproving him, "I shall make you a present."

"What of?" asked the boy, eagerly. "But I am better now!"

"No, no, you must do what the doctors tell you and not vex them."

"And what will you give me then?"

Othomar looked at him long and firmly.

"What shall I have then?" repeated the child.

"I mustn't tell you yet, Berengar; it's really rather big for you still."

"What is it then? A horse?"

"No, it's not as big as a horse, but heavier. Don't ask any more about it and also don't try and guess what it is, but be obedient: then you'll get better and then you shall have it."

"Heavier than a horse and not so big!..." Berengar pondered, with glowing cheeks.

With his head bowed on his breast, dragging his footsteps, Othomar returned to his room. He stayed there for hours, sitting silently, gloomily, in the same attitude; as usual, he did not appear at dinner and hardly ate what Andro brought him. Then he went to lie down on his couch, took up a book to read, but put it down again and raised himself up, as though with a sudden impulse:

"Why not now?" he thought. "Why keep on postponing it?..."

Night fell, but the upper corridors of the palace were not yet lighted; dragging his fatigue through this dusky shadow, Othomar went to the emperor's anterooms. The chamberlain announced him.

Oscar sat at his writing-table, pen in hand.

"Am I disturbing you, papa? Or can I speak to you?"

"No, you're not disturbing me.... Have you been to see mamma?"

"Yes, this afternoon; she was pretty well, but Berengar's temperature was higher."

The emperor glanced up at him:

"Worse than this morning?"

"I don't know: he was rather feverish."

The emperor rose:

"Do you want to talk to me?"

"Yes, papa."

"Wait a moment, then. I've not been to Berengar yet to-day."

He went out, leaving the door ajar.

Othomar remained alone. He sat down. He looked round the great work-room, which he knew so well from their morning consultations with the chancellor. Lately, however, he had not attended these. He thought over what he should say; meanwhile his eyes wandered around; they fell upon the great mirror with its gilt arabesques; something seemed strange to him. Then he rose and walked up to the glass:

"I was under the impression there was a flaw near the top of it," he thought. "I can't well be mistaken. Has it been renewed?"

He was still standing by the looking-glass, when Oscar returned:

"Berengar is not at all well; the fever is increasing," he said; and the tone of his voice hesitated. "Mamma is with him...."

Absorbed as he was in his own meditations, it did not strike Othomar that the little prince must have become worse for the empress, who was herself ill, to go to him.

"And about what did you want to speak to me?" asked the emperor, as the prince remained silent.

"About Berengar, papa."

"About Berengar?"

"About Berengar and myself. I have been contrasting myself with him, papa. We are brothers, we are both your sons. Which of us, do you think, takes most after you ... and ... our ancestors?"

"What are you driving at, Othomar?"

"At what is right, papa: right and just. Nature is sometimes unjust and blind; she ought to have let Berengar be born first and me next ... or even left me out altogether."

"Once more, what are you driving at, Othomar?"

"Can't you see, papa? I will tell you. Is Berengar not more of a monarch than I am? Is that not why he's your favourite? And ought I to deprive him of his natural rights for the sake of my traditional rights? I want to abdicate in his favour, papa. I want to abdicate everything, all my rights."

"The boy's mad," muttered Oscar.

"All my rights," repeated Othomar, dreamily, as though he foresaw the future: his little brother crowned.

"Othomar, are you raving?" asked the emperor.

"Papa, I am not raving. What I am now telling you I have thought over for days, perhaps weeks; I don't know: time passes so quickly.... What I am telling you I have discussed with mamma: it made her cry, but she did not oppose me. She looks at it as I do.... And what I tell you holds good; I have made up my mind and nothing can make me change it.... I am fond of

Berengar; I am glad to give up everything to him; and I shall pray that he may become happy through my gift. I am convinced—and so are you—that Berengar will make a better emperor than I. What talent do I possess for ruling?..."

He shrugged his shoulders in helplessness, with a nervous shudder that jolted them:

"None," he answered himself. "I have no talent, I can do nothing. I do not know how to decide—as now—nor how to act; I shall always be a dreamer. Why then should I be emperor and he nothing more than the commander-in-chief of my army or my fleet? Surely that can't be right; that can't have been what nature intended.... Papa, I give it him, my birthright, and I ... I shall know how to live, if I must...."

The emperor had listened to him with his elbows on the table and his hands under his chin and now sat staring at him with his small, pinched eyes:

"Do you mean all this?" he asked.

"Yes, papa."

"You're not delirious?"

"No, papa, I'm not delirious."

"Then you're mad."

The emperor rose:

"Then you're mad, I tell you. Othomar, realize that you're mad and return to your senses; don't become quite insane."

"Why do you call me insane, papa? *Can't* you agree with me that Berengar would be better than I?"

His father's cruel glances stabbed Othomar through and through:

"No, you're not insane in that; you're right there...."

"And why, then, am I insane because I wish, for that reason, to abdicate in his favour?"

"Because it's impossible, Othomar."

"What law prevents me?"

"My will, Othomar."

The prince drew himself up proudly:

"Your will?" he cried. "Your will? You acknowledge that I am nothing of a prince except by birth? You acknowledge that Berengar does possess your capacity for ruling and you will not, you *will* not have me abdicate? And you think that I shall fall in with that will?..."

He uttered a hoarse laugh:

"No, papa, I shall pay no heed to that will. You can carry through your will in everything, but not in this. Though you called out your whole army, you could not prevail against me here. There is a limit to the power of human will, papa, and nothing, nothing, nothing can prevent me from considering myself unfit to reign and from *refusing* to wear a crown!"

The emperor seized Othomar's wrists; his hot breath hissed in Othomar's face:

"You damned cub!" he snarled between his large, white teeth. "You wretched nincompoop! You're right: there's nothing of the emperor in you; there never will be. If I didn't know better, I'd say you were the son of a footman. You're right, you're incompetent. You're nothing: our crown doesn't fit you. And yet, though I had to lock you up in a prison, so that no one might hear of your baseness, you shall *not* abdicate your rights. My will extends farther than you can see. Do you hear? You shan't do it, you shan't resign, though from this moment onwards I have to hide you, as a disgrace, from the world. Your slack brain can't understand that, can it? You can't understand that I'm fonder of Berengar than of a poltroon like you and that nevertheless I won't have him as my successor in your stead? Then I shall have to tell you. I won't have it, so as not to let the world see the degeneration of our race. I will not have the world know how pitiably we have deteriorated in you; and I would rather ... I would rather murder you than allow you to abdicate!"

Fiercely Oscar took the prince by his shoulders, pushed him backwards on a couch, on which Othomar sank in a huddled attitude, while his father continued to hold him like a prey in the grip of his strong hands:

"But I tell you," continued the emperor, "I tell you, you are *not* the son of a footman, you are my son; and I shall not murder you, because I am your father. I will only say this to you, Othomar: you might have spared me this. I believe you have a high opinion of your own delicacy of feeling, but you have not the very least feeling. You do not even feel that you have been contemplating a villainy, the villainy of a proletarian, a slave, a pariah, a wretch. You have not felt even for an instant the pain you would cause me by such an infamy. You saw that I was fonder of your brother; you thought that I should approve of your cowardly proposal. Not for a moment did the thought occur to you that, with that cowardice of yours, you would give *me* the greatest pain that I could ever experience!..."

Othomar, utterly crushed, had fallen back upon the couch. He was no longer able to distinguish what was just and what was true; he no longer knew himself at that minute; his father's words lashed his soul like whips. And he felt no strength within him to resist them: the insulting reproaches kept him down, as though he had been thrashed. Infamy and disgrace, insanity and degeneration: he collapsed beneath them; he gulped down the mud of them, till he felt like suffocating. And that he did not suffocate and continued to breathe, continued to live, that the light was bright around him, that things remained unchanged, that the outside world knew nothing: all this was despair to him. For a moment he thought of his mother. But he wished for darkness, for death, to hide himself, himself and his shame, his degeneration, the leprosy of his pariah-temperament.... It flashed through him in the second after that last lash of reproach, flashed across his despondent soul. He knew that Oscar always kept a loaded revolver in an open pigeon-hole of his writing-table. His brain grew tense in the effort of thinking how to reach it. He rose, approached the pigeon-hole; suddenly he sprang towards it, stretched out his hand and seized the pistol....

Did Oscar believe that his son had been driven mad by his last words and now wanted his father's life? Did he perceive this ecstasy of suicide in his offspring, was his quivering brain penetrated by the horrible thought that self-destruction would be the pariah's last refuge? Be this as it might, he rushed at Othomar. But the prince lightly leapt out of his reach, pointed the revolver, with wild eyes, with distorted features, in senseless despair, upon himself, upon his own forehead, on which the veins swelled blue....

"Othomar!" roared the emperor.

At this moment hurried footsteps were heard outside, confused words sounded in the anteroom and the Marquis of Xardi, the emperor's aide-de-camp, alarmed and flurried, threw the door wide open....

"Sir!" he exclaimed. "The empress asks if your majesty will come to Prince Berengar this instant...."

The shot had gone off, into the wall. Blood dripped from Othomar's ear. The emperor had caught hold of the crown-prince and torn the revolver, still loaded in five chambers, from him; a second shot went off in that brief moment of struggle, into the ceiling, Othomar remained standing vacantly.

"Marquis!" the emperor hissed out at Xardi. "I don't know what you think, but I tell you this: you've seen nothing, you think nothing. What happened here before you came in ... did not happen."

He pointed his finger, threateningly at Xardi:

"Should you ever forget, marquis, that it did not happen, then I shall forget who you are, though your pedigree dates back farther than ours!"

Xardi stood deathly pale before his emperor:

"My God, sir!..."

"What do you mean by entering your sovereign's room in this unmannerly fashion? Even the Duke of Xara has himself announced, marquis!"

"Sir...."

"What? Speak up!..."

"Her majesty...."

"Well, her majesty?"

"Prince Berengar ... the fever has increased ... he is delirious, sir, and the doctors ..."

The emperor turned pale:

"Is he dead?" he asked, fiercely. "Tell me at once."

"Not dead, sir, but...."

"But what?"

"But the doctors ... have no hope...."

With an oath of anguish the emperor pushed the aide aside and darted out of the room.

The prince remained standing. Life returned to him: a reality full of anguish, born of nightmare. His eyes swam with tears:

"Xardi," he implored, "Xardi ... your house has always been loyal to our house; swear to me that you will be silent."

The marquis looked at the crown-prince in consternation:

"Highness...."

"Swear to me, Xardi."

"I swear to you, highness," said the aide, subdued; and he stretched out his fingers to the crucifix hanging on the wall.

Othomar pressed his hand:

"Did Prince Berengar...." He could scarcely speak. "Did Prince Berengar become so ill suddenly?..."

"The fever is increasing every moment, highness, and he is delirious...."

"I will go to him," said Othomar.

He wiped the blood from his ear with his handkerchief and held the cambric, which was at once soaked through, against it.

In the last anteroom he passed the chamberlain and looked at him askance.

Xardi stopped for a moment:

"The Duke of Xara has hurt himself slightly," he said. "He was examining the emperor's revolver when I went in and he started: two shots went off."

"I heard them," whispered the chamberlain, pale as death.

"There might have been an accident...."

They were silent for a moment; their glances were full of understanding; a shudder crept down their backs. The chill night seemed to be descending over the palace as with clouds of evil omen.

"And ... the little prince?..." asked the chamberlain, shivering.

Xardi shrugged his shoulders; his eyes grew moist, through innate, immemorial love for his sovereigns:

"Dying," he answered, faintly.

6

The crown-prince passed through the anteroom: one of the doctors stood dipping poultices into a basin of ice; a valet was bringing in a pail of fresh ice. The door of the bedroom was open and Othomar remained standing at the door. The little prince lay on his camp-bed, talking in a low, sing-song tone; the empress, pale, suffering, bearing up in spite of everything, sat beside him with Princess Thera.

The emperor exchanged brief words with the two other doctors, whose features were overcast with a stark hopelessness; a mordant anguish distorted Oscar's face, which became furrowed with deep wrinkles:

"My God, he doesn't know me, he doesn't know me!" Othomar heard the emperor complain.

"Nor me," murmured the empress.

"What can it be? What, what, what can it be?" sang the little prince; and his usually shrill little voice sounded soft as a bird's melody: it was as though he were playing by himself. "I'm to have a present from my brother, from my brother, something nice!" he sang on.

The empress could distinguish his words, but she did not understand; and when he went on to sing the name of the crown-prince, with his title:

"Othomar, O Othomar of Xara, of Xara!..." she turned to the door and gently implored:

"Othomar, he's calling your name; come, perhaps he will know you!"

Othomar approached; he went past the emperor and knelt down by the bed; a smile lit up Berengar's little face.

"He is becoming calmer," said the kind doctor, whose tears were running down his cheeks, to Oscar. "Does your majesty see? The prince recognizes his highness the duke...."

A note of gladness sounded in his voice.

But a violent jealousy distorted the emperor's features:

"No, no," he said.

"Certainly, sir, only look," the doctor insisted, his hope reviving.

"O Othomar, O Othomar of Xara!" sang the little prince: he had recognized his brother, but did not see him in the flesh, saw him only in his waking dream, through the mist of his fever.

"What do you bring me that's nice? Smaller than a horse, but heavier? Heavier? Oh, how heavy it is, how heavy, heavy, heavy!..."

His little voice came as though with an effort, as though he were lifting something; his convulsive, small, broad hands made a gesture of laborious lifting.

"Berengar," said the crown-prince; and his voice broke, his heart sank within him....

"Othomar," replied the child.

A cry of anguish escaped the emperor.

"Yes, you're always so good to me," continued the little prince in his sing-song. "You always give me such nice things. You know, those lovely guns on my last birthday? And that pistol? But mamma's afraid of that!... Are you dying, Othomar? Look, there's blood on your ear.... But when people bleed they die! Are you dying, Othomar? Look, blood on your coat...."

The empress remained sitting straight upright; she glared from Berengar at the bleeding wound of her eldest son....

"Blood, blood, blood!" sang Berengar. "Othomar is dying! Yes, he always gives me so many nice things, does Othomar. I have so many already, many more than all the other children of Liparia put together! And what am I to have now?... Still more?... That nice thing: what is it? I can feel it: it's so heavy; but I can't see it...."

The doctor had come from the anteroom and approached with the poultices.

"I can't see it!... I can't see it!..." the boy sang out, painfully and faintly.

When the doctor applied the poultices, Berengar struggled, began to cry, as though a great sorrow was springing up in his little heart:

"I can't see it!" he sobbed. "I shall never see it!..."

A violent paroxysm succeeded the sobbing: he struck out wildly with his arms, pulled off the poultices, threw the ice off his head, stood up mad-eyed in his bed, flung away the sheets.... Othomar rose, the empress also. The emperor sat in a chair, his face covered with his hands, and sobbed by Princess Thera's side. The doctors approached the bed, endeavoured to calm Berengar, but he struck them: the fever mounted into his little brain in madness.

At this moment Professor Barzia entered: he was not staying in the palace; he had been sent for at his hotel.

"What is your highness doing here?" he said, point-blank, to Othomar.

The crown-prince made no reply.

"Your highness will retire to your own rooms at once," the professor commanded.

"Save my boy!" exclaimed the emperor, broken, sobbing.

"I am saving the crown-prince first, sir: he is killing himself here!"

"Very well, but next save *him!*" shouted Oscar, fiercely.

The other doctors had given orders: a tub was brought in, filled with lukewarm water, regulated by a thermometer.... But Othomar saw no more: he rushed away, driven out by Barzia's stern glances. He rushed along the corridors, through a group of officers and chamberlains, who stood anxiously whispering and made way for him. He plunged into his own room, which was not lighted. In the dark, he thought he was flinging himself upon a couch, but bumped upon the ground. There he remained lying. Then, as though crushed by the darkness, he began to croon, to moan, to sob aloud, with sharp, hysterical cries.

Andro entered; his foot struck against the prince. He lit the gas, tried to lift his master. But Othomar lay heavy as lead; fierce and prolonged, his nervous cries came jolting from his throat. Andro rang, once, twice, three times; he went on ringing for a long time; at last a footman and a chamberlain appeared together, at different doors.

"Call Professor Barzia!" cried Andro to the footman. "Excellency, will you help me lift his highness?" he begged the chamberlain.

But, when the footman turned round, he ran against the professor, who could do nothing for the little prince and had followed the crown-prince. He saw Othomar lying on the floor, moaning, screaming....

"Leave me alone with his highness," he ordered, with a glance around him.

The chamberlain, Andro, the footman obeyed his order.

The professor was a tall old man, heavily-built and strong; he approached the prince and lifted him in his arms, notwithstanding the leaden heaviness of hysteria. Thus he held him, merely with his arms around him, upon the couch and looked deep into his eyes, with hypnotic glances. Suddenly Othomar ceased his cries; his voice was hushed. His head fell feebly upon Barzia's shoulder. The professor continued to hold him in his arms. The prince became calm, like a quieted child, without Barzia's having uttered a word.

"May I request your highness to go to bed?" said the professor, with a gentle voice of command.

He assisted Othomar to get up and himself lit the light in the bedroom and helped the prince off with his coat.

"What has made your highness' ear bleed?" asked Barzia, whose fingers were soiled with clotted blood.

"A revolver-shot," Othomar began, faintly; his closed and averted eyes told the rest.

The professor said nothing more. As though Othomar were a child, he went on helping him, washed his ear, his neck, his hands, with a mother's gentleness. Then he made him lie down in bed, covered him over, tidying the room like a servant. Then he went and sat by the bed, where Othomar lay staring with strange, wide-open eyes: he took the prince's hand and sat thus for a long time, looking softly down upon him. The light behind, turned down low, threw Barzia's large head into the shadow and just glanced upon his bald cranium, from which a few grey locks hung down his neck. At last he said, gently:

"Your highness wishes to get well, do you not?"

"Yes," said Othomar, in spite of himself.

"How does your highness propose to do so?" asked the professor.

The prince did not answer.

"Doesn't your highness know? Then you must think it over. But you must keep very calm, will you not, very calm...."

And he stroked Othomar's hand with a gentle, regular motion, as though anointing it with balsam.

"For your highness must never again give way to nervous attacks. Your highness must study how to prevent them. I am giving your highness much to think about," continued Barzia, with a smile. "I am doing this because I want to let your highness think of other things than of what you are thinking. I want to clear your brain for you. Are you tired and do you want to go to sleep, or shall I go on talking?"

"Yes, go on," whispered the prince.

"There are days of great grief in store for the Imperial," the doctor resumed, gently. "Your highness must think of those days without permitting yourself to be overcome by the grief of them.... The little prince will probably not recover, highness. Will you think of that ... and think of your parents, their poor majesties? There are days like these for a nation, or for a single family, in which grief seems to pile itself up. For does not this day, this night seem to mark the end of your race, my prince?... Lie still, lie still, don't move: let me talk on, like a garrulous old man.... Does your highness know that the emperor to-day, for the first time in his whole life, cried, sobbed? His younger son is dying. Between this boy and the father is a first-born son, who is very, very ill.... Is not all this the end?"

"Yet, if God wills it so," whispered Othomar.

"It is our duty to be resigned," said Barzia. "But does God will it so?"

"Who can tell?..."

"Ask yourself, but not now, highness: to-morrow, to-morrow.... After the saddest nights ... the mornings come again...."

The professor rose and mixed a powder in a glass of water:

"Drink this, highness...."

Othomar drank.

"And now lie quiet and close those wide eyes."

"I shall not be able to sleep though...."

"That is not necessary, only close those eyes...."

Barzia stroked them with his hand; the prince kept them closed. His hand again lay in the hand of the professor.

A hush descended upon the room. Outside, in the corridors and galleries, perplexed steps approached at times, from the distance, in futile haste; then they sounded away, far away, in despair. A world of sorrow seemed to fill the palace, there, outside that room, until it held every hall of it with its dark, tenebrous woe. But in this one room nothing stirred. The professor sat still and stared before him, absorbed in thought; the crown-prince had fallen asleep like a child.

7

Next morning the day rose upon an empire in mourning. Prince Berengar had passed away in the night.

Othomar had slept long and woke late, as in a strange calm. When Professor Barzia told him of the young prince's end—the apathy of the last moments, after a raging fever—it seemed to him as if he already knew it. The great sorrow which he felt was singularly peaceful, without rebellion in his heart, and surprised himself. He remained lying calmly when the professor forbade him to get up. He pictured to himself without emotion the little prince, motionless, with his eyes closed, on his camp-bed. Mechanically he folded his hands and prayed for his brother's little soul.

He was not allowed to leave his room that day and saw only the empress, who came to him for an instant. He was not at all surprised that she too was calm, dry-eyed: she had not yet shed tears. Even when he raised himself from his pillows and embraced her, she did not cry. Nor did he cry, but only his own calmness astonished him: not hers. She stayed for but a moment; then she went away, as though with mechanical steps, and he was left alone. He saw nobody else that day except Barzia: not even Andro entered his room.

Outside the chamber, the prince, judging from certain steps in the corridors, certain sounds of voices—the little that penetrated to him—could divine the sorrow of the palace; he pictured sad tidings spreading through the land, through Europe and causing people to stand in consternation in the presence of death, which had taken them by surprise. Life was not secure: who could tell that he would be alive to-morrow! Vain were the plans of men: who could tell what the hour would bring forth! And he lay thinking of this calmly, in the singular peacefulness of his soul, in which he saw the futility of struggling against life or against death.

Not till next day did Barzia give him leave to get up, late in the afternoon. After his shower-bath, he dressed calmly, in his lancer's uniform, with crape round the sleeve. When he saw himself in the glass, he was surprised at his resemblance to his mother, at seeing how he now walked with the same

Majesty | 173

mechanical step. Barzia allowed him to go to the empress' sitting-room. He there found her, the emperor, Thera and the Archduke and Archduchess of Carinthia, who had arrived at Lipara the evening before. They sat close together, now and then softly exchanging a word.

Othomar went up to the emperor and would have embraced him; Oscar, however, only pressed his hand. After that Othomar embraced his sisters and his brother-in-law. Then he sank down by the empress, took her hand in his and sat still. She looked attenuated and white as chalk in her black gown. She did not weep: only the two princesses sobbed, persistently, again and again.

The family dined alone in the small dining-room, unattended by any of the suite. A depression had descended upon the palace, which seemed wholly silent at this hour, with but now and then the soft footsteps through the galleries of an aide-de-camp carrying a funeral-wreath, or a flunkey bringing a tray full of telegrams. After the short dinner, the family retired once more to the empress' drawing-room. The hours dragged on. Night had fallen. Then the Archbishop of Lipara was announced.

The imperial family rose; they went through the galleries, unattended, to the great knights' hall. Halberdiers stood at the door, in mourning. They entered. The emperor gave his hand to the empress and led her to the throne, whose crown and draperies were covered with crape. On either side were seats for Othomar, the princesses, the archduke.

In the middle of the hall, in front of the throne, rose the catafalque, under a canopy of black and ermine. On it lay the little prince in uniform. Over his feet hung a small blue knight's mantle with a great white cross; a boy's sword lay on his breast; and his little hands were folded over the jewelled hilt. By his little head, somewhat higher up, shone, on a cushion, a small marquis' coronet. Six gilt candelabra with many tall candles shone peacefully down upon the lad's corpse and left the great hall still deeper in shadow: only, outside, the moon rose in the distant blue, nocturnal sky; here and there it tinged with a white glamour the trophies and suits of armour that hung or stood like iron spectres in niches and against the walls. At the foot of the catafalque, on a table like an altar, with a white velvet cloth, a great gilt crucifix spread out its two arms, between two candelabra, in commiseration.

With drawn swords, motionless as the armour on the walls, stood four blue-mantled knights of St. Ladislas, two at either side of the catafalque.

A soft scent of flowers was wafted through the hall. All round the catafalque wreaths of every kind of white blossom were stacked in great heaps; the fragrance of violets outscented all the others.

They sat down: the emperor, the empress and their four children. Slowly the archbishop entered with his priests and choir-boys. Then the imperial party knelt on cushions placed before their seats. The prelate read the prayers for the dead; and the chanted *Kyrie Eleison* and *Agnus Dei* besought mercy for Berengar's little soul amongst the souls in purgatory, quivered softly through the vast hall, were wafted with the scent of the flowers over the motionless, sleeping face of the imperial child....

The rite came to an end; the prelate sprinkled the holy water, went sprinkling around the catafalque. The princes left the hall, but Othomar stayed on:

"I want to lay my wreath," he whispered to the empress.

The priests also departed, slowly; the crown-prince expressed to the four knights, who were waiting to be relieved by others, his wish to be left alone for a moment. They too withdrew. Then he saw Thesbia appear at the door, with a large white wreath in his hand. He went to the aide-de-camp and took the wreath from him.

Othomar remained alone. The hall stretched long and broad, with darkness at either end. The moon had risen higher, seemed whiter, cast a ghostly glamour over the suits of armour. In the centre, as though in sanctity, between the pious light of the tall candles, rose the catafalque, lay the prince.

The crown-prince mounted two steps of the catafalque and placed his wreath. Then he looked at Berengar's face: no fever distorted it now; it lay peaceful-pale, as though sleeping. All sounds had died away in the hall; a deadly silence reigned. Here the world of sorrow which had filled the palace and the country seemed to have become sanctified in an ecstasy of calm. And Othomar saw himself alone with his soul. The uncertainty of life, the vanity of human intentions were again revealed to him, but more clearly; they were no longer black mystery, they became harmony. It was as though he saw the whole harmony of the past: in all Liparia's historic past, in the whole past of the world there sounded not one false note. All sorrow was sacred and harmonious, tending more closely to the lofty end, which would be in its turn a beginning and never anything but harmony. Resignation descended upon his mood like a spirit of holiness; his strange calmness became resignation. It was as though his nerves were relaxed in one great assuagement.

And his resignation contained only the sadness that never again would he hear the high-pitched little commanding voice of the boy whom he had loved, that this little life had run its course, so soon and for ever. His resignation contained only the surprise that all this was ordered thus and not as he had imagined it. He himself would have to wear the crown which he had wished to relinquish to Berengar. And it now seemed to him as though he himself were receiving it back from the dead boy's hands. This no doubt was why he felt no touch of rebellion in his soul, why he felt this peace, this sense of harmony. His gift was returning to him as a legacy.

Long he stood thus, thinking, staring at his motionless little brother; and his thoughts became simplified within him: he saw lying straight before him the road which he should follow....

Then he heard his name:

"Othomar..."

He looked up and saw the empress at the door. She approached:

"Barzia was asking where you were," she whispered. "He was uneasy about you...."

He smiled to her and shook his head to say no, that he was calm.

She came close, climbed the steps of the catafalque and leant against his arm:

"How peaceful his little face is!" she murmured. "Oh, Othomar, I have not yet given him my last kiss! And to-morrow he will no longer belong to me: all those people will then be filing past."

"But now, mamma, he still belongs to us ... to you...."

"Othomar ..."

"Mamma ..."

"Shall I not have ... to lose you also?"

"No, mamma, not me.... I shall go on living ... for you...."

He embraced her; she looked up at him, surprised at his voice. Then she looked again at her dead child. She released herself from her son's arms, raised herself still higher, bent over the little white face and kissed the forehead. But, when the stony coldness of the dead flesh met her lips, she drew back and stared stupidly at the corpse, as though she understood for the first time. Her arms grew stiff with cramp; she wrung her fingers; she fell straight back upon Othomar.

And her eyes became moist with the first tears that she had shed for Berengar's death and she hid her head in Othomar's arms and sobbed and sobbed....

Then he led her carefully, slowly, down the steps of the catafalque, led her out of the hall. In the corridor they came across Barzia; the prince's calm and quiet face, as he supported his mother, eased the professor's mind....

So soon as the empress and crown-prince had left the knights' hall, four knights of St. Ladislas entered in their blue robes. They took up their positions on either side of the catafalque and stood motionless in the candle-light, staring before them, watching in the night of mourning over the little imperial corpse, on which the blue light of the moon now descended.... The priests too entered and prayed....

The palace was silent. When Othomar had consigned his mother, at the door of her apartments, to the care of Hélène of Thesbia, he went through the galleries to his own rooms. But, on turning a corridor, he started. The great state-staircase yawned, faintly lighted, at his feet, with beneath it the hollow space of the colossal entrance-hall. Upholsterers were occupied in draping the banisters of the staircase with crape gauze, for the time when the coffin should be carried downstairs. With wide arms they measured out the mists of black, threw black cloud upon cloud; the clouds of crape heaped themselves up with a dreary flimsiness, up and up and up, seeming to fill the whole staircase and to rise stair upon stair as though about to conquer the whole palace with their gloom....

The upholsterers did not see the crown-prince and worked on, silently, in the faint light. But a cold thrill passed through Othomar. In deathly pallor he stared at the men there, at his feet, measuring out the crape and sending clouds of it up to him. He recalled his dream: the streets of Lipara overflowing with crape till the very sun reeled.... His blood seemed to freeze in his veins....

Then he made the sign of the Cross:

"O God, give me strength!" he prayed in consternation....

8

Next day, through the guard of honour of the grenadiers, the people filed past the little prince's body. The following morning, it was removed to Altara and interred in the imperial vault in St. Ladislas' Cathedral. Princes Gunther and Herman of Gothland had come over for the ceremony, but the Duke of Xara was forbidden by Professor Barzia to take part in it: he remained at Lipara.

The Gothlandic princes and their suite returned with the Emperor Oscar to the capital, where, at her sister's pressing request, Queen Olga had also come, with Princess Wanda. And, in the mourning stillness of the Imperial, the family drew together in a narrow circle of intimacy. After her first tears, the Empress Elizabeth had lost her unnatural calm and constantly gave way to violent fits of sorrow, which Queen Olga or Othomar had difficulty in allaying. The emperor was inconsolable, indulging his grief with childish vehemence. Nobody had ever seen him like that before, nobody recognized him. The fact that he had lost his favourite child aroused his soul to rebellion against God. In addition to this, he had very much taken to heart his last conversation with Othomar, in which the prince had spoken to him of abdicating. The emperor had not returned to the subject, but it was never out of his thoughts. He feared that he would have to discuss it with Othomar again. He was furious when he felt how powerless he was to prevent the crown-prince from taking this desperate resolution. And he pictured the legal results if the prince maintained his purpose: the Archduchess of Carinthia empress, the archduke prince-consort and the house of Czyrkiski no longer reigning in the male line on the throne of Liparia. The possibility of this contingency, taken in conjunction with his sorrow at Berengar's death, made the Emperor Oscar suffer with that very special suffering of a monarch in whose veins still flows all the hereditary attachment to the greatness of his ancestors and who hopes to see this endure for all time. And he was also inconsolable for the loss of the child whom he loved best, more profoundly but also more silently, in greater secrecy, since he did not speak of it; and this probably made him feel more bitterly the thought of the future which he saw imaged before him. He had not even mentioned it to the empress, because of a certain superstitious dread.

And with this mental sorrow—that his robust soul, which had always retained a touch of childishness, was allowing itself to feel weak, as though it were the soul of any other mortal instead of his, a monarch's—there was mingled his substantial annoyance about the army bill. There would be three hundred millions needed: one hundred millions had already been voted for the increase of the infantry; the other two hundred, for the artillery, Count Marcella, the minister for war, had not yet succeeded in obtaining. The majority of the army committee was against this colossal arming of the frontier-forts; the minister already expected a violent opposition in the house of deputies and was fully prepared for his fall. None of the three—Oscar, Myxila or Marcella—was willing to make the least compromise. And Oscar moreover was prepared to support his minister to the point of impossibility.

It was at this time that Othomar made General Ducardi teach him the question, thoroughly, that he studied the staff-charts and military statistics and reports of the committee, that he followed the parliamentary discussions from out of his solitude. He held long deliberations with the general. He had, however, not for months attended the morning conferences in his father's room. But one morning he dressed himself—as was now no longer his regular habit—in uniform and sent a chamberlain to ask Oscar whether the emperor would permit him to be present at Count Marcella's audience. The emperor shrugged his shoulders in surprise, but combated his antipathy and sent word to his son that he might come. So soon as the minister and the imperial chancellor were with the emperor, Othomar joined them. He had grown still more slender and the silver frogs of his lancer's uniform barely sufficed to lend a slight breadth to his slimness; he was pale and a little sunken in the cheeks; but the glance of his eyes had lost its former feverish restlessness and recovered its melancholy calm, together with a certain stiffness and haughtiness. He refrained at first from taking part in the discussion, let the emperor curse, the chancellor shrug his shoulders and rely on the impossible, the minister declared that he would never give in. Then, however, he asked Oscar for leave to interpose a word. He took a pencil; with a few short, decided lines of demonstration on the maps, with a few simple, accurate indications on the registers, with a few figures which he quoted, correctly, by heart, he showed that he was quite conversant with the subject. He expressed the opinion that, in so far as he could gather from the reports of the committee, from the mood of the house of deputies, it remained an undoubted fact that the two hundred millions would be refused ... and that the minister would fall. He repeated these last words with emphasis and then looked firmly first at his father and then at Count Marcella. Then, in his soft voice, which rose and fell in logical tones, with serene words of conviction, he asked why they should not submit to circumstances and make the best of them. Why not accept the one hundred millions for the infantry as so much gained and—for this after all would be possible without immediate danger—endeavour to·distribute the other two hundred over a period of four or five years. He felt certain that an increase of twenty millions or so a year would not meet with such violent opposition. By this arrangement Count Marcella would be able to maintain himself in office and to be supported by the emperor....

When he had ceased, his words were succeeded by a pause. His advice, if not distinguished by genius, was at least practical and made the most of this critical situation. Count Myxila slowly nodded his head in approval. The emperor and Count Marcella could not at once adhere to Othomar's idea and were obstinate, as though they still hoped to force the army bill through, unchanged as conceived at first. But the chancellor took the same view as the crown-prince, proved still more clearly that an arrangement of this sort would be the only one by which his majesty would be able to retain Count Marcella's services. And the end of the matter was that the Duke of Xara's proposal should be taken into consideration.

When Myxila and Marcella had gone, the emperor asked the prince to wait a moment longer:

"Othomar," he said, "it gives me great pleasure to see you once more occupying yourself with the affairs of our country...."

He hesitated an instant, almost anxiously:

"What conclusion may I draw from this ... for the future?" he continued at last, slowly.

The crown-prince understood him:

"Papa," he said, gently, "I have had my moments of discouragement. I shall perhaps have them again. But forget ... what we were discussing just before Berengar's death. I have given up all thought of abdicating...."

The emperor drew a deep breath.

"I am religious, papa, and I have faith," continued the prince. "Perhaps an almost superstitious faith. I plainly see, in what has happened, the hand of God...."

He passed his hand over his forehead, with a meditative gaze:

"The hand of God," he repeated. "I had a presentiment that one of us would die within this year. I thought that I myself should be the one to die. That is perhaps why, papa, I did not see how monstrous it was of me to take the resolution which I did. I was not thinking of myself, who was bound to die in any event; I thought only of Berengar. But now he is dead and I am alive; and I shall now think of myself. For I feel that I do not belong to myself. And I feel that it is this that should support us through life: this feeling that we do belong not to ourselves but to others. I have always loved our people and I have wished to help them vaguely, in the abstract; I threw out my hands, without knowing why, and when I did not make good, it drove me to despair...."

He suddenly stopped and looked timidly at his father, as though he had gone too far in delivering his thoughts. But Oscar sat calmly listening to him; and he continued:

"And I now know that this despair is not right, because with this despair we keep ourselves for ourselves and cannot give ourselves to others. You see—" he rose and smiled—"I cannot manage to cure myself of my philosophy, but I hope now that it will tend to strengthen me instead of enervating me, as it now flows from quite a different principle."

The emperor gave a little shrug of the shoulders:

"Every one must work out his own theory of life, Othomar. I can only give you this advice: do not be carried away by enthusiasm and keep your point of view high. Do not analyse yourself out of all existence, for such abnegation does not last and inevitably harks back to the old rights. I do not reflect so much as you do; I am more spontaneous and impulsive. But I will not condemn you for being different: you can't help it. Perhaps you belong to this age more than I do. I only wish to look at the result of your reflections; and this result is that you're giving yourself back to ordinary life and to the interests of your country. And this rejoices me, Othomar. Nor do I wish to look too far into the future; I dare say that later too you will not have my ideas, I dare say that later you will reign with a brand-new constitution, with an elected upper house. I expect you will encounter much opposition from the authoritative party among the nobles.... But, as I say, I do not wish to go into that too far and I am content to rejoice at your moral convalescence. And I am very grateful to you for the advice you gave us just now. It was quite simple, but we should never have thought of it by ourselves. We are too conservative for that. I think now that what you propose will be the best thing to be done and that it can't be done otherwise...."

He held out his hand; Othomar grasped it.

"And," he continued with the great magnanimity which, for all his despotic haughtiness, lay at the very root of his soul, "do not bear any malice because of ... of the words I used to you, Othomar. I am violent and passionate, as you know. I was fonder of Berengar than of you. But you yourself loved the boy. Bear me no malice, for his sake.... You are my son too and I love you, if only because of the fact that you are my son and the last of my race.... Forgive my candour."

Then he pressed Othomar in his arms. It struck him painfully to feel the frailty of the prince in his firm embrace, so immediately upon his words: "the last of my race...." A strange, bitter despair shot through his soul; yet he clearly divined the mystery of this frailty: an unknown moral spring, which he himself lacked, in the direct simplicity of his nature, but which, to his great surprise, he felt in his son. When the prince was gone and Oscar, left alone, thought of this and sought that spring in what he knew of his son, he did not find it, yet felt that, whatever it might be, it was something to be envied, a strength tougher than muscular strength. He looked about him; his eyes fell upon a portrait of the empress on his writing-table. How often had he not stared at it in irritation because of their successor, who was so wholly her son! But, as though a gleam of light passed before his eyes, he now looked at the delicate features without the old annoyance; and a grateful warmth began to glow within him. Whatever it were, Othomar had derived this mysterious strength from his mother. It saved him and spared him for his country, for his race. And—who knew?—perhaps this mystery was just the element which their race needed, a necessary constituent of its new lease of life.... He did not seek to penetrate any farther; the future—even though it was now emerging more clearly out of its first dimness—had no attraction for him. He loved the past, those iron centuries with their heroes of emperors. But he felt that everything was not lost. In his pious belief in the Almighty, he thought, as did his son, of the hand of God. If it must be so, it was right. God's will was inscrutable.

And grateful to the empress, grateful for the light that shone before him, he bent his knees to the crucifix on the wall and prayed for his two sons. He prayed long for the son who was to bear his crown, but longer for the soul of the child of his own blood, whose loss would be the grief that would always be as wormwood in the depths of his soul, which was now outpoured in gratitude....

9

From the Diary of Alexa Duchess of Yemena, Countess of Vaza.

"—November, 18—.

"The crown-prince has not come with the emperor. Professor Barzia forbade it, because he considered that the big hunting-parties with which the emperor wishes to divert his thoughts from his grief for our little prince would be too fatiguing for my sweet invalid. Still, I hear from Dutri that he is making distinct progress and has already resumed his daily morning rides.

"It is all over with me. Poor sinful heart within me, die! For, after this last flower of passion that blossomed in you, I wish you to die to the world. For the sake of the purity of my imperial flower, I wish you now to die. Nothing after this, nothing but the new life which I see lifting before me....

"And yet I am still young; I look no older in my glass than I did a year ago. I have no need to abdicate my feminine powers unless I wish to. And that is how every one looks at it, for I know that they whisper of the Duke of Mena-Doni, as though he would be happy to replace my adored crown-prince in my affections. But it's not true, it's not true. And I'm so glad of it, that they do not realize me and do not know anything, that they do not understand that I want to let my imperial love fade away in purity and wish to cherish no earthly love after it.

"Dear love of my heart, you have raised me to my new life! You were still a sin, but yet you purified me, because you yourself were purified by the contact of that sacred something which is in majesty. Oh, you were the last sin, but already you were purer than the one before! For I have been a great sinner: I have immolated up all my sinful woman's life to consuming passion; and it has left nothing but ashes in my heart! Great scorching love of my life for him who is now dead—may his soul rest in peace!—I will not deny you, because you have been my most intense earthly pleasure, because through you I first learnt to know that I possessed a soul and because you thus brought me nearer to what I now see before me; but yet, what were you but earthliness? And my chaster imperial love, what were you too but earthliness? Gentle sovereign of my soul, what will God have you be but earthly? An empire awaits you, a crown, a sceptre, an empress. God wills it and therefore it is good, that you are earthly, while your earthliness is at the same time consecrated by your pious faith. But I, I have been less than merely earthly: I was sinful. And now I wish that my heart should wholly die within me, because it is nothing than sin. Then shall my heart be born again, in new life....

"I have prayed. For hours I lay on the cold marble in the chapel, till my knees pained me and my limbs were stiff. I have confessed my sinful life to my sainted confessor, his lordship of Vaza. Oh, the sweetness of absolution and the ecstasy of prayer! Why do we not earlier feel the blessed consolation that lies in the performance of our religious duties! Oh, if I could lose myself utterly in that sweet mystery, in God; if I could go into a convent! But I have my two stepdaughters. I must bring them into society; it is my duty. And the bishop thinks that that is my penance and my punishment: never to be able to withdraw into a hallowed seclusion, but to continue breathing the sinful atmosphere of the world.

"I will give my castle in Lycilia, where we never go—my own castle and estate—to our Holy Church for a convent for Ursulines of gentle birth. I went there with the bishop the other day. Oh, the great gloomy rooms, the shadowy frescoes, the sombre park! And the chapel, when the new windows are added, through which the light will fall in a mystic medley of colour! My dearest wish is to be allowed to grow old there, and to die far away from the world: but shall I ever be permitted? Holy Mother of God, shall I ever be permitted?

"Am I sincere? Who knows? What do I myself know? Do I truly feel this purification of my soul, or do I remain the woman I am? A dreadful doubt rises in me; it is Satan entering into me! I will pray: Blessed Virgin, pray for me!

"I have become calmer; prayer has strengthened me. Oh, full of anguish are the doubts which tear me from my conviction! Then Satan says that I am deluding myself into this conviction, to console myself in my destitution, and that I have become religious for want of occupation. At such times I see myself in the glass, young, a young woman. But, when I pray, the doubts retire from my sinful mood and I look back shuddering upon my wicked past. And then the new life of my future once more shines up before me....

"Beloved prince, sovereign of my soul, here in these pages which none shall ever read I take leave of you, because it was not vouchsafed me to bid you farewell at a moment of tangible reality. Oh, I shall often, perhaps from day to day, still see you in the crush of the world, in the ceremonial of palaces; but you will never again belong to me and so I take leave of you! Whatever I may be—a twofold sinner perhaps, longing only for Heaven because the earth has lost its charm for me—I have been true to you, as I always have been, in love. I have seen you bowed down, you so frail, beneath your heavy yoke of empire; and I have felt my heart brimming over with pity for you. I have tried to give you my poor sinful consolation as best I could. May Heaven forgive me! I met you at a moment when the tears were flowing from your dear eyes with bitterness because people hated you and had dared with sacrilegious hands to strike at your imperial body; and I tried to give you what I could of sweetness, so as to make you forget that bitterness. Ah, perhaps I was even then not quite sincere; perhaps I am even not so now! But that would be too terrible; that would make me despise myself as I cannot do! And I will at least retain this illusion, that I was sincere, that I did wish to comfort you, that, sinful though it was, I did comfort you, that I did, in very truth, love you, that I still love you now, that I shall no longer love you—because I must not—as your mistress, but that I shall do so as your subject. The blood in my veins loves yours, your golden blood! And, when I myself have found peace and no longer doubt and hesitate, my last days shall be spent only in prayer for you, that you also may receive peace and strength for your coming task of government. I feel no jealousy of her who will be my future empress. I know that she is beautiful and that she is younger than I. But I do not compare myself with her. I shall be her subject as I am yours. For I love you for yourself and I love everything that will be yours. You are my emperor; you are already my emperor, more than Oscar! Farewell, my prince, my crown-prince, my emperor! When I see you again, you will be nothing more to me than my emperor and my emperor alone!

"To HIS IMPERIAL HIGHNESS THE DUKE OF XARA,

"LIPARA.

"CASTEL VAZA,
"—November, 18—.

"MY BELOVED PRINCE,

"Pardon me if I venture to send you the accompanying pages. I meant at first to send you a long letter, a letter of farewell. And I did write you many, but did not send them to you and destroyed them. Then I wrote to you only for myself, took leave of you for myself. But can I trace what goes on within me, what I think from one moment to the other? I did miss it so: my sweet farewell, which would still bind me in some intimate way to you! And so I could not refrain—at last, after much vacillation of mind—from sending you these pages, which I had written only for myself. At your feet I implore you graciously to accept them, graciously to read them. Then destroy them. Through them you will learn the last thoughts that I have dared to consecrate to the mystery that was our love....

"I press my lips to your adored hands.

"ALEXA."

CHAPTER VI

1

The Empress Elizabeth rode with Hélène of Thesbia in a victoria, preceded by an outrider, from St. Ladislas to the Old Palace, which, together with the cathedral and the Episcopal, formed one gigantic building. Here, at Altara, the Archduke Albrecht and the Archduchess Eudoxie, with the imperial bride, had taken up their abode on the previous day. From the tall fortress—a broad mass of granite with crenulated plateaus and squat towers, overlooking Altara—the road wandered downwards, indistinguishable beneath the old chestnut-trees, in tortuous zig-zags. The dust flew up under the wheels; on both sides lay villas, with terraces gay with vases and flowers and statues, sloping lower and lower towards the town. The villas blazed with bunting; the blue-and-white flags with the white crosses revelled in all their gaudy newness among the dusty foliage of the old trees and acacias.

It was June, six months after the death of the little prince; but the mourning had been lightened because of the approaching nuptials of the Duke of Xara, which the emperor wished to see celebrated as early as possible. The empress, however, still wore heavy mourning, which she would not lay aside before the day of the wedding; Hélène was in grey; the liveries were grey.

Many pedestrians, horsemen, carriages passed along the road and stopped respectfully; the empress bowed to left and right; she received cheers and salutations from the balconies of the villas. In this warm summer weather a mellow welcome, a soft gaiety reigned all along the road; the road, with its villas where the people sat in groups, emitted a friendliness which affected the empress pleasantly and made her heart swell in her breast with a gentle melancholy. Children ran about and played in white summer suits; they stopped suddenly and, like well-bred children, accustomed to seeing members of the imperial family pass daily, they bowed low, the boys awkwardly, the girls with new-learnt curtseys. Then they went on playing again.... And the empress smiled at a large family, old and young people together, who sat on a terrace, doubtless celebrating a birthday, and laughed and drank, with many glasses and decanters before them, the children with their mouths full of cake. So soon as they saw the outrider, they all stood up and waved, some with their glasses still in their hands, and the empress, laying aside her usual stiffness, bowed back with a winning smile.

And it was as though she were driving through a huge, luxurious village; for a moment she forgot the light obsession that depressed her, forgot why she was this day going to Valérie and allowed herself to be lulled by her delight in the love that she divined all round her. It was the love of the old Liparian patrician families—noble or not noble—for their sovereigns. It was a caress which she never felt at Lipara. And she remembered Othomar's letter, at the time of last year's inundations:

"Why are we not oftener at Altara?"

She could not for a moment desist from bowing. But she was now approaching the town: the old houses shifted like the wings at a theatre; the whole town shifted nearer, gay with flags, which threw an air of youth over its old stonework. The streets were full: thousands of visitors, native and foreign, were at Altara; there was not a room to be had in the hotels. And the empress could scarcely speak a word to Hélène; she could do nothing but bow and bow, perpetually....

In the fore-court of the Old Palace, the infantry composing the guard of honour of the Austrian bride were drawn up and presented arms as the empress drove in. The Archduchess Eudoxie was awaiting the empress.

"How is Valérie?" Elizabeth at once asked.

"Better, calmer," replied the archduchess. "Much better than I dared hope. But she will receive no one...."

"Do send to ask whether I can see her...."

The archduchess' lady-in-waiting left the room: she returned with the message that her imperial highness was expecting the empress.

Elizabeth found Valérie lying on a sofa, wearing a white lace tea-gown, looking very pale, with great, dark, dull eyes; she rose, however:

"Forgive me, ma'am," she said, in apology.

Elizabeth embraced her with great tenderness; the archduchess added:

"I was not well, I felt so tired...."

But then her eyes met Elizabeth's and she saw that the empress did not expect her to exhibit superhuman endurance. She nestled up against her and cried softly, as one cries who has already wept long and passionately and is now exhausted with weeping and has not the strength to weep except very, very softly. The empress made her sit down, sat down beside her and caressed her with a soothing movement of her hand. Neither of the two spoke; neither of the two found words in the difficult relation which at that moment they bore one to the other.

Two days ago, the day before that fixed for the bride's journey to Altara, the news had arrived that Prince von Lohe-Obkowitz had shot himself in Paris. The actual reason of this suicide was not known. Some thought that the prince had taken much to heart the disfavour of the Emperor of Austria and the quarrel with his own family; others that he had lost a fortune at baccarat and that his ruin was completed by the bohemian extravagance of his wife, the notorious Estelle Desvaux, who herself had been ruined more than once in her life, but had always retrieved her position by means of a theatrical tour and the sale of a few diamonds. Others again maintained that Prince Lohe had never been able to forget his love for the future Duchess of Xara. But, whatever might be suggested in Viennese court-circles, nothing was known for certain. Valérie had by accident read the report, which they had tried to conceal from her, in the same newspaper in which, now almost a year ago, she had, also by accident, on the terrace at Altseeborgen, read the news of Prince Lohe's proposed marriage and surrender of his rights. Her soul, which had no tendency to mysticism, nevertheless, in the shock of despair that now passed through it, became almost superstitious because of this repetition of cruelty. But when, months ago, she had combated and worn out her sorrow, it had been followed by an indifference to any further suffering that she might yet have to experience in life. The death of her illusions was a final death; after her betrothal she had as it were found herself with a new soul, hardened and girt about with indifference. It was strange that in this indifference the only thing to which she continued sensible was that exquisiteness in Othomar's character: his delicacy in sparing her at Altseeborgen, against Oscar's desire; his wide feeling of universal love for his people; all his gentle nature and simple sense of duty.... But, however indifferent she might generally think herself to be, this second incident struck her cruelly, as though a refinement of fate had chosen the moment for it. The official journey from Sigismundingen to Altara had been a martyrdom. Valérie had endured like an automaton the receptions on the frontiers, the welcome at the Central Station at Altara, with the greeting of her imperial bridegroom, who had there kissed her, and the addresses of the authorities, the offering of bread and salt by the canons of the chapter of

St. Ladislas. She had swallowed it, their bread and salt. And then the drive through the town, gay with bunting and with triumphal arches erected from street to street, to the Old Palace, in the open landau with the emperor and her bridegroom, amid the cheering of the populace which cut her ears and her overexcited nerves as though with sharp-edged knives! Then, at the palace, it had struck Othomar how like a hunted fawn she looked, with her frightened eyes. Prince Lohe's death was known at Altara; and, though the people had cheered, cheered from true affection for the future crown-princess, they had stared at her because of that tragedy, curious and eager to see an august anguish shuddering in the midst of their festivities, hunted through arches of green and bunting. They had seen nothing. Valérie had bowed, smiled, waved her hand to them from the balcony of the Old Palace, standing by Othomar's side! They had seen nothing, nothing, for all their tense expectation. But then Valérie's strength had come to an end. Her part was played: let the curtain fall. Othomar left her alone, with a pressure of the hand. For hours she sat lifelessly; then night came; she could not sleep, but she was able to sob.

Now it was next day; she was lying down exhausted, but really she had shed her last tear, fought her last fight, recovered her indifference: no sorrows that were still in store for her could ever hurt her now!

Yet the fond embrace of Othomar's mother softened her; and she again found her tears.

They exchanged barely a few words and yet they felt a mutual sympathy passing between them. And through the midst of her sorrow Valérie could see her duty, which would at the same time be her strength: no bitter indifference, but an acquiescence in what her life might be. Oh, she had imagined it differently in her dreams as a young girl: she had pictured it to herself as more agreeable and smiling and as finding its expression more naturally, more spontaneously and without so much calculation! But she had awakened from her dreams; and where else should she seek her strength but in her duty?... And she conquered herself, whatever might be destroyed in her soul, by an unsuspected vitality—her real nature—even more than by her thoughts. She dried her eyes, mentioned that it was near the time when a deputation of young Liparian ladies was to come and offer her a wedding-present; and the empress left her alone, that she might dress.

She appeared presently, in a white costume embroidered with dull gold, in the drawing-room where her parents sat with the empress and with Hélène of Thesbia and the Austrian ladies-in-waiting. Shortly after,

Othomar came too, with his sisters and the Archduke of Carinthia. And, when the deputation of young ladies of rank was announced and appeared, with Eleonore of Yemena in its midst, Valérie listened with her usual smile to the address recited by the little marchioness, with a gracious gesture accepted from the hands of two other girls the great case which they caused to fly open, showing, upon light velvet, a triple necklace of great pearls. And she was able to find a few pretty phrases of thanks: she uttered them in a clear voice; and no one who heard her would have suspected that she had passed a sleepless night, bathed in tears, with before her eyes the lifeless body of a young man with shattered temples.

The young ladies of the deputation were permitted to see the wedding-presents, which were displayed in a large room; Princess Thera and the ladies-in-waiting accompanied them. There, in that room, it was like a sudden gleam of brilliancy, flashing in the daylight from the long tables on which the presents stood surrounded by flowers: the heavily-gilt candelabra, gilt and crystal table- and tea-services, gilt and silver caskets from various towns, an Altara Cathedral in silver, silver ships with delicate, swelling sails from naval institutions and jewelled gifts from all the royal friends and relations in Europe. On a satin cushion lay, like a fairy trinket, a sparkling duchess' diadem of big sapphires and brilliants, one of the presents of the bride's future parents-in-law. And very striking was Princess Thera's present: the Duke of Xara's portrait, a work of art that had already been seen at exhibitions in both capitals. But it had little likeness to the original left and was therefore the despair of the princess. It was younger, more indecisive, feebler than the prince looked now: a little thinner than of old, but with a fuller moustache and a lightly curling beard on his cheeks. The melancholy eyes had acquired more of the Empress Elizabeth's cold glance; in other respects too Othomar resembled his mother more than before. But what was still noticeable in the young prince, in his nervous refinement, was the look of race, his trenchant distinction, his air of lawful haughtiness. He had lost much of his rigidity, his stiff tactlessness, and had gained something more resolute and assured; and, in spite of his colder look, this inspired more confidence in a crown-prince than his always winning but somewhat feeble presence of former days. The thoughts seemed to be more sharply outlined on his features, the words to come more pointedly from between his lips; he seemed to have more self-reliance, to care less for what others might think of him. It was, although not yet quite consciously, that unique princely feeling awakening within him: his simple, proud, innate confidence in the single drop of golden blood which ran through his veins and gave him his rights....

It was Professor Barzia especially who, attached as he was to Othomar and treating him personally every day, had aroused this self-confidence with his words, which were prompted both by his knowledge of mankind and by his love for the dynasty, as well as by a personal affection for the crown-prince. The cold-water douches had braced the prince up, but the suggestions of the professor, who had aroused Othomar's latent practical qualities as it were from their subconscious hiding-place, had probably been a still more efficacious remedy. The prince had learnt to govern himself and had become dearer to the professor than ever....

This devotion, born of a discovery of what others did not know to exist—high qualities of temperament—was enhanced by Barzia's fostering of those same qualities; and, when the prince's marriage could be fixed, the professor looked with as much pride as affection upon his patient, whom he declared to be physically cured and considered, in his own mind, to be morally cured as well....

2

Two days later was the day of the imperial wedding. The town swarmed from early morning with the people who had streamed in from the environs and who noisily thronged the narrower streets. For already at an early hour the main thoroughfares had been closed by the infantry, from the fortress to the Old Palace and the cathedral. And Altara, usually grey, old, weather-beaten, was unrecognizable, gaudy with flags, fresh with festoons of greenery, decked with draperies and tapestries hanging from its balconies. A warm, southern May sun shed patches of light over the town; and the red and blue and white and green of the waiting uniforms, with the even flash of the bayonets above them, drew broad lines of colour through the city, with a gaiety almost floral, right up to the Castle of St. Ladislas.

Through the streets, closed to public traffic, court-carriages drove to and fro, filled with glittering uniforms: royal guests who were being carried to St. Ladislas or the Old Palace. There were Russian, German, British, Austrian, Gothlandic uniforms; briskly, as though preparing for the ceremonial moment, they flashed through Altara, through its long, empty streets lined with soldiers.

Beneath the chestnuts on the Castle Road the villas also teemed with spectators, sitting or moving in the gardens and terraces; and, in the sunbeams that filtered through the foliage of the trees, the ladies' light summer costumes and coloured sun-shades cast variegated patches: it was as though garden-parties were taking place from villa to villa, while people waited for the procession of the bridegroom, who, in accordance with Liparian etiquette, was to drive from St. Ladislas to fetch his bride from the Old Palace.

Eleven o'clock. From the Fort of St. Ladislas booms the first gun; other guns boom after it minute by minute. A buzz of excitement passes along the whole of the Castle Road. On the almost imperceptible incline appear trumpets and kettle-drums, preceding heralds on horseback. Behind them come the slashing throne-guards, round the gilt and crystal gala-carriages. The court chamberlain, the Count of Threma, in the first; in the second, with the imperial crown and the plumed team of eight greys caparisoned in scarlet—and the cheering from the villas rises higher and higher—the emperor with the Duke of Xara by his side; in the following coaches the assembled majesties and highnesses of Europe: the Empress of Liparia, the German Emperor and Empress, the King and Queen of Gothland, Russian grand-dukes, the Duke of Sparta and the Prince of Naples.... The imperial chancellor, the ministers, the robed members of the house of peers.... And the endless procession passes slowly amid the roar of the cannon down the Castle Road, through the main streets and into the heart of the city. There, in the Old Palace, the bride is waiting with all her Austrian relations: the emperor and empress, the Archduke Albrecht and the Archduchess Eudoxie....

It is here that the marriage-treaty is signed, on the gilt table, covered with gold brocade, upon which the emperors and empresses of Liparia have written their signatures since centuries, upon which, after the imperial bride and bridegroom, the august witnesses sign the contract....

Now the whole procession goes through gallery after gallery to the New Sacristy. It is a ceremonious parade of some minutes' duration: the trumpeters, the heralds, the masters of ceremonies; the blue-robed knights of St. Ladislas: the white-and-gold throne-guards; the Emperor Oscar with the Duke of Xara, the Emperor of Austria with the bride.... Slowly she walks by her uncle's side, her head a little bent, as though beneath the weight of her princess' coronet, from which the lace veil floats, lightly shading her bare neck, which is studded with drops of brilliants. Her gown is of stiff, heavy satin brocade, embroidered with silver-thread in front and smothered in emblematic patterns of pearls; great, white velvet puffed sleeves burgeon at her shoulders; the train of silver brocade and white velvet is so long that six maids-of-honour bear it after her, swaying from its silver loops. Behind the maids-of-honour follow the bridesmaids, dressed all alike, carrying similar bouquets: they are Princess Thera, Princess Wanda, German,

English and Austrian princesses. And the majesties and highnesses follow; the procession flows into the New Sacristy; here the cardinal-archbishop, Primate of Liparia, with all his mitred clergy, receives the bridegroom and the bride....

In the cathedral waits the crowd of invited guests. Despite the beams of the summer sun, a mystic twilight of shadow hovers through the tall and stately arches of the cathedral and the daylight blossoms only on the motley windows of the side-chapels; in the vaultings it is even dark. But the high altar is one blaze of innumerable candles....

The imperial chancellor, the ministers, the ambassadors, the whole diplomatic body, the members of both houses of parliament, the judges of the high court have entered; they fill the tiers that have been erected to right and left. And the whole cathedral is filled: one great swarm of heavy, rustling silks—the low-necked dresses of the ladies, whose jewels twinkle and flash—and one blaze of gold on the glittering military and diplomatic uniforms, which like great sparks light up the twilight of the cathedral.

Then the trumpets sound, the organ peals its jubilant tones in the solemn festival-march; the first procession enters through the sacristy: the German Emperor with the Empress Elizabeth of Liparia, the Archduchess Eudoxie and a long retinue.... Now the trumpets sound, the organ peals unceasingly; and the invited majesties with their suites and the representatives of the foreign powers enter in group after group. The canopied spaces to right and left of the choir begin to fill up.

Soon the second procession follows: the dignitaries in front, with the insignia of state; the Emperor Oscar, leading the Duke of Xara: both wear over their golden uniforms the long draped blue robes of St. Ladislas, with the large white cross gleaming on the left arm; four crown-princes follow as the bridegroom's four witnesses: the Duke of Wendeholm, the Czarevitch, the Duke of Sparta and the Prince of Naples; the knights of St. Ladislas, the officers of the throne-guards, equerries and pages follow after....

And suddenly a choir of high voices vibrates crystal-clear and proclaims a blessing on the bride, who cometh in the name of the Lord.... The third procession has entered the cathedral: the Emperor of Austria and the Archduke Albrecht, leading the bride, with her maids of honour and her bridesmaids; and she seems to be one white wealth of illustrious maidenhood among her white and floral-fragrant retinue. And the anthem scatters its notes as with handfuls of silver lilies before her feet; her solemn advent arouses an emotion that quivers through all that whirl of splendour, through the whole cathedral. Now, at last, appears the fourth procession: the cardinal-archbishop, Primate of Liparia, with his bishops and canons and chaplains; the high ecclesiastics take their seats in the tall carved choir-stalls; the rite begins....

The sun seems to have waited till this moment to come shooting down, through the tall, party-coloured, pointed windows, in which the life of St. Ladislas glitters with its small, square, gem-like pictures, shooting down in a slanting sheaf of rays upon the choir, upon the priests, upon the canopies under which the majesties are sitting, upon the bride-groom and bride.... And all the colours—the old gold of the altar, the new gold of the uniforms, the brocades, the crown-jewels—flame up as though the sun were setting them ablaze: one fire of changing sparks which, together with the numberless candles on the altar, suddenly irradiates the church. The diadems of the princesses are like crowns of flame, the orders of the princes like a firmament of stars. The acolytes swing incense which is wafted misty blue, delicate, transparent in the sunshine; the sunshine filters through the blonde lace veil of the kneeling bride, lights a glowing fire over her white-and-silver train, illuminates her as with an apotheosis of light that reflects a maidenly pallor upon her. Her bridegroom kneels beside her, wholly enfolded in his blue robe, with on his arm the sheen of the white cross. Both now hold long tapers in their hands. And the primate, with his jewelled mitre and his stiff gold dalmatic covered with jewelled scrolls, raises his eyes, spreads his hands on high and stretches them in benediction above the bent imperial heads....

The chant swells high again: the *Te Deum laudamus*, as though the waves of the voices were rising upon the waves of the organ, higher and higher, up through the cathedral to the sky in one ecstasy of sacred music. The old, granite, giant fabric seems to quiver with emotion, as though the music became its soul, and sends forth over Altara from all its bells a swelling sea of sound, bronze in the depths and molten out of every metal into gold of crystal purity in the highest height of audible sound....

An hour later. On the closed Cathedral Square movement begins again, among the waiting gala-carriages. Now the procession returns to St. Ladislas, but behind the Emperor Oscar's carriage Othomar and Valérie now ride together. And the city cheers and shouts its hurrahs; the houses groan with the clamour among all the flags and trophies. The guards present arms; and amid this festive uproar it passes unperceived how yonder in the smaller streets fighting goes on, arrests are made, a well-known anarchist is almost murdered by the imperialistic populace....

With its costly pageant, now heightened by the white presence of the young Duchess of Xara and her own retinue, the endless and endless procession returns, through the town, up the Castle Road; and there too the villas now obtain a sight of Valérie and cheer and cheer and cheer....

It is in the white throne-room that Othomar and Valérie hold their court; one and all defile before them: the ministers and ambassadors, the members of both houses, of the courts of justice, corporations and deputations. After the court, the breakfast, at which the table glitters with the ceremonial gold and jewelled plate, used only at imperial weddings. After the breakfast, the last observance: in the gold hall—a vast low hall, Byzantine in architecture and decoration, ages old and unchanged—the torch-dance; the procession of the ministers, who carry long, lighted links in gilt handles, while Othomar and Valérie keep on inviting the highnesses according to rank, invite all the highnesses in turns and march round behind the ministers.... It is a monotonous ceremony, continually repeated: the ministers with the torches, Othomar with a princess and surrounded by the Knights of St. Ladislas, Valérie with a prince and all her white suite; and it is a relief when the function is finished and the newly-married couple have withdrawn to change their dress. Then they appear: Othomar as commanding officer of the Xara Cuirassiers, Valérie in her white cloth travelling-dress and hat with white feathers; and they make their adieus. An open landau awaits them; and with a compact escort of Xara Cuirassiers they drive anew through the town, drive in every direction, showing themselves everywhere, bowing to one and all, and at last drive out to the castle where they will spend the first days of the honeymoon: Castle Zanthos, quite near the town, on the broad river....

And the old weather-beaten capital, which remains full of majesties, which still flutters with pennants, which in the evening is one yellow flame and red glow of fireworks and illumination, seems all the same, without the newly-married couple, to have lost the attraction which turned it into a centre of festivity and splendour and imperial ceremony; and in the evening, despite the illuminations and fireworks and gala-performances, the Central Station is besieged by thousands who are leaving....

3

It was months after the wedding of the Duke of Xara that the Emperor Oscar, entering his work-room very early in the morning and moving towards his writing-table, caught sight of a piece of cardboard, with large, black letters pasted on it, lying on the floor by the window. He did not pick it up; though he was alone, he did not turn pale, but on his low forehead the thick veins swelled with rage to feel that he was not safe from their treason even in his own room. He rang and asked for his valet, a trusted man:

"Pick up that thing!" he commanded. And he roared, through the silence, "How did it get here?"

The valet turned pale. He read the threatening words of abuse, with their big, fat letters, on the ground before stooping and taking the card in his trembling hand.

"How did it get here?" repeated the emperor, stamping his foot.

The valet swore that he did not know. In the morning no one was allowed to enter the room except himself; he had come half an hour ago to open the windows and then had seen nothing:

"The only explanation, sir, is that some one must have stolen into the park and flung it through the window...."

This doubtless was the only explanation, but it was an explanation that irritated the emperor greatly. It was not the first time that the emperor had found such notices in the intimacy of his writing-room. The result was the sudden arrest of servants, of soldiers belonging to the various guards in the Imperial; but arrests and enquiries had brought nothing to light and therefore made an all the more painful impression. The guards of the palaces, the guards at the gilt railings of the park, where this merged into the Elizabeth Parks — the public gardens of the capital — were already increased; the secret police, the emperor's own police, even kept a sharp watch on the guards themselves.

The Emperor Oscar looked fixedly at the valet; for a moment the thought rose in him to have the man himself examined, but he at once realized the absurdity of any such suspicion: the man had been his personal servant for years and years, was entirely devoted to him and stood answering Oscar's long stare with calm, respectful eyes, evidently pondering the mystery of the strange riddle.

"Burn that thing," commanded the emperor, "and don't talk about it."

Subsequently Oscar had a long interview with the head of his secret police, with whom he had lately had every reason to be satisfied: secret printing-presses of anarchist papers, which were continually being distributed, had been ferreted out; a plot to wreck the imperial train on its way from Castel Xaveria, the summer-palace in Xara, to Lipara had been frustrated; suspicion of being connected with anarchist committees had fallen upon a clerk in one of the government-offices and even upon a young officer and it was proved that the suspicion was correct in both cases. Quite recently the police had discovered a workshop in which men were taught how to manufacture dynamite-bombs and infernal machines. But who the insolent miscreants were who succeeded in flinging their threatening letters into the emperor's own room: this they had not been able to discover. For a whole week the windows had been watched from the park and all that time nothing had been seen; it was now a couple of days since that secret watch had been given up. The head of the secret police felt convinced that the culprits were lurking in the Imperial itself and acquainted with the emperor's private habits. Sudden visits were paid to the rooms of any servants at the Imperial of whom there was the least doubt; and, when a groom was found to be in possession of an anarchist leaflet containing words of insult directed against the emperor, the man was banished to one of the convict sections of the eastern quick-silver-mines. This banishment was the introduction to numberless other banishments; they followed one another in quick succession; the victims were soldiers, sailors, many minor provincial officials: the press had even ceased to report all the banishments. The censorship was rendered more severe; newspapers were continually being suspended, their editors fined and imprisoned; the imperialist papers, Count Myxila's organs, almost despotically indicated the required tone. A socialist meeting was dispersed by hussars with drawn swords; serious disturbances followed in the capital and infected the other large towns, Thracyna, Xara, even Altara. A strike of dock-labourers filled Lipara for weeks with rising insubordination; policemen were cruelly murdered at the docks in broad daylight.

The Duke of Mena-Doni was the Emperor Oscar's right hand during this period; and his rough displays of force kept the capital so far in subjection that no riot burst out, that the everyday life of sunny, laughing luxury went on, that the elegant carriages continued every afternoon at five o'clock to stream to the Elizabeth Parks, where the Empress or the Duchess of Xara still showed themselves daily for a moment. But thousands of protecting eyes were secretly supervising this apparent carelessness; the troops were confined to barracks; gleaming escorts of cuirassiers accompanied the imperial landaus.

The empress also had asked Othomar to abandon his solitary morning rides and never to show himself unattended. The Duke and Duchess of Xara inhabited the Crown Palace, a comparatively new building on the quays, where they kept up an extensive court; and in this palace the emperor also caused domiciliary visits to be made and it appeared that there were anarchists lurking among the staff.

This treason within their very palaces kept the empress in a constant shudder of terror: she lived in these days an unceasing life of dread whenever she was separated from the emperor. For she was least terrified when she showed herself by Oscar's side, at exhibitions, at public ceremonies, at the Opera; and this was strange: she did not at such times think of him, but, if they were not with her, thought rather of her children, as though the catastrophe could happen only at some place where she would not be present.

The empress saw in Othomar so very much her own son that, in the intimacy of their morning conversations—for the crown-prince still paid his mother a short visit every morning—she was surprised not to find in him her own dread, but on the contrary all her own resignation, which was the reverse side of it. But since his marriage she had found him altogether changed, no longer, in these short moments of their private intercourse, complaining, hesitating, searching, but speaking calmly of what he must do, filled with an evident harmony that gave a restful assurance to his words, his gestures and even his actions. With this assurance he retained a quiet, dignified modesty: he did not put his views forward at all violently; he continued to possess that receptiveness for the views of others which had always been one of his most prominent and attractive qualities. He was undoubtedly old for his young years: any one who did not know better would have given him more than his twenty-three years, now that he was allowing his crisp beard to grow…. And yet, yet, especially in these troubled days, his old fears would often well up within him and he would remain sitting alone for minutes at a time, staring at a vague point in his room, listening to the murmurs of the future, as he had listened in that haunting night among his forefathers at Castel Vaza. He then felt that, suddenly, as with a garment, all his new resignation in life was slipping from him, falling from his shoulders. But he had learnt so to govern himself that nobody, not his father, not his mother, not even the crown-princess, noticed anything of this mental dizziness, which left him ice-cold in his short periods of solitude, doubting his right, full of strange, soft compassion for his people….

It was, actually, the old illness which thus, periodically, seethed in him again like an evil sap, flowing through his veins, enfeebling his nerves, crushing him internally, as though he would never be cured of it. But he grew accustomed to it, no longer felt despair because of it, even knew, during the few minutes that the malady lasted, that it would pass and afterwards regained that sense of harmony which above all constituted his resignation.

It was in these days of silent fermentation that there was talk of a marriage between Princess Thera and the Prince of Naples; nothing was yet decided between the two families, but the young prince was invited to Lipara to attend the great autumn manoeuvres. Shoots were arranged; different festivities followed one upon the other. Othomar had in these days to combat those sudden weaknesses more than ever: a strange feeling, a shivering, a mysterious terror remained with him and no longer left him, a terror which he dared not analyse, for fear of discovering motives which would cause him to lose his calmness entirely. There revived within him the recollection of the fact that shortly after his marriage he had dreamt a dream more or less similar to his former dream: the sinister capital filling with crape. It happened while he was still residing with his young wife at Castel Zanthos and he had attached no importance to it, because he considered that this second dream was only a shadow of the former one, only the remembrance of what had already happened and nothing more. But now, in these days of busy celebrations in honour of the prince who was visiting their court, with the ferment of popular discontent like a turbid, gloomy element beneath the surface brilliancy of all their imperial display, the memory of it revived and the terrors and shudders became more and more plainly defined in his imagination and at one moment he felt his former nervous weakness come over him to such an extent that he found an excuse to summon Professor Barzia from Altara and had a long interview with the specialist of which he did not even speak to the Duchess of Xara. When the professor had gone, Othomar felt relieved and strengthened; only the thought lingered within him that it was not right for a future sovereign to be so much under the influence of a stronger mind as he was under that of Barzia; and he proposed next time not to call in the professor's power of suggestion, but to cure himself, in the privacy of his own soul. This plan, to rely on his own strength in future, made him find himself again for good and all....

The day after his interview with Barzia, he spent the whole morning and afternoon in the company of the Prince of Naples, with whom he visited different places and, in so doing, displayed a gaiety and liveliness which were rarely witnessed in the Duke of Xara. The members of their suite were astonished at this radiant cheerfulness of the crown-prince, in whom they had grown used to perceiving always a strain of melancholy. That evening there was a great state-banquet at the Imperial. After dinner, the imperial family were to accompany their guest to the Opera, where a gala-performance was to take place and a famous tenor was to sing.

In these days, whenever the imperial family appeared in public, severe precautionary measures were taken under the guise of glittering display. A strong and close-packed escort of cuirassiers pranced round the carriages which drove that night to the great opera-house. The street at the side of the building containing the emperor's private entrance was closed off; a guard of honour lined the staircase; the secret police mingled with the expectant audience, which included all the smart society of the capital....

The imperial box, with its dark-violet draperies and gold tassels, was just over the stage of the colossal theatre. The first act was finished—they were playing Aïda—when the trumpet-blasts clanged out from the orchestra and the august personages appeared: the emperor, the empress, the Prince of Naples, the Duke and Duchess of Xara, Princess Thera. And their entry seemed to electrify the hitherto dull, waiting, nervously indifferent mood of the crowded house, as though, upon their appearance, the light in the lustres shone more brilliantly, the house blazed out with all the changeful flickerings of its jewels, all its flashing gilt, all the curiosity of the bright eyes that gazed at the imperial centre-group; as though the ladies' costumes suddenly blossomed out with one rustle of heavy silken fabrics, while the unfurled fans fluttered to and fro as though a breeze were blowing through many flowers in unstinted light....

Then the curtain rising on the second act, with all its melodrama of royal Egyptian state: the victory after the war and the consequent dances; the hero's love for the Ethiopian slave; and the Pharaoh's jealous daughter and the procession of the gods with the sackbuts: all sung, orchestrated, swelling symphonically in a square frame against a painted background; a stirring picture of royal Egyptian antiquity chanted before the eyes of modern royalty, of a modern audience, indifferent to the rest so long as they met wherever society decided that they should meet at the moment, under the eyes of the emperor and his family and his illustrious young guest.... The passions on the stage unbridling themselves in swelling bursts of music, a world of music, of love and despair, of war and triumph and priestly ambition in music, all music, as though life were music, music the soul and essence of the world.... And, beneath the glamour of this music and of this factitious life, the visible acting of the players, the glory of the famous tenor, with his too-modern head, his dress marked by unreal because unwarlike splendour, his bows and his smile aimed at the real world outside his small, framed world of make-believe, aimed at the audience that applauded after the emperor had deigned to clap his hands....

It was at this moment, this moment of ovation, this moment of lustrous triumph for the tenor, of applause led by the imperial hands. It was at this moment: the Emperor Oscar turning to his aide-de-camp, the Marquis of Xardi, behind him ... the aide listening respectfully to his majesty's command that he should summon the singer to the withdrawing-room of the imperial box ... the Empress Elizabeth and the Duchess of Xara, glittering in their gala, their jewels, in smiling conversation with the young foreign crown-prince who was their guest ... Othomar still with his gaiety of the afternoon, jesting with Thera and the ladies-in-waiting ... the whole house gazing, when the curtain had fallen for the last time, at all of them, in their blaze of luxury and light....

At this moment, in the topmost gallery a sudden tumult, a struggle of soldiers and police with one man.... A sudden rough scrimmage up there in the midst of the most mundane expansion of aristocratic pageantry. And all eyes no longer directed to the imperial box, but upwards.... Then, the man, struggling, releasing himself with superhuman strength from the grasp of his assailants, surging forwards, from out of their throng, like a black lightning-flash of fate: dark, curly head, eyes flashing hatred, fixed and fanatical, one arm suddenly outstretched towards the imperial grandeur below, as though at a target, with inexorable aim. The whole house one tumult, one shout, one shriek; wide gestures of helpless arms: all this very quick, lasting barely a second.... A shot ... and yet another shot....

The emperor is hit in the breast; he falls against the empress, whose bare, jewelled bosom he suddenly soils with blood, which at once soaks his gold uniform through and through ... not golden blood: rich red blood.... But the empress throws up her arms in despair; her strident scream rings through the house. She falls back into the embrace of the Duchess of Xara. The emperor has sunk into the arms of Xardi and of Othomar; a furious oath forces its way through his tight-clenched teeth, while he tears open his gory uniform so fiercely that the buttons fly around him....

4

Outside, the Opera Square, brightly lighted with many-armed, monumental lamp-posts, had at once become dark and swarming, filled with a vast mob; the whole town poured into it from every street; the alarm drew everybody thither, as though with a magnet. Detachments of hussars were already moving through the town, keeping order among the excited populace; the Duke of Mena-Doni was everywhere at once, trampling down the revolution with the military at his command in whatsoever corner it seemed to lift its head. The sky above was dark and frowning. It began to rain....

The rumour sped that the emperor had died. It was not true. Wrestling for breath, the sovereign lay in the crush-room of the opera-house, amidst the panic of his family, of his suite, of the hurrying doctors. He must not be moved, they said. He insisted. He refused to die here. He was set on returning to his Imperial. And, straining the springs of his energy, he commanded, he drew himself up, with the blood spurting from his throat; Othomar and the aides supported him....

Outside, in the square, the mob grew in numbers, the panic increased, riot seethed up from among those black clusters of people. Continual fights burst out between groups of men, dock-labourers, and the guard in front of the building, the police. The court-carriages returned empty, under escort, to the palace.

Other carriages, cabs, tried here and there to force a way through the people; they were surrounded by cuirassiers, who protected them with drawn swords. Volumes of curses and abuse spattered up against them, against the vaguely transparent windows, behind which were patches of light colours, flashing sparks of jewels. Women's scared eyes peered out fixedly, askance, without moving.

In the corridors, on the huge, monumental staircase of the opera-house, people hustled one another, fought to get through; then suddenly all eyes, staring wide, looked up above: the emperor was passing, bleeding, panting for breath, surrounded by his kin.... A feeling of awe stopped the crush for a moment; then they pressed on again.... Ladies fled till they found themselves behind the scenes, where they mingled their aristocracy with the bohemianism of the actors and actresses, all mixed up, confused, amidst the terrified, humming crowd of ballet-girls, priestesses of Isis. Gratuities were lavished: anything for a carriage, a cab....

The Duchess of Yemena stood there with her daughters; they were looking out for their carriage, which they had sent for at least ten times.... A stage-carpenter shrugged his shoulders indifferently: he did not know where to get a carriage from.

"I won't wait any longer," said the duchess, shuddering.

The girls clung to her, sobbing hysterically. She obtained a leather bag from an actress; she hastily took off her jewels, ordered the girls to do the same. They crammed them into the bag. She slipped a gold coin into a dresser's hand, asked her to pin up their trains, to pin them high, asked her to find them some black shoes. Other ladies, waiting and half-swooning with fright, looked at her, saw her thus, strangely practical. She succeeded in buying three long black cloaks and three black hats from a group of chorus-girls, flung one cloak over herself, flung the others over the sobbing little marchionesses.

"I'm frightened, mamma!" sobbed Eleonore.

The duchess was determined to get home somehow:

"Come, come along!" she urged, driving the two girls before her.

The other ladies, in alarm, watched them disappear through a back-door into a side-street....

The duchess pressed the bag with the jewels to her:

"For God's sake, don't cry; keep your heads!" she ordered her daughters. "Walk on quietly and not too fast. Wrap your cloaks well round you."

She walked on, tall and erect between the two little trembling marchionesses, in those chorus-girls' clothes; rain poured down. Clusters of people ran up against them; they mingled with them; for a moment she lost Hélène:

"Wait a moment!" she said to Eleonore.

And they remained standing amid the press of people; troops came jogging on; socialistic songs of triumph carolled up coarsely.... Then she went back with Eleonore, pushing, shoving, giving Hélène an opportunity to get back to her:

"Now both give me an arm: here!..."

They did as they were told; thus, seemingly calm, slowly, slowly, as though they were sight-seers who had also come to look, they reached the Opera Square, where the mob was swarming up against the guards. Carriages passed, at a walking-pace, escorted by soldiers. A wretched old hired growler, with a gaunt hack, pushed a muddy wheel right up against her, grazing her knees; a cuirassier of the escort raised his sword threateningly against her....

"My God!" she cried, awe-struck, clutching the children.

She had first recognized the driver, in a dirty coat: a footman from the Imperial, whose face she remembered. Then, with a swift glance into the cab, she recognized—just close to a lamp-post with a number of ornamental branches—the emperor leaning against Othomar and her own stepson, Xardi. But the marquis did not recognize her, for, startled by the great light, he quickly turned his face away and bent, sombrely, protectingly, over the emperor and the crown-prince....

The girls had seen nothing; the duchess said nothing, afraid of betraying them.... She felt all her pluck and assurance forsake her; she shuddered from head to foot. She could not restrain her tears for her poor emperor, who was dying, who was returning to his palace in such a guise. A great, dark terror took possession of her. The rain trickled over her bosom....

"Keep your cloaks round you!" she again admonished her daughters.

Then she went on, dragging herself along and the girls as well, beside her, stumbling on their feet...

But a whirl of people swept across the Opera Square; there seemed to be a fight in progress: a heap of men, surrounding a group of police-constables and soldiers, in whose midst a madman wrestled with forcible gestures; a coarse clamour rose on high. At the lighted, open windows of the opera-house, above the perystile, still decked in its bright, festal illumination, face after face, appeared, actors still in costume looked on....

"Mamma, we shall never get through!" sobbed Eleonore, softly.

The duchess thought in despair of the great Empress Avenue in which their town-house stood; it was so far away: how would they ever reach it, how would they ever get home?...

"They're murdering him, they're murdering him, they shan't murder him!" bleated the people round them.

Then the duchess understood, then she saw and the girls also saw: the mob, furious, foaming at the mouth—avengers now, though at first malcontents, perhaps even anarchists: such were the Liparians!—the mob pressing against the soldiers and constables, in the midst of whom the emperor's murderer still made fight with his large, frenzied gestures. And the avengers stormed this circle of protecting police; they dragged the man out.... They dragged him right under the eyes of the duchess, of her daughters....

"Ugh, ugh, ugh!" they roared brutally, men and women alike.

They tore the clothes from his body, they beat him; and he howled back. They struck him to the ground with cudgels and trampled on him with coarse shoes; his blood flowed; his brains spattered from his crushed skull....

Then, at the sight of blood, they became like wild beasts; they grinned and smacked their lips with delight.

Eleonore fell back fainting against the duchess, but Alexa shook her by the arm:

"Keep up, keep up, for God's sake keep up, can't you?" she cried out aloud. "I can do nothing with you if you faint!"

Her strong hands goaded the little marchioness back into life and again she dragged them on, staggering....

5

The emperor, who refused to die, lived by sheer energy for two days longer, with his perforated lungs, panting for breath.

And such were the Liparians: the man, the murderer, seized in the opera-house, despite the police and the guard, had been battered into a shapeless mass by the malcontents themselves....

And such is life: the emperor of a great country was shot dead by a fanatic in the midst of his kith and kin and life went on.... The country was as extensive as before: a rich, naturally beautiful, southern empire; tall, snow-clad mountains in the north; medieval and modern towns, lying in broad provinces; the residential capital itself, white in its golden autumn sunshine, with its Imperial, beneath a blue sky, close to the blue sea, round which circled the quays....

And such is the life of rulers: the emperor lay dead, killed by a simple pistol-shot; and the court chamberlain was very busy, the masters of ceremonies unable to agree; the pomp of an imperial funeral was prepared in all its intricacy; through all Europe sped the after-shudder of fright; every newspaper was filled with telegrams and long articles....

All this was because of one shot from a fanatic, a martyr for the people's rights.

The Empress Elizabeth stared with wide-open eyes at the fate that had overtaken her. Not thus had she ever pictured to herself that it would come, thus, so rudely, in the midst of that festivity and in the presence of their royal guest; thus, glancing past her, striking only her husband and not crushing them all, at one blow, all their imperial pride! It had come to pass and ... she still feared, she still went on fearing, more now than before: for her son!... It seemed to her as if she were fearing for the first time....

It was the day before the funeral of the Emperor Oscar, when the Duchess of Xara, now the young empress, was seized with indisposition and the doctors declared that she was *enceinte*.

The emperor's remains had already been removed in great pomp to Altara. At St. Ladislas the Altarians were to see him lying in state between thousands of flaming candles, with the brilliant insignia of the supreme power at his feet; after that he was to be removed to the imperial vault in the cathedral....

On that day too at Lipara, whose whiteness took tones of sombre twilight beneath mourning decorations and flags flown at half-mast, the salutes from Fort Wenceslas echoed over the town, thundering in dull tones their regular, heavy, monotonous bombardment of farewell. Lonely, majestically, in the town resounding with the salutes, stood the Imperial, empty, with its caryatids staring with gloomy, downcast eyes. The young emperor, Othomar XII., was at Altara, leading the solemn procession. The empress-mother was at the Crown Palace, with the young Empress Valérie.... Over their glamour, still shining, shone new glamours, in life which had continued, which was continuing still....

The two empresses sat side by side. Valérie held Elizabeth gently in her arms; at regular intervals the guns boomed from the fort, through the palace...

Then Elizabeth drew herself up painfully from her daughter-in-law's arms and spoke in low, oracular tones:

"If it's a son ... it will be a Duke of Xara.... He would so much have liked to see a Count of Lycilia...."

The guns boomed; the two empresses, in deep mourning, wept and sobbed. And now for the first time after a long interval—as there had also been a long interval at Berengar's death—Elizabeth realized all her loss, her sorrow, her misery, her despair; and she felt that that emperor, to whom, as a very young princess, now four-and-twenty years ago, she had been given in marriage, without love, she had come to love in this quarter of a century of their life in common on his high pinnacle of sovereignty....

That evening Othomar returned and, alone with his wife, with his mother, he sobbed with them, the young emperor, whom no one had seen weeping in the cathedral at Altara. For the Empress Elizabeth had repeated yet once more:

"If it's a son ... it will be a Duke of Xara...."

And then the Emperor of Liparia had lost his self-restraint. In one lightning-flash, one zig-zag of terror, he saw again his life as crown-prince, he thought of his unborn son. What would become of this child of fate? Would it be a repetition of himself, of his hesitation, his melancholy and his despair?

And then with irrepressible sobs, suddenly overwhelmed by the menace of the future, he sobbed out his grief for his father who had been and his son who was to be! He sobbed, with his head in the arms of his young empress, who, suddenly realizing that she must comfort him, had grown calm and looked calmly down upon him, taking their life of majesty upon her shoulders as though it were an oppressive, heavy mantle of purple and ermine and nothing more, taking it up so valiantly because there flowed in her veins as in his one single drop of sacred golden blood, common to all of their order, their might upon earth and their right before God....

6

"To HER IMPERIAL AND ROYAL HIGHNESS EUDOXIE
"ARCHDUCHESS OF AUSTRIA,
"SIGISMUNDINGEN.

"ST. LADISLAS,
"ALTARA,
" —May, 18—.

"MY DEAR MOTHER,

"I cannot tell you how your letter pained me. For God's sake, do not excite yourself so and say such terrible things. We too regretted intensely that you could not be present at our coronation and that your rheumatic fever obliged you to remain at Sigismundingen; but why need you, dear mother, look upon that fever as a punishment from God? And why need you look upon it as a punishment from God that you did not see your fondest illusion fulfilled and were not able to be present in our old cathedral when Othomar, after being crowned by the primate, with his own hands crowned me Empress of Liparia? You were not there, but yet it came about: your illusion is truth, after all. And I tell you this without the least, oh, believe me, without the *least* bitterness!... A punishment for forcing me, against my will? You must be ill indeed, ill in body and mind, poor mother, to be able to write like that: it makes me smile a little, I no longer recognize you. And let my smile bear witness that I am not unhappy: oh, far from it! Our happiness is hardly ever what we ourselves intend it to be and what we regret that it is not....

"If you were to see me, you would see that I am not unhappy. It is May, the sun is shining, the oriel-windows are open. In the distance, when I look out, I can see the Zanthos winding away in a broad, gleaming expanse of water. Close by my writing-table stands your beautiful big silver cradle; and through the closed lace curtains I can see my little Duke of Xara slumbering.... I don't know how to write all this to you, I have no command of words in which to express it fully to you; but what I feel, with this wide river landscape before me and this precious little child by my side: oh, mamma, it is not unhappiness! It is a feeling which hides a great deal of melancholy, but which hides nothing more sombre than that. And really why should it, in spite of that melancholy, not be even happiness? I am young, I am empress and I see life before me! Round about me, I see my country, I see my people: I want it to become the people of my heart, of my soul, entirely. I don't yet know how, but I want to live for this people, I want to live together with Othomar. Oh, I grant you, how I am to do that I don't yet know, but I shall find a way, together with him! And, having a husband and a child and a people, an emperor, a crown-prince and an empire, have I then no aim in life? And, having an aim in life—and such a tremendous aim!—have I not then also happiness? Is happiness anything other than to have found a lofty, a noble aim in life?

"I am so anxious to convince you. And, if you saw me here, at our quiet St. Ladislas, now that all the agitation of the coronation-festivities is past, you would believe me. Othomar loves St. Ladislas and proposes to come here every year for a month in the spring. It is considered a good omen that my child was born here, for you know the feeling of the Liparians, their wish to see the crown-prince of their country born at St. Ladislas, under the immediate protection of the patron saint.

"Othomar, however, is not here at the moment: he has gone for a few days to Lipara—of course, you know this from the papers—and writes to me twice a day. I asked him to do this so that I might be fully informed as to his state of mind. The tragedy of his father's death, the Emperor Oscar's two days' death-agony affected Othomar so violently, so violently: my God, how can I find words to describe that terror to you! How can I still live in hope, after all that I have already suffered in my short life and seen around me in the way of terror! And yet, yet it is like that, for youth is so strong and I, I am strong, I *must* be strong....

"I admired my young emperor, in those terrible days, for his outward calm, through which the storm-flood of all his emotions never burst loose before the eyes of the world. Directly after the funeral, the ceremony of signing the five sacred deeds; the immediate agitation of the accumulated affairs of state.... A month later, the new elections, the constitutional majority in the house of deputies, the resignation of the ministry.... All this you will have seen in the papers.... After that, the birth of our son and then our coronation, at the moment when Liparia seemed shaken to its foundations! And now Othomar is at Lipara, because of the new constitutional ministry.... Then Count Myxila, who does not agree with Othomar's modern ideas and who has even ventured to reproach him with some vehemence for abandoning all his father's views upon government so shortly after his violent death and who is now tendering his resignation.... Othomar will make an effort to keep him, though he himself realizes that it will not be possible.... And the revision of the constitution in the immediate future, with so many drastic changes, probably with the inauguration of the upper and lower chambers, while the house of peers will continue its outward existence, but will be actually nothing more than an honorary consulting body. These are concessions, if you will have it so, but then, you know, Othomar has quite different ideas from his father's and, when he makes these concessions, he undoubtedly makes them to the past and not to the future nor to himself....

"Life is cruel, cruel in its changes and cruel even in its renascences; and for us rulers all this is perhaps even more cruel; but the world belongs to the future....

"The Empress Elizabeth is still here: she has suddenly grown so old, so grey and very dull and depressed; and she does not know what to do: whether to remain with her household at the Imperial, to stay on here at St. Ladislas, or to retire to Castel Xaveria.... All the imperial palaces and castles are whirling through her poor head: her private properties and the crown domains; she does not know where she wants to go; we of course continue to urge her not to leave the Imperial: it is large enough to enable her to retain almost all her own military and civil household....

"Dearest mother, I will write to you again soon: my head is still too much in a whirl; I have touched on too many topics; my woman's brains are not capable of thinking that all out logically and coherently and writing it down.... And I have only been empress for such a short time and I am only twenty-two, though I no longer feel so young.... This letter is but a hurriedly-written reply to your doleful self-reproach, which I now beseech you in Heaven's name to put aside *entirely*. Now that I write this to you, the evening of my betrothal-dinner at Sigismundingen rises before my mind. We were such a strange engaged couple, Othomar and I! I asked him—smile at this, mamma, and don't cry about it—whether he loved anybody. He said no. He told me he loved his people and he stretched out his arms, as though he would have embraced them. His people! The dawn of a new idea—old no doubt to thousands and ages old, but new to me, as a new day is new—shone out before me, threw light over my gloomy sufferings, brightened a road before me....

"That road, mamma, I now see stretching before me clearer and clearer every day; and I mean to follow it with my husband and my child, with my emperor and my crown-prince ... my crown-prince, who is waking and crying for me!

"May God grant me strength, mamma!

"VALÉRIE."